The Pink Forest

A Woman's Intimate Confessions

Dana Dorfman

Banderae Publishing

Disclaimer: All the characters and places in this book are fictitious and intended solely for the purpose of entertainment.

Printed in the United States of America

ISBN 13: 978-0-9798592-0-5

Library of Congress Control Number: 2007907188

To my parents

I sat down with my laptop and in your magical light,
The Pink Forest appeared!

Thank you for your wisdom.

Dear Dezerae,
You are etched in me forever.
We are one.

I love you.

A distinguished soul eyed me once.
He said be brave. Accept it all graciously.
Thank you Dad.

There will always be Bandit.

You were a thought-reader, an ardent communicator,
and my good friend.
I will miss your wagging tail and
will wait for your kisses from Heaven.

Byron, I will miss you padding around in your
chocolate socks and your soothing purr for a very long time.

Foreword

The bookstore has knotty pined walls. It looks like it has been carved by the wind. The shelves carry waves of peaceful feelings. It has recently opened on the other side. A muse crouches on the edge of the stone fireplace, reading.

Floating above a light wood floor it makes another selection. There is a blank book and quill next to a reading list. Pressing gently on the cover its pen comes alive and I begin to write.

My first one hundred nights with you are without resentment although your rousing me at 4 am to reveal the spirit world was a bit unsettling. At first I thought you were a dream in the middle of the night but in the morning I was covered with book dust so indeed you awakened my mind. I hope I have redone *The Human Masquerade* to suit your needs.

Perhaps what I have said is not easy to take or, for some not something to take seriously but the muse on the other side is not complaining about lack of attention. It is whispering softly and I am listening.

I am not sure if I am sliding with astonishing ease into the spirit world or if I am just earth-side in interpretive range. For those who have no understanding of this language, reach beyond these pages and you will, no dx-oubt, glimpse flying silk.

This is not about a meditative beginning. This is about allowing a voice to soar that is not my own.

Kneeling in *The Pink Forest* I thank the heavens that there is no writers block on the other side.

And to the muse who mystically-lights my pages, I will continue to follow the breadcrumbs . . .

Contents

Contents

Introduction

At first I stood on the outskirts of the pink forest too shy to venture in. And so it went for some time. But then I blew out the light of fear and in the curves of the vine-draped woods I inched further. My painted toes blush the earth as I move through the sultry winds of emotion. "The pink forest is more than a bundle of ferns," I think as I give a shy glance to the timelessness fluttering the trees.

Flying silk draws me further into the mist-shrouded haven. I pause and look around. Through the haze I see a delicate figure feathered in infinite layers of lace. "Do you carry the Earth's shadow?" I call. Clouds of Lady Slipper orchids float past me in a land that looks like it has just been kissed by a rose. "These woods have the power to tease reality," I say to the amorous creatures unfolding my presence.

A sprinkling of woven leaves caress me and I greet them on dancing feet. "My little toes are upon the clouds!" I cry. "I am fingered in twilight!" My eyes gleam with excitement as the wind spells my name. Like a flame on top of a candle my body flutters in a language I've never known. "I am in the touch of silk," I whisper. A magic comes forth and I smile shyly behind the trees.

The pink forest is untamed. This is my story.

Dipping my quill into the heat
of passion
I unbutton my pages and elicit
my intimate confessions.

Chapter 1

Passion's Admirer

A blushful aura obscures my face. I am a travel weary woman locked in a maze of button pink curlers. Unmercifully I grab for my silver clippies. Rows of bobby pins hide under my flossy scarf. They banish all thoughts of me making my plane on time. I give myself a tired smile while my astonished eye scrutinizes my face. I am almost ghostly as I grip the edge of the fluffy pink canopy costuming my head.

Picking the bobby pins out of my hair a swoop of wet locks fall on my face powdered cheeks. I lunge at the slippery strands. They are like thousands of strangers offering me an invitation to play. "Feel free to be as imaginative as you please," they say teasingly. But it is the pink setting tape across my bangs that has me wincing at the frizz factor.

And then just when I think there is no hope for this bobby pin queen, the heat blowing monster rises! It tumbles my hair in the diffuser bowl down the tunnel of mousse where I vanish into the light scent of lilies, lift my hair with my large toothed comb, and cross my fingers for a taxi encounter.

A yellow car pulls up in a puff.

"Are you really a cabbie?" I ask peering inside.

A cantankerous driver greets me and I hop in with my bags. Gliding over a double yellow line my commute to the airport begins. I hold my stomach. He slips over a few more lanes of city roadway and a hundred backlights come into view. "This looks like a good spot for tofu," I think as we sit idly in traffic. A group of passers-by peer in at the restaurant window. They give the impression they want to taste every dish imaginable.

A few cars inch up ahead and we slowly pass a storefront window of scantily clad mannequins. They stare at me and I find myself ogling them back. "What is behind your purse-shaped lips?" I wonder. "Is it a quick glimmer of human perfection?" Once again my cab lurches forward and I take a quick, backward glance at the lifelike mannequins seductively posed. They stare at me from behind the glass and I am caught in their blinking eyes.

Turning into the airport terminal a row of yellow taxis idle at the curb. Outside is a mob scene. I eye the cabbie. He makes a few impolite taps on the meter and I unroll his fare. He gives me the briefest of nods. Gathering my baggage I jump out of the cab with clouded wisdom and stand at the edge of the crowd. I bite my lip. And then, in a quick moment's panic I turn into an emotional spectacular and run for the departure gate. Upon entering the magical kingdom of chaos the unthinkable happens.

Someone in front of me lets out a baleful "Uh, oh!" and the pandemonium begins. It is hard to enjoy the hustle and bustle of a cancelled flight. News of it alone sparks Armageddon. Like wildly rearing horses the terminal becomes strewn with ear-pricked, disgruntled inhabitants stampeding in mayhem over their unconventional manners. Emotionally heightened conversations detonate my travel bubble, and I am quickly dispersed into the dispiriting scene. The realm of pure noise is hardly a soft landing as I careen into the bedlam of luggage-toting figures. Stumbling my way further and further into the sodden gloom, I search for a spot to stretch my legs for I too am an emotional casualty. Not finding an empty seat, I crouch on my baggage and resign myself to my fate.

Drifting high above the airport chaos, I think of the sunlight caressing my comforter, and I realize I miss my bedroom. Perched somewhere off in my dreams are my fuzzy bunny slippers and the smooth corners of my blanket and sheets. It had been an erratic two days of air kissing, and I was looking forward to getting back to L.A. Although working for Kenmar Studios comes with boutique hotels and smart suits, it is hardly a spell of awe.

My career at the studio had accidental beginnings. I would like to say that while traveling the icy tundra or wading in lush rain forests, the concept of movie production illuminated me, but it was hardly the case. Ironically, it was while waiting at a traffic signal at the intersection of Hollywood and Vine in the City of Angels that the throes of life fell upon me. Inspired by a flier with the buzz word "employment," I gave in to the tug at my ankles and sought the subversive pleasures of movie making.

Despite my lack of "biz" experience, I was richly received by the gifted industry giant, JB, who turned me into a pile of flutters. Amid gusts of paper swirling, I was hired as her loyal jet-setting assistant. But now, in an amusing moment, the sweet scent of irony swaggers up to me and catches a gleam. I shake my head. It is this award-winning diligence of mine that has me currently stranded in a freak snowstorm's utter mayhem!

Turning into an airport artifact I lean back on the wall behind me and fume quietly. Never considering myself an iron-clad traveler, I kick off my heels and massage my aches and pains. A mismatched posse of newly formed traveler vigilantes charges past me and catches my attention. They are seeking runway justice and I wave them on by. Their scorched-Earth attitudes and clenched fists have reduced them to shouting pathetically. They are a catalog of horrors that cannot come to terms with the fact that we are for the moment life's unintended consequences. I watch another conglomeration of altered images storm past me, and in their faces I choose to observe myself.

"Hey you in there, stuck in the folds of your existence, I can see you. Have you ever fanned the flames of life?"

"What?" I ask. "Who are you?"

"I am your wild side. Sound seducing?"

"My wild side?" I ask, blushing.

"Stop controlling your erogenous zones," I command, my voice echoing in my ears. "Are you a mystery unexplained?"

I tap on my shoulder. "Excuse me, but there is an untamed fever within you."

I don't answer.

"Pardon the intrusion," I continue politely, "but your fire is racing."

Still, I cannot seem to get my attention, for I am too busy tiptoeing through love's minefields, bashfully exploding in erotic thought.

Continuing along on my fabled route, I stop and nod respectfully to the ancients. They greet me with open palms and we exchange pleasantries. "Do you know the way to ecstasy?" I ask. "I am trying to find my tantalizing vision."

The ancients sally forth and cast me critical glances.

"No disrespect intended but I am tired of dressing in your morals and ethics. I'm looking for a life a little less traditional." Taking in a deep breath, I casually glance at my surroundings. "You have outdated notions," I shout. "Tell me, do you ever kiss here in your jungle of virtue? You know impulsiveness might do this place some good!"

Morality's eccentric defenders are not amused by my question. They tap their feet with impatience and demand my intentions.

"I have an intimate confession," I whisper. "I want to run through the moonlight. And there is more."

The ancients lean in toward me and all falls silent in the jungle of virtue.

"I lust for a night tussle. My spirit has awakened!"

The ancients raise their brows.

"Is it so wrong to be a bit mischievous at times?"

The scowling ancients are without answer.

"I am ready to engage hotly with life."

The ancients shudder and immediately crumple my desires. Clearly my confession has disturbed their calm and I wonder why the outrage. They stare at my compelling image.

"I am a woman after some playful fun! Heaven knows I've had enough moral sense handed down to me over the years to drive me crazy. What is so wrong with some simple longings? I am ready to hunt for life's scandalous pleasures."

Instinctively the ancients nudge one another as they catch the gleam in my eyes.

"I want to sprawl out in the world of sensual loitering. I want to be captured by animalism. Is there any animalism running around in this jungle of yours? If there isn't, there should be. It would lighten this place up if you all were a little bit playful."

They cross their arms in front of them, and I know I will not be getting their nods of approval.

"I want to romp in the world of play. I'm human. You know, chemistry hotly percolates the soul. Have you had your soul hotly percolated lately?"

The ancients wipe their brow.

"I want to feel life from the inside," I whisper. "I want to be teased."

The ancients dust off their spectacles and pretend that they don't see me.

"I want dimpling cheeks," I say, blushing.

The ancients are sullen.

"Forgive me, I don't mean to make you ill natured. I just want a few moments packed with some thrills. The modern world is passing me by," I wail.

The ancients shake at my honesty.

"I find you to be unreasonable protectors of virtue," I clamor. "I have come here hoping to gain your support, not to defend my feelings. You know, just once I'd like to search myself for some sin and find some! It's not like I want to peek out of my neckline! I just want my cheeks to get a little pink, that's all. Lusting for the fiery cosmos doesn't make me less of a human being; it makes me more of one. It is not a crime to want to feel passion. I have had intimacy only with love and commitment. It has been ho-hum. I want my lips to have a fluttery glow!"

The ancients appear hypnotized and I carry on with my spell.

"I have found my feminine assertiveness. I'm ready to romp!"

The ancients gasp and lock themselves in a battle pose. My promiscuous notions are an unwelcome guest and they stare at me worriedly.

"Hey, I'm not aiming to be a sex goddess."

They wipe their brow with relief and shafts of sunlight fill their smiles.

"I am not hunting for shameless exploits. I am just a woman who desires a bit of spontaneity. You know, it wouldn't be so bad if there was a little hanky-panky here in your jungle of virtue."

My truthful admissions have stunned the defenders of decency. They stare at me as if I were an exhibit in the gallery of the absurd.

I thumb my nose at their judgment. "You can look at me in any fashion, but I want to take a stroll through enchantment."

The ancients are angry and I continue to hurl my thoughts at them like lightning bolts.

"Journey through my promiscuous thinking," I shout at them. "I promise it will be an exhilarating ride."

The ancients are sullen and I know that I have skipped across ethical lines. They have buried my notions in their taboos.

"You know, these peer-judged honors you have bestowed upon me are hard to live up to. Curiosity arms human beings."

The ancients stand with their hands on their hips and look at me disbelievingly.

"Listen, we all try to make wonderful choices in life. I don't mean to duck under your traditional ethics, but I have made my decision. I choose to seek passion."

The ancients shirk back from my soul-shaking mix and dab the air with their critical thinking. They fear that my provocative notions will have me enter the tomb of error. Their disenchantment hovers over me. But I am not discouraged. Restless with intrigue I continue stumbling away from my conscience.

"I am tired of being passion's admirer. Rapture is a wondrous place far away. Explore the details of my face. Can't you see that I am quietly affected?"

The ancients wink at one another

"I am not attracted to the dark and ghoulish, but really, what defines the forbidden?" I ask, addressing the unmentionable. "I mean I'm just trying to speak directly about my emotions. Is that a bad thing?"

Fearful glimpses frame the ancients as they slowly recede into their darkened hollow.

I giggle. "What is so wrong with wanting a rip-roaring time?"

The ancients stare at me as if I were an immoral nomad trekking by camel to some secret sexual oasis. I smile and flirt dangerously with the idea.

The ancients cross their arms. They are defensive and reserved in their mood.

"You know, I just want to cuddle up to an ear whisper."

The ancients rub their eyes with disdain.

"I am not here to cradle my emotions."

My openness has angered the ancients. They are suspicious of my ambitions, and I feel the need to explain.

"Mine is not a story about getting lost in a dream." I lower my eyes. "I want to tingle."

The ancients cover their ears. They are not interested in hearing my lunacy any longer.

"I want to take a tantalizing peek at life. I think there is more out there than righteousness."

The ancients hold their breath.

"I want to be an erotic warrior," I say with a devilish twinkle in my brown eyes. "Everyone flirts with madness. Why not me?"

The ancients point me a lecturing finger. They are concerned that my mythic adventure will journey me through cads and philanderers and frauds and cold-hearted sexual adventurers.

"You read too much," I laugh.

My message falls on deaf ears. "You lack the voracious appetite for understanding a different perspective. Your traditional values have survived for thousands of years, but the world is changing. Didn't you get the memo?" I ask, winking. "There is an unspoken side of sensuality."

The ancients stare at me.

"I know I am acting with great surprise, but I am tired of being a coffee run. I want to live my vision."

The ancients gaze at me behind bottle-thick glasses. Their sloping posture has the uncanny ability to project their wounded image.

"Do you know I long to be fanned by a million heated breaths?"

The ancients blush as I reveal yet another intimate confession.

"I am tired of my quiet Friday nights," I whisper. "I want a life encounter."

With fury the ancients wave me away. I have fallen out of step with them, yet there is no turning back. Peering into their ominous clouds, I persevere.

"Life can be perfect sometimes," I say, shyly.

The ancients gaze at me as if I should be righteously fined. They are appalled by all they have heard.

"I want to get into some serious ear smooching," I say, blushing.

Exhaling audibly, I can see the ancients are out of patience.

"I have another intimate confession," I whisper. "I want to slip into Eden but I don't know how."

A sensual mist begins to fall and the ancients step from their cloaks. They come forth and give me bunny hugs. "We are passionate spirits," they whisper.

Hugging the space in which they dwell, I gaze into their sacred entrails. "You are a fire that I want to warm myself in," I utter.

They smile and I know they are granting me my rite of passage.

"I hope to throw you a blushing rose someday," I call to them.

The ancients hold out their hands and in a sweet breeze, my sensual spirit falls softly on earth.

Reality nudges me. It is just another day of personal uprising.

With my senses hardly marauded, I am splashed by absurdity. Why must it be just another day of personal uprising? I cling to a smile as I glance around at my sodden jungle. The crowd for the most part has dwindled to angry mutterings and idle chitchat. A few melancholy rebels with pulsing temples stream past me. They are in denial of the knowable truth. As I join the gaggle of airport hopefuls waiting at the information desk, the fantasy gods greet me and my imagination roves.

"Excuse me," I say, approaching the customer service counter, "I'm looking to book an opening to my soul. You see, my sensual spirit has landed."

The agent is soft-spoken. "We apologize but all flights out of the airport are significantly delayed due to bad weather. I can book your ticket on standby if you'd like."

I twiddle my thumbs. "You don't understand I want to pass into a whisper-light excursion."

The wistful agent studies my demeanor.

"Listen please," I beg. "I want a magical kiss to put a soft blush in my cheeks."

The wistful agent is quiet. She senses she is on to something interesting.

"I am not a security risk. I am spellbound."

The wistful agent nods understandingly, a slight smile dances upon her lips.

"You see, I've decided to try to find passion, and I am wrestling with conflicting ideals. I guess I am a saga of emotion right now who just wants to breathe in a little euphoria."

"This is the proper forum for your concerns. I have the ability, thanks to my extensive training, to meld sensitive observation with clear explanation. And believe me I completely understand the complexity of your situation. Unfortunately, the best I can offer you at this time is standby."

"May I explain my nonstop ambiguity? I want to establish credible thinking."

"Take all the time you need. A well-trained customer service agent must be a good listener. I am very dedicated. I am required to make my presence felt by boosting your spirits. Please proceed. And by the way you don't need to authenticate yourself. We are all human."

"Thank you," I say, feeling a sense of mortal camaraderie. "You see, my lust has been stuck at the gate for a long time. I need to pursue my impassioned destination at all costs. There is something exotic locked inside of me." My eyes quickly scan the departure monitor. "It is important that I be booked on a flight immediately cleared for takeoff. You see, I am looking for a sudden change in direction. Can't you help me? I seek the wisdom of someone who knows."

"Of course, we are here to service your every need. It is our policy to promote good will," replies the wistful agent. "I have had extensive training on that. But we are very understaffed right now. We ask that you please bear with us."

Feeling frustrated, I walk away and bounce around in lines that are wrapped around forever. Once more I return to the wistful agent.

"You, again," she says.

"Yes. I am back."

"May I remind you that we are still understaffed?"

"I know, but my transgressions are growing in leaps and bounds. I am resurrecting a notion, and if I don't get to passion quickly, I may lose my nerve to seek it. I may even become a doomed lover! And then, how could I get lost in a good smooch?"

"I have on many occasions assisted passengers to retrieve lost items from inbound aircrafts. Of course, losing one's nerve is horribly traumatic. Federal regulations require us to be commiserative. Just in case you fall into the tragedy of doomed lovers, please accept the airline's most sincere sympathies."

"Thank you. I just want to book a flight in an untraditional direction."

"Booking a direct flight anywhere right now is quite challenging," says the wistful agent sympathetically. "But I assure you that you won't have any trouble flying in untraditional directions through connector flights. We take pride in being an on-time airline."

"I am not trying to camouflage my mischief with all sorts of connector flights. I just want to zoom into some fun!"

"I understand that. But let me just emphasize to you that our connecting flights are not in any way unendurable commutes. Our connections are ensured."

"Look," I say, hunching over my words, "I have erotic tastes."

The wistful agent shifts uneasily.

"I don't think it is being immoral to have erotic tastes. But I cannot help but wonder if this is just the intensity of my womanhood coming forth or if this is truly the flaring of my own fever-crazed nature. Please don't call security," I say. "I am a sensible passenger. My entire life I've tried to do things the right way. Now, I just want to curl up in the echoes of a sunset."

The wistful agent nods. "Confusing policies and procedures breed an atmosphere of anxiety, something we don't like to evoke upon our passengers. We want you to have a pleasant experience with us. However, I must be truthful. I don't think this airlines has clearance to fly off into the sunset."

"You see, I am not here to set my limits on exploration, nor do I want to taxi these sensations and find out I can't go anywhere with them. I need to book a direct flight to passion. It must be a confirmed reservation. I am ready to romp."

"When our engines are revved up and we are in full power to take off, we cannot have anything unusual noted," says the wistful agent, "including petals of enchantment."

I shrug. "I just want to peep above the sky."

"And do you know that you can do that with us? We proudly offer atmospheric refuge to our passengers and not just during take-off. We fly above storms and clouds and everything. Of course, we follow the strict code of regulation and so forth. You see, as our passenger your needs are foremost in our minds. We guarantee attentiveness as well as sufficient leisure. It is an important part of our policy."

I take in a deep breath. "What I'm trying to say here is that the sensual genie just won't go back into its bottle."

"Oh, so there will be two of you flying?" asks the wistful agent.

"No," I clarify. "Just me!"

"I see. The sensual genie is just a shadow of you then?"

"Yes."

"How nice," she chimes.

Smiling bashfully, I turn red in the face.

"Okay. Just so that you understand that we are not allowed to take the passenger who arrives on a dead run five minutes before departure. Of course, from a service view, that's great! It is one more customer with a revenue ticket. But you understand we are a well-respected airline and we have no tolerance for someone who is attempting to flaunt the rules. Please know we have a ten-minute cut-off. Traveling is a privilege, you know."

"Oh yes. I know."

"I see. Well, there is also always a chance that your flight will get rerouted for some reason. In the event this should occur, we can always issue you a voucher."

"Thank you. You see, my sensual spirit has landed and I am frightened."

"May I say that we all bubble inside with discontent, insecurities, and obsessions from time to time? New situations bring out the best in us. Please remember that on behalf of the airline."

"Can you expand a bit on that please? I am feeling vulnerable."

"Sure. No one can control the climate of fear," says the wistful agent. "Fear taxis in and out of our everyday existence."

"You see, I am hardly venturesome. Actually I'm not used to going out in the world, I mean except for business trips. Really I've been known to hide when my spirit moves me. And now in this airport ruckus I find I need to courteously apologize to myself for my quiet, reasoned approach."

"We in the airline industry freely apologize. It is our policy to collect information with compassion. And may I say if you are flying out of your character, we suggest that you allow plenty of time to arrive at your destination. A word of warning, passion can have you soaring at unusual altitudes. Make sure you fasten your emotional seatbelt."

"Well, my sensual spirit fuels me and gives me hope for a tantalizing future." I blush. "It is rustling my corporate attire."

"May I say that the rustling could be due to head winds?" chimes the wistful agent. "They can most certainly have that effect on attire. Just on the tarmac alone it can get quite gusty."

"I don't believe head winds can have this type of an effect," I say, my cheeks turning a rosy pink.

The wistful agent stares at her display monitor. "I would like to be able to offer you a lavish travel package of pillows, aromatic oils, and candles along with your ticket, but unfortunately those types of offerings must be booked ahead of time. Are you budget-minded?"

"I will take anything at this point."

"I have booked you one ticket to paradise. It is a direct flight and an aisle seat, first class. Plenty of room to sprawl out for sensual loitering," she says, grinning. "In the event that paradise is not what you have envisioned, I must warn you that this is a non-refundable ticket. No exceptions."

"Yes. I understand."

"Congratulations! Your flight to passion has been cleared for takeoff," says the wistful agent. "May humankind welcome you warmly and may you find the turbulence you are searching for."

"I am a soaring emotional enthusiast," I shout happily. "I am ready to rock!"

"Will you be checking in baggage?"

"Yes," I answer. "I will be traveling with luggage packed with my utopian ideals."

The wistful agent fidgets with last-minute fixes.

"Allow me to stamp your passport to pleasure. May passion greet you at the gate!"

"Thank you," I reply.

"Enjoy your layover," says the wistful agent, "and your jet lag, and thank you for flying the sensual heavens."

The word "next" oscillates my ears and I am nudged to take my turn at reality. I leave the line of weary travelers waiting to be helped and step up to the information desk. The customer service representative behind the counter is curt and not into personal listening.

"Can you tell me what time flight 3260 departs to Los Angeles?" I politely ask.

"That flight has been cancelled," she says. "We suggest you book a new flight."

"That was my new flight," I say.

"There are no flights out tonight," she claims, her haughty sarcasm shooing me away from her counter. Dispirited, I make my way back to reclaim my sacred spot on the floor. Time has silenced the terminal's mayhem with a myth-like quality and I grasp at its elusiveness. Impulse sneaks into the limelight and in a room swallowed up by sleepy shadows I lift my shroud and gather around my life.

Extending my hand I introduce myself, for sometimes I appear to be a stranger. Checking my soul, I confirm it is me and kindly comment on how fashionable I am looking. "Thank you," I respond, "but you know this is not really me. The real Jenna Weyburn is simplicity's adorer and then I murmur something about "appearances."

"Have you ever truly let yourself go?" I ask, pulling up a stool outside my existence.

"Come to think of it, all of my decisions have been done with dainty deliberation. There has never been a speck of promiscuity in my world," I say, looking myself in the eye.

"Have you found that to be a bit unsettling?" I ask.

"Yes. Stealing some kisses would have been a nice spirit for me to confirm that I am alive. I've never felt life dip its tongue in my ear."

"So you've always been like this then?"

"I have never allowed myself to be seduced."

"Perhaps then, it is time to leave your comfort zone."

"Well, I must admit I want my neck to tingle."

"Ah, so you want to be a thrill enthusiast?"

"Yes! I want life to sweep me off of my feet!"

"There are times when one must hunch a shoulder against the trappings of society and wait for guidance from the wind."

A crimson blush roses my cheeks as I dream of doing something daring. The moment entices me. I inhale a quick, icy whiff of cowardice and then breathe normally as my quest for fire flames.

"So are you thinking I should take some time off to find passion? I've never played with fire before."

"Yes. It is time for your tiny toes to tingle."

"You mean its time for me to have my hair caressed at the nape of my neck?"

"I mean it is time life reflects warmly from your eyes."

"You mean get touched by a real caress?"

"Yes. It is time to brush the lips of the sun."

"I am trembling."

"Why are you scared?"

"The border between fantasy and reality is erasing and I am frightened."

"Allow the amorous creature in you to disrobe."

"It is acting out of my nature."

"Close your eyes."

"I will have to crawl out from under heaps of conservatism to do so."

"Mingle with your heated breaths."

"Does magic float in the air?" I whisper.

"Close your eyes."

"My emotions are flying all over the place," I say, flailing my arms. "It is a shivery world."

"Close your eyes."

"I am in the mood for the unfamiliar. I want to glide the skies. Am I a vague wish?"

"Don't be a story never explored. You cannot get to your feelings by being shy."

"I'm scared."

"Do you want to be a fire breather?"

"Yes." I whisper. "What do I do?"

"Catch the twinkle in your eye. Breathe deeply. Allow life to peck your ear."

Bringing life to my lips, my former self departs. "A vast world awaits you," calls my flickering image.

And so, in squishy sneakers and with a bag full of morals slung over my shoulder, I set out for passion. Of course, the first step is to get out of La Guardia.

I laugh.
I cry.
I sigh.
I experience confusion.
It is all a part of what I am,
For I am only human.

Chapter 2

My Bedroom Oasis

I am a barefoot, flannelled reveler, twirling around and around in my bedroom! It is 3 a.m. Los Angeles time and I am home! Thank God it is not my imagination. I give myself a disbelieving shrug while eyeing my reading lamp and the books on my dresser. "I'm really here," I shout, throwing my teddy bear up in the air! Impishly I bounce on my bed and sing to the top of my lungs while the sweet lunatic within me dives under the covers. Filled with an exhilarating sense of freedom my weariness slowly recedes. I'm home. I'm safe.

My delayed flight landed at LAX in angry sheets of rain. I was stuck in the very last row in an aisle seat on a bumpy, uneasy, nighttime ride, and I am not someone who is immune to fear. After feeling the thunder of hundreds of jumbo jets and being jostled by what seemed like millions of people at La Guardia, landing in the rain almost felt serene. Of course, in a city where the sky is often blue and the days typically warm, I had anticipated being greeted by sunshine. Instead, I was dodging water puddles and berating myself for not having the foresight to bring an umbrella. However, I did make a promise that on the off chance I survived my business trip, I would remind myself to do so the next time.

Sleepy, after hellish days of hypnotic shuffles, I joyously reunite with my lacy pillows. Visions of passengers in La Guardia wreaking havoc still exhaust me. I hug my teddy bear. I definitely am an overly sensitive 'poof' of a human being.

Stretching my arms above my head, I close my eyes and listen to the Pacific storm I flew into. I sigh contentedly. Wrapped in my blanket I swing my legs over the edge of the bed and run to look out the window. I press my nose to the glass. It is raining sideways. My flannel pajamas make me a comfortable ensemble and are pampering as I pause to watch the rain. Jumping back in my bed I pull my comforter way up under my nose and look at my rain-soaked clothes hastily strewn over the back of my chair. I smile and turn my face into my pillow. Behind my curtained windows it is a scene of earthly paradise.

Sitting cross-legged on my bed in the early dawn I am a soft pile of blankets surrounded by my bell-shaped lampshades. They have been with me for ten years and are not going anywhere any time soon. I eye my clunky bedroom furniture with its glass top and deep drawers strewn with personal renderings. It is hardly orderly. I reach over for the crumpled magazine on my nightstand. In my dutiful boredom it is always at my side.

Sheltering me from pandemonium, my bedroom is my tranquil retreat from the world. It is a warm, inviting place that cradles me to sleep, sends my anxieties fleeing and gives me a sense of belonging. It is my adoring crowd of warm embraces that cheers my breaths to Heaven and graciously receives my most cherished thoughts. In it I am never fumbling or unconvincing. I am beyond perception and appearance. My eccentricity is vindicated and I can uninhibitedly run past my "moments." But there is more.

Behind my bedroom curtains the whims of intrigue purr. My fantasies expand and I am no stranger to passion. In my darkened editing room I embrace the exotic and quiz myself on the world I inhabit. Drifting off in fantasy, I smile. Searching for sensual reality makes me want my belly kissed.

In my earthy cave I am a conjurer of imagination and reality. I reinvent myself and magically I reappear! I am a soulful nurturer and an emotional chemist. I overcome obstacles, make significant sacrifices and imagine my dreams. Here I never am empowered to confront reality. Here I am in a different place than I would ordinarily be. In here, I am marvelous in my own eyes.

In my bedroom I am famously written and instantly famous. I am master of the plausible and filled with possibility. I am the producer of ideas and a productive critic. The world never passes on my theories, and my moments in the spotlight never pass. I am a treasure trove of artifacts and treasured in dusty ledgers. On Fiction Street my heroic exploits control my surroundings and I never cease to mesmerize the world. On Fiction Street I am the stuff of a legend, always a genius, and eternally an identifiable human figure.

When I am on the fringes of darkness, my bedroom becomes my hero. It is my gallant protector and comforts me with nods of approval. In my bedroom oasis, I swat at chaos from under the covers and find hope in sadness. The truths I refuse to speak are freely released in my tranquil abode. Here I speak with convincing authenticity. Here I am neither misunderstood nor a violator of common sense. In my bedroom I am the founder of admirable intentions and the keeper of sentimentality. In here, I matter. In here, my ideas are forever validated and I remain inescapably myself.

In my bedroom I am a mop of hair and a yawning face. I am an untied bathrobe moving in slow motion, in floppy slippers with a steaming cup of coffee leading the way. In a room strewn with scattered newspapers, a pair of reading glasses peers over a bowl of cereal and catches the headlines. I look at the clock and discard my half-eaten French toast. It's time to get civilized.

After experiencing bedlam with the shower curtain, I head out in the early-morning darkness to face my day. "Who can possibly go out on a day like today?" I ask myself, sloshing through puddles. I cannot say that I love bundling up and walking fast to keep warm.

Under an unusual, Los Angeles winter sky, I quickly become adept at the art of scarf tying and umbrella juggling. Rainy air licks at my face as I run to my rain-sodden convertible. I laugh for a moment as lightning streaks the skies. I live in L.A. and I haven't had the top down for years. With shivery hands I fumble with my keys. Jet lag kindly opens the door for me and settles behind the wheel. I am a soaking mop top as I back out of the driveway. It is 6 a.m. on a pitch-dark, pouring morning, and I realize I have not slept in the last 24 hours. My left eyeball hurts and I'm feeling a little irritable. No doubt I've got the jet-lag blues.

Getting back to my freeway instincts are a bit rusty as I hop on the highway. The normally early morning commute is a jammed stretch of chaos. Thunderclouds drop buckets of rain upon my windshield. My breath rolls hard. Immersed in the rumble of traffic my mind does a boggling dance with my life.

Although my business trip was anything but a magical journey, the enduring ordeal gave me a chance to revisit my character. With renewed eyes I was able to see my life in the confusion of La Guardia's bedlam. The decision to take some time off to pursue passion may make me unusual but where in someone's composition are the human guidelines that they must follow? Perhaps my eccentric self is emerging, but I must admit, the impulse to do something daring is exciting!

This puffed-up feeling of elation is wonderful and I am grinning from ear to ear. After forty-five minutes of freeway pandemonium, butterflies escort me to my flooded off ramp and to the studio's palm-lined, colonial entrance doused with rain. Blustery winds lash at the rain-slicked guard at the gate. He smiles and motions me through. I turn into the wet parking structure, parallel park, and then with flagging energy climb a flight of stairs to the normally sunshine-bathed courtyard. Jet lag is furious and comes at me red-faced with temples of bulging veins. Rounding the fountain, I take the elevator to the executive production offices and wonder if I am bordering on madness.

Striding past the perky receptionist, I grumble at my apprehension. I don't know if JB is going to shrug me off and poke fun at my notions or if she will choke my attempt at pursuing something that is important to me. I take another deep breath and prepare myself for her tension-inducing talents.

Hypnotically paced, Jackie Berman is an intrepid studio executive sitting in the sizzling seat of motion picture production. Sleekly polished with the power of celebrity she makes it rain in the rivers and snow in the slopes. But being part of JB's motion picture enclave has unjustly consigned me to hide from my intimate confessions. Heaven knows, there are no storied clashes of good versus evil here. I've spent eternity applauding her inspiration without once vying for the limelight. Still I am exploding with a passionate sense of personal entitlement. I want to explore my wild side. I want to tingle.

It has always been part of my personality to be painfully shy. Pictures of my childhood sweep my mind as I remember myself as a skinny little brown-haired girl hugging her dogs. I smile. I've always been my most at peace when I'm with my animals. My present situation fills me with panic. I don't know how I am going to explain myself. I bite my trembling lip. I will be okay once I get past the initial wave of dry-throated moments. Fueled by human spirit, I charge into JB's office and clumsily stand before her. There is no time to compose myself. Her blue eyes are already staring at my trench-coated figure and bedraggled umbrella.

"Welcome aboard, troubled soul," chimes the money-minting studio queen. Stirring her café latte, she sits curled up in her leather swivel chair in black sweat pants and a thick black jacket. "I have just come in from a session of coffee-shop scribbling at Jerico's Coffee Emporium," she says, rising. "The winds are screaming over the sets!"

Pivoting gracefully, she hands me a cup of hot coffee and gestures for me to sit down. I wrap my cold hands around the warm china cup. The steam from the coffee gently rises. It is the calm before the storm.

My body is on the wings
Of tantalizing sirens.

Chapter 3

Lounging in Eroticism

I push my rain-soaked hair back from my face and bring the piping-hot java to my lips. "I am not used to being late," I vent, taking a sip. "What a fine impression I am making on you this morning, stumbling in on my heels."

"Life doesn't always run with exact precision," says the soft-spoken champion of civility.

I allow her fix-it-all statement to escort me out of my apology.

"I gather you didn't land in sunlit swoops at LAX," she jokes.

"No. To say the least! And we actually took off in a swirl of snow flurries at La Guardia after a grueling delay."

"A day like that can make you mad with desire," she says, and my breathing quickens.

A tall woman with tousled blonde hair, JB had been in her office for hours while I was still under the covers hugging my teddy bear. Hollywood's hotshot film producer tends to burst upon the imagination of the world pretty early. But at any time of the day JB is a potent image. Nibbling on a cookie, she motions again for me to sit down. As my jittery soul sinks into her marshmallow-like couch, the thick cushions embrace me. I fold my hands in my lap as the rain-drenched city below calls my name.

"I'd hate for you to think that what I am about to say is the consequence of jet lag," I begin.

JB grins. "Is this about unread newspapers piling up in yellow heaps around your house?" she asks playfully.

"No," I sullenly reply.

"Is it about not having the time to take your bright red Christmas stockings out of their crammed cardboard boxes?" She snaps her fingers as if the light bulb of life has just gone off. "I've got it! This is about enduring rounds of airports and hotels right?"

"It really is not about being time-deprived. I just am in despair." I pause. "JB, is the art of seduction carried out with plumes of smoke?" I ask, rubbing my forehead.

JB's lips twitch in a smile.

"Brace yourself for my emotional whims, JB, for I have thrown on the light switch of life."

"I'm ready, Jenna. You are creating mental mayhem. What's the word on the streets of your soul?"

"I want to step into the land of the living."

"Not the mad world of the living," she exclaims.

"Yes." I blush.

"I see," she says. "Isn't this a retreat from your image?"

"I'm hoping to revive myself with a leave of personal freedom."

JB winks. "It sounds like you want to lounge in eroticism," she says and I lower my eyes.

"JB," I whisper, "I am a faceless drone."

JB inches her chair back. Her brows furrow. "If I were smart, I'd cover up my ears and urge you to fret about a more serious dilemma. But instead my mind is a geyser full of thoughts," she says and I bite my trembling lip.

"So you've reached into the backpack of life and pulled out a faceless drone. That's what you are telling me. Are these the whims of a woman hunched in thought?"

"JB, it's time to allude to the days of lying dispirited on my living room sofa. I am lifeless and wonder how I address this with you without sounding like I'm losing my mind."

"You are looking to ride in the bubble of intrigue. That doesn't make you a figure of ridicule. That just makes you human."

"I want to slip beyond my lips. I want to see myself in soft candlelight," I whisper.

A smile starts on her mouth. "Life can easily seem otherworldly. I am a studio filmmaker. I can make passion drift in the air! I can make a featherlight kiss fall from the sky and I can make a lighthouse wildly twinkle a night! Talk to me!"

"Well, JB, I am perplexed."

"Don't try to make sense of the world," she says, nibbling her cookie.

"I seem to have the lifelike realism of an eccentric."

"Maybe you're just a little quixotic," she jokes.

I smile but she senses I am ill at ease, and for the moment, changes a subject that I know she will get back to.

"I don't think anyone will be going out for a bikini wax in this weather," she chuckles. "I fear that the sun is permanently obscured by a shroud of whiteout!"

I look into JB's eyes. They are bluer than the typical California sky.

"You know, Jenna, the clouds are usually so perfect over Los Angeles they look as if they are painted onto blue air." She gives her galoshes a quick glimpse under her desk and sighs. "I'd give just about anything right now to stretch under the glowing sunlight and nap right through the sunset!" Her eyes glitter.

This trough of low pressure makes me miss sitting under the soft filters of West Hollywood's café umbrellas, shoulder to sunburned shoulder, sipping my Piña Colada and looking at the parade of spiky-haired, hip-hugging, shoulder-padded rage lovers, soaking up the hazy rays with their crazy, asymmetrical shades. You know, it's all about image," she remarks, gazing placidly out the window. I nod, wondering if she has ever explored her dreams.

"In sprawling Los Angeles, a place where the sun's magnetic presence is an alluring part of its aromatic landscape, this weather is hard to handle. Why, it compounds one's ordinary existence! This morning, yesterday's car-washed windshield got sluiced with hail, and it made me want to skip my annual skiing vacation to Vermont. But that would indeed break Ronnie's heart. Being in Southern California has had her living in snowy silence unless we take a trip to Mammoth or something. She misses her breath billowing in the thin cold air and longs for her face to turn scarlet in the breeze. Ronnie craves for us to be a pair, huddled together, wrapped in long winter coats with the wind snatching our scarves." She sips her latte.

"I travel with my electric blanket wherever I go, but you best keep that in the vault," she says. "You know, Ronnie and I have so much in common, yet we are so different. She loves being on skis, gaping over the edges of slopes. Me, I am just a red-nosed onlooker, content watching surfers skim head-high waves in ninety-degree temps. I'll take a set of avalanche-carved slopes on a warm studio lot any day."

JB has been "out" since she first began with Kenmar Studios twenty-some years ago. As a native Southern Californian, she met Ronnie Gillespie eating a celery stick at an outdoor café in Palm Springs. She overheard Ronnie say she was from Vermont and had never been in warm temps in November. According to the headstrong executive, the next few hours gabbing with Ronnie remain a high point in her life.

JB sits back in her chair. "You see, Jenna, the rain seeks no permission to fall, not even from the Hollywood gods! Seriously though, it is atmospherically barbaric out there," she moans with the affectionate exasperation of a native. "The hillsides are saturated." She pauses. "It's interesting. A longtime repository of lost-cause romanticism, L.A.'s wayward allure is its cackling rarity. A city of gargantuan appeal, filled with the hustle and bustle of the notoriously imaginative, L.A. demands that its flaws be forgiven. It is a city filtered through the lens of valet parking, stretch limos, aspiring actors, and the sinkholes of success. The signs of celebrity are everywhere, as are the signs of affluence and power." She takes another sip of her latte and continues.

"L.A. is a setting of glimmering attitudes and green-lit dreams. It is a haven of scripts scrawled on café napkins and the rallying cries of talents yearning to be discovered. Even the disillusioned are charmed by L.A.'s twinkling allurement."

Leaning forward on her marshmallow-couch, elbows on my knees, holding my chin, I stare at her and wait for her humor to come into play.

"Los Angeles is a Mecca of promising edge. It rests on its own starry mystique, and its unique twinkle is known throughout the world. L.A. is the home of star sightings and rescued fantasies. Beneath its sparkling special effects, its aura of infinite creativity allows one to touch the sky; yet there is no other place that is so easily disturbed by falling rain," she says, smiling.

"I suppose driving in L.A. in falling rain reveals still another one of the city's unique glories," I jest.

"Indeed, we tend to hover on the sun's fringes, enjoying its calming pulse most of the year for weather here is predictably tranquil." She winks. "The L.A. sun is swarmed by paparazzi," she says and I giggle.

"You see, Jenna, L.A. courts the future without a steady eye on the past for Los Angeles is restless to discover new traces, new starlets, and new trends."

"JB, I want to be an untidy mass of hair," I blurt.

At first JB is taken aback by my bold admission and then her eyes twinkle. "You don't want to be a kitten anymore? You want to be a tigress?" she asks.

"Yes. I want to whisper into life's ear."

JB grins. "I didn't know you were prone to erotic encounters."

"Promiscuity has set down and bit the wild woman in me," I whisper.

"I thought you were going to tell me that you want to paint yourself in skimpy leotards," she chuckles.

"JB, I have an intimate confession. I want to feel life play upon my tongue."

JB tilts her chin. "There is nothing wrong with wanting to be served some tantalizing bits of life. You have the right to touch upon your secrets." JB lifts her gaze to the heavens. "Passion seems to be the bridge that you fear to cross," she softly chides. "I've never seen you as voyeuristic."

"These purring sensations have emerged out of nowhere."

"Keep reality in mind when you seek the pleasure puzzle. You are after amazing intrigue."

"Me?" I exclaim.

"Your sensual spirit will bring you to your knees if you continue to be an icicle trying to bloom. Perhaps you thrive on the thrill of the hunt."

"Me?"

"The thrill of the hunt is within every human being who inhabits the Earth. But the deepest quest is when we rummage through our soul. That is life's most torrid affair," she says, smiling. "You see, the highway of desire is a tricky one. It is a stranglehold of heart-fluttering charms."

"This is not about love, JB. This is about passion."

"Love and passion are jewels of fire. Both allow you to see life through golden eyes."

"I have another intimate confession, JB. I want to be a fire-breather."

"You want to be a rapturous spectacle."

"I want to give the earth the light brush of a butterfly kiss."

JB grins. "You want to run towards the sun."

"I want to giggle in rose-scented bath water from lips caressing my neck."

"You want to feel rapture roam your face."

"I want my wrists to tingle."

"You want to feel limitless."

"I want to feel the butterflies in my soul."

JB rubs her palms together. "So tell me, what made you crave to be a sensual heroine? What made you want to roar?"

"The moonlight suddenly came in through my window. It caressed my cheek and kissed me lightly on my nose. Suddenly I found it hard to breathe. I tossed and turned in bed until a thought touched my lips. I want to be covered by moonlight. I want to be moon splashed. I want to feel passion," I whisper.

JB's eyes flash. "Passion is the fire of the soul. It touches your senses and keeps you in a state of daze. Feeling passion is embracing mystery! The only thing better than passion is a tickle fight," she chuckles.

"What about sex?" I whisper.

"Sex is a moment's whim. At times it is not even a desire, just a mere idea. People speak most loudly through sex. They scream and moan, surfing through their sexual adventures with curled toes and grasping hands. The mind is an esoteric blend of odyssey."

"I just know that I am a slumbering woman. And I know that my request arrives at a rather inopportune time."

"Yes, Jenna, it is Oscar season and we are stunningly set in chaos. Ears perk up at elusive queries. Suspicious eyes scan copious notes. Snoops are all over, no one immune to their fascinations. It is a dubious time when truth becomes sought after and questioned. It is a time to be team-spirited and intuitive. Imitator invaders are in disguise everywhere."

I nod my head in agreement.

"Oscar season is an insanely driven time for everyone in the industry. But with that said even the wind and sun would drive you crazy if I were to ignore your request." She winks. "It's okay to be playful."

My eyes twinkle and a wolfish grin falls over L.A.

Incensed by the prowl of
playfulness,
I greet life with intoxicating lips.

Chapter 4
Smooching Behind Virtue's Back

"I turned my head to look behind me once and I grinned like I had won a prize. I smiled under its full weight. Its lips drew upward and brushed the inside of my ear. Shaken to life I shivered with sensation. I squeezed its hand as its fingers deeply caressed my shoulders. Tickling the nape of my neck with its heated breaths, I turned over and do you know what I learned? Passion was straddling my back with fiery-hot kisses." She smiles. "May your ardent aspirations be realized, Jenna, and may you pursue life with intoxicating lips."

I stare at JB. "Is it wrong to play out our fantasies?"

"Just be careful you don't break your soul."

I shiver.

"Passion is life's charm, Jenna, but it can make even the best of us sloppy thinkers."

"I am ready to be realized," I whisper.

"Jenna, are you saying that you no longer want to bartend any off-hour amours?"

"I am ready to smooch behind virtue's back. I want to be enticed."

"No. You want to be enchanted."

"I long for my lipstick to be smeared and my body to be rapturously traced by the hunger in someone's eyes."

"Jenna, I believe you crave mass adoration! You yearn to be adored! You are not unique. Affection makes us feel good. But remember nothing great is created in an instant." She pauses. "Your quest is not a casual decision. It is superb heroism to stand up for what you want. I admire you for doing so. After all, life is one of intrigue."

"So have I cleared a date with destiny?" I ask, gazing into her soul-baring eyes.

"I suppose that remains to be seen. But your leave is approved." Her lips curve slightly. "Oscar season is hardly a season of slack. Yet, you also have an obligation to yourself that must be fulfilled. If I were to deny your request, I fear you would be lost forever in the figment of your wishful imagination," she says and my tummy flutters.

"More realistically, you would waltz around in cheery falseness, but deep inside you would be mean-spirited, with a perpetually hung-over scowl lurking inside. You are a fawnlike creature venturing into the heat of your being. Denying you your request would have you infinitely aching for your fantasies. Longing messes with the mind as nothing else does," she says and the room spins.

"Now, putting this aside you will need to go through the administrative mumbo jumbo with Roy. He and Darcy are having an impromptu anniversary party. With their troubled marriage it is a nice occasion for them. I won't be able to attend because Ronnie has me committed to one of her weekend adventures so I'd like you to go in my place."

Like most everyone at the studio I, too, was aware of Roy's philandering. At first the gossipmongers had him portrayed as an impassioned madman who was swept away by inescapable rapture. But as depraved sexual sinners go, he shed the image of a pitiful adulterer. Armed with ethical lessons he cast aside his roving eye and came forth as a wedded hero deeply devoted to matrimony.

"After you make the necessary arrangements with Roy, your leave will be effective. You are dead weight now, Jenna. You are a huntress of smoldering eroticism," she says with a wink.

She shuffles the papers on her desk. "Begin your rapturous pilgrimage. I fear it is the only way for you to put your world back together." She smiles. "I am craving a cheeseburger, slathered with ranch dressing and stuffed into toasty, sesame-seed, buttered buns. Can you go to Dion's Bar and Grill to get me one?"

"Sure. I can use the air. Jet lag appears to be gaining on me," I say rubbing my temples.

"Jenna, before you leave I have a news flash for you. Ross Heaverton will be joining Kenmar Studios. According to Brass Green, Kenmar's head-honcho entertainment chief, Ross is a carefully calculated step for the studio to stay at the top. I think Brass selected him because he needs very little sleep and he knows everyone wherever he goes. I will want you to meet him before your official return."

"JB, you know I get nervous meeting the big wigs."

JB leans back in her chair. "Although an industry maverick, Heaverton's history is nothing more than that of an unknown actor appearing in a few third-rate films. This is not just another Hollywood studio-execs meeting. Meeting with Ross will be a major meeting of the minds. It is all about unity, Jenna. There is value to collaboration. Sometimes it has to take the place of our dreams." She pauses. "Your leave will bring you back here at a challenging time."

I nod.

She speaks quietly. "Be careful when your eyes close with pleasure."

I cock my head.

"The language of heat cannot be interpreted. Nothing passion utters is decipherable. Are you emotionally daring enough to embark on this quest for fire? It's not too late to change your mind."

"Is passion a distant threat?" I ask.

"Human beings are elusive creatures. Beware of imaginary friends. Passion can be a snake across your lips!"

I shiver. "I want to be caressed through silk."

"It sounds like you want to strip down to your pasties," she jokes, and I cannot control my girlish blush.

"Jenna, passion doesn't always have a soft landing," says JB quirking a brow. "It can be an odd, almost eerie dimension. Facing rapture's tentacles can have you looking at yourself through the telescope of life. Through it you will know what it is to be human."

I swallow hard.

JB lowers her voice. "Passion gropes your mind. It rubs provocatively against your skin. Humankind cannot break the kiss of destiny. Just remember anything can be made to look convincing, even the truth."

Her words squeeze the air from my soul.

She puts her arm around my shoulders. "The tale of your quest is yet to be seen," she whispers. "You are at the point of your departure. May there be a logical end to your quest for fire. And may your lips loosen the ties of life."

Rapture ahoy! I cry.
Let the ardent waves of life
devour me.

Chapter 5
Audible Sniffles

With shrieking winds nearly ripping me from my broken umbrella, I slosh across the soggy boulevard as a spectacle of audible sniffles. I left the studio's executive offices fearlessly following my intuition, yet feeling effusively sensitive. Something deeply real is happening to me. I let out another sonic sniffle. But it is self-centered L.A. and nobody notices. And anyone who did notice would probably think it the norm.

As rushing cars speed past me, I think about my conversation with JB. There shouldn't be this air of desperation I feel. She granted my request. But she didn't exactly preach paradise, and it has me wondering if I am in search of villains or if passion is going to huff and puff and blow me down! Not one to menace the world, I am a bit nervous embarking on my blistery excursion. It is not easy closing the door on your silent soul and letting the wild woman out. A shy smile crosses my face. I can't believe I told her I want to be a rapturous spectacle! Feverish emotion ricochets through me, coloring my cheeks with another intimate confession. "I want to dance in unexpected places," I muse and for a moment, I stand in the rain, blushing under my broken umbrella.

Approaching myself with a playful attitude is quite new for me. I haven't allowed life to tickle my ear. Instead, my dead-serious eyes always seem lost in some internal crisis and my dark-suited figure roves through my existence as a petite bundle of nervous energy. This is not how I want to be chronicled for all time. I'm done staring glumly into space.

A kiss lands on my cheek. "It is time to get frisky," calls a voice.

"Do I know you?" I ask, glancing around.

"Not yet. I'm the wild woman inside of you. I wiggle with fury and passion."

"Oh wow! I'm scared as hell of you."

"Don't worry. I don't wear a red loincloth, gold armlets, and anklets. My hair is not held in place with gold beads either. Do you have an appetite for those types of things?"

I gulp. "No, I don't think so. I really don't know what I have an appetite for. Where are you?"

"I'm in you, waiting to emerge."

"I'm frightened of you."

"Don't be. Do you know you have a captivating smile?"

"Me? Why, thank you."

"You are a sexy woman."

"Me?"

"Yes. Your large brown eyes sparkle. You should allow your body to swim in silk."

"Oh wow!"

"You should wear hipster panties."

"Oh, I don't know about that," I say turning crimson.

"You should wear exotic dancewear and black tights. It is nice to feel sexy."

I smile.

"Do you have a mesh bra?"

"No."

"You need to get one. And a lace halter bodice, as well."

I giggle.

"You are a hidden beauty. Now, you need to get some thong panties and rhinestone danglers."

I blush.

"The time will come when you burst into fire. Wild with desire, wild with passion you will not be able to hold me back. There will be a fiery explosion and I will emerge."

I tremble. "When will I know I am ready?"

"Your body will sizzle."

Visually audacious, I sniffle into Dion's to get JB her cheeseburger slathered in ranch dressing. My hair is blowing three feet ahead of me as I open the door.

"Hey, Jen! Over here!"

It is Roy Saxton waving to me from a booth by the window. He is instantly recognizable. Boyishly professional, his pleasantly disheveled hair looks suave in his yellow rain slicker. "Over here, Jen," he shouts again.

With soaked shoes I swash over to him.

"It is impossible to maintain any sophistication in this soggy air," he says. "Do you agree?"

I smile and self-consciously touch my frizzed-up hair.

"So where are the wild and crazy street performers today? I fear they are appearing in some sunlit venue far away."

I can't help but grin. Roy crackles with good humor.

"Sit down," he gestures. I scoot into the seat across from him. "I'll buy you some lunch," he says, shooting a menu across the table.

"I'm actually picking up some lunch for JB. I'm not really hungry," I say, quickly scanning the entrees.

"I just talked to JB on the phone."

Putting the menu down, I gape at him with surprise.

"Where would we be if cell phones were blocked and phone lines were cut? Back in the dark ages for sure!

We've grown accustomed to devices. They are the electronic umbilical cords for life. Why, they are the strings that control the world. It is rather delicious to eavesdrop on behind-closed-door situations," he says, chuckling.

I inhale deeply.

"JB said you seemed a little stressed. She wants you to take a few deep breaths. Let me buy you lunch. Why don't you have the long-standing tradition? The double cheeseburger with fries. I know it is hardly a match made in culinary heaven, but it will do."

"I'll just have soup and a salad," I say, giving in.

"Nonsense! Live a little, Jen. She'll have the double cheeseburger with fries and a shake," he says to the approaching waitress.

"Soup and a lettuce wrap would have been fine," I say, sniffling.

"Are you coming down with a cold?" he asks, ignoring my preference. "This weather will do it for sure."

I rummage through my purse for a tissue. For a moment there is stillness and then a tremendous thud! My already shattered umbrella drops to the floor, startling a few fellow booth herders. They turn around and roll their eyes in my direction. My cheeks redden. Roy leans down and picks it up, propping it against his sleek, collapsible black one. Feeling embarrassed, I hope he refrains from comment.

"You know, Darcy and I were running all over the house this morning trying to find my yellow hooded windbreaker. Darcy finally found it in the linen closet, of all places. This rainy weather has completely upset my routine. I haven't been to the gym since the looming gray skies first shrouded the city. I suppose your plane didn't land in sunlit swoops!"

I sigh.

"It is interesting. We don't need an apology for an unseasonably warm afternoon, but as a native of sunny

California I need to know the story behind an ink black sky. I miss L.A.'s fun-in-the-sun image. Do you know, Jenna, these storms have dumped tons of snow at Mammoth? I can't wait to take Darcy up there after our bash this Friday night. You are coming by, right?"

"I don't know, Roy. I'm not feeling very sociable."

"It is just a cozy, spur-of-the moment anniversary bash Darcy and I have rustled together, celebrating ten years of off-and-on hell. You know our marriage has been rocky. A nice house party might do Darcy and me some good. We're trying to stitch our relationship back together. An impromptu gig might help do the trick. I'd kind of like you to come by. Of course there won't be any fancy people in ritzy attire driving up in their personal limos. But there will be a good group of people laughing at witty exchanges, a well-stocked buffet and a chance to wine taste. It is a good sense of occasion."

I let out a deep breath.

"Looks good, huh Jen?" says Roy as the waitress sets down our plates.

"Yes," I mumble, picking up a straw to put in my shake.

"So, I hear you are out to conquer the erotic universe," trumpets Roy, salting his fries.

"What?" I gasp, dropping my straw on the floor.

"I hear you are ready to swap your job for some intrigue! JB told me about your wild notion of desire. It sounds as if you are yearning for a touch of magical whimsy."

I knit my brows.

"Pretty bold move, asking for a leave during the thick of Hollywood's Oscar season. I've got to tell you, your pursuit of life's unexpected pleasures sounds exciting! Do you long for companionship, Jen? Craving is universal. That is for sure!"

I look at him in amazement. I can't believe my ears.

"JB clued me in on your quest for fire," he expresses matter-of-factly, popping a straw into his shake.

"Oh yes, I spoke to JB at length about it," I respond, "and in confidence."

"JB and I bounce everything off each other all day long. You know that! I am a major part of her daily briefings," he says, trying to tranquilize the moment. "Your noble attempt to find passion is stirring, but this is Oscar season, Jen! This is the time for strategy lunches, not for dreaming of erotic adventures!"

I gulp. His words are strong.

"Why, we are front-runners in the Oscar race for best picture. This is the time when anchors and reporters swap trivia and anecdotes as news crews trail past whispered worriers. Everyone is suspect and in the limelight now. It is a period of fraudulent reportage, biased sources, and egomania. Soon hordes of people will be gathering in clusters yearning for our handshakes and cheek kisses. Why the cinematic universe is ours!"

I take a few puffs of anxiety.

"Jen, get the recurring image of you in the unemployment line out of your mind. There is no need to feel anxiety on your horizon, but did you define a moment of pride by asking for your leave during this period of time," he asks, scratching his head in confusion, "or do you have hidden aspirations?"

"I can't find justification for this Roy, but I can assure you that you don't need to call my motives into question."

"I didn't think so," he says, rubbing the stubble on his chin, "but you have to understand that my job is to play devil's advocate. I'm personnel, remember? But I'm also a trusted co-worker of yours, and your friend." He leans toward me. "Your leave is in the middle of a gaggle of nervous studio execs who are frantically trying to be the recipients of the winning bid. It is otherworldly right now!" He lowers his voice to a whisper. "Has reality collided with your imagined life, Jen?"

I take a deep breath. "I know it sounds outlandish, but the unthinkable happened. I realized I have more guts than I imagined."

Roy grins. "And so you have become an emotional activist!"

"I suppose I was feeling uncommonly brave when I approached JB."

"But that is hardly you, Jen, to be a stirring blend of courage."

"I know and now I'm worried. I really like my job. Life feels deadly still."

"Jen, let me reassure you that you will not be fired by brooding, executive, money-making icons. You are safe. But as head of personnel I do have to know all that is involved with the employees at the studio. There is no nightmare potential here. No one is out shooting production of your somewhat provocative concept. At least not yet anyway," he chuckles. "But you must admit the reason for your leave is a bit unorthodox, and one cannot help, but associate it with personal ambitions. I've always found you to be rather timid," he says and I wince.

He leans in closer to me. "You know, in this journey of life there should be no rules for living. Of course that might require a wee bit of explanation." He winks. "But I mean how can we learn what is important to us unless we live a little? Bitter, distraught, unsatisfied people go to hell, not hell-raisers. Talk to me! I've been there before. Your craving is on the loose, right?"

I blush.

"Come on, Jen, I want to be useful here. My life is a homemade flip book filled with fantasy as well."

"I want life to fold with a ruffle," I whisper.

"You have caught my ear, Jen. You are after sheer madness. But an erotic traveler looking for passion in the real world could rightfully feel swindled. You can lug across the globe and never find it."

I frown.

"Hey, what do I know? Sometimes our fanciful ideas are sounder than our reasonable ones! I can see a hidden normalness to your quest and I've got to tell you, I am pretty impressed by it actually."

"I know my quest for fire is a little outlandish," I say, shyly.

"Way out there would be more accurate, but I am impressed by it nonetheless. It is daring and playfully inviting. It is a most inspired hunt! I am peppered with extensive questions about it. I mean it is not often when you know someone who has nerve enough to channel their erotic spirit."

I take a sip of my shake and place it back on the table.

Roy grins.

"What?" I ask.

"You may want to wipe your lip. You have a milk moustache!"

"How embarrassing," I say as I grab for a napkin.

"It looks cute! You wear it well."

I wipe my upper lip. "Talk about sophistication," I mutter.

"You know, Jen, you have a sweet innocence about you that is not seen very often."

I look down at my shake but hesitate to take another sip.

"Relax! This is an off-the-record conversation."

I smile. "I just had one of those with JB."

"Well, I am not an authority figure or an influential filmmaker. You can relax with me. But then again you can be totally at ease with JB. She plays with soft-spoken wit.

Poet-warriors are like that. JB has the ability to see into the window of one's soul. She can also see into the land of wild dreams. She is my mentor."

"Mine too," I add.

Guzzling down his shake, he returns to the subject at hand.

"Jen, when craving is on the loose, it is like the wind. It cannot be stopped. We can only lick our lips with intrigue." He picks up a French fry and studies it for a moment. "For eons human beings have been on this Earth salted by personal pursuit and filled with the exuberance of curiosity. Defined by daily commitments the ache of desire often goes on the back burner. And there it remains until our human torch illuminates within us the thrill of discovery. There is nothing wrong with wanting to trace someone's lips until they quiver."

"There isn't?" I ask, taking a small bite of my cheeseburger.

"No! And may there never be a cure for wonder," he chortles. "Talk to me."

I look down at my fries. "I've discovered myself in dead ends."

"I detect your restlessness. You want to embrace the wonders of being human."

"I don't know," I muse, twirling my hair. "I feel as if I have been living life in its abbreviated form."

"Well, that happens to all of us especially when we are on the never-ending ladder of career utopia."

I smile.

"What is that smile for, Jen?" Roy asks, coyly.

"Well, I've known you to be playful, but I've never known you to be philosophical."

"Under darkly swelling rain clouds you see that I crackle with enlightenment!" He chuckles. "Seriously Jen, I hope you realize I am not some sex-crazed wolf, eagerly chasing shapely women and looking for thrills on beer-drenched weekends. Although, I have cupped temptation's ear in the still of the night and have had fuzzy moments of curling toes!"

"Well, you do crackle with enlightenment. Do you have a degree in philosophy?" I ask.

"I am human. That is my degree. As human beings we are all philosophers." He strokes his chin. "What is beneath one's leggings, Jen? Is it dark magic pulling shirttails loose from the waistband? Under rolled up sleeves are we fragile or haunting? What really lurks behind one's shirt buttons?" he asks and I shiver.

"You have dynamited familiarity with your quest," he says, pushing his empty plate aside. "Are you a woman in peril or are you an erotic stripper with deep secrets?" He chuckles. "So, what shall we call your pursuit, an inspired romp? I don't mean to be a Doubting Thomas, but you must admit, Jen, the reason for your leave is somewhat unusual. I mean who requests such a thing?" he asks with a tone of absurdity and I lower my eyes.

"And the timing," he says, running his fingers through his hair. "This is hardly the time for personal adventure." He shakes his head. "Your quest arouses dubious speculation even though it is an extraordinary idea. But I am sure there are wilder escapades out there than yours. This is Hollywood!"

I sigh.

"Jen, are you in the wishing stage of life? Perhaps you are unsettled by the mystery of yourself."

"How does one balance desire, Roy?"

"By opening both eyes to a shoulder rub," he says, winking. "I can see your adventuresome twinkle, Jen. Talk to me."

"Holding my history in the palm of my hand, I hear the scrape of something haunting. I probe deeper. It is the tip of life's tongue flirting with my earlobe. Sitting on my groaning bed, I part my lips and greet the erotic flurries falling upon my limp pillow." I pause. "I am so tired of yawns splitting my face, Roy. I want to curl up to my wild side."

His hand reaches out to touch my shoulder. "I know what you mean. I brushed my fingers against the lips of life once. It was a natural thing for me to do. Like slow bubbles teasing my flesh, my body exploded in a thunderous clap. It had a mysterious name to it. It was called passion and I will never forget how I rolled in its flames. It is a wolfish world, Jenna."

His words set me in flight and my travel fantasy begins.

As I crank the handle of life,
I ease into being human.

Chapter 6
Roaming Hands

"Jen, rap insistently on the window to get his attention! That S.O.B. owes me twenty bucks!"

Tucker Richmond stands outside of the eatery in the filtered gray daylight of a rain-drenched boulevard. A jock-like figure whose friendly face and dimpled chin sets him apart from the typical jocks of the world peers through the window and smiles.

Roy motions for him to come in.

Bestowed with an odd sort of grace, he approaches our table wearing snazzy winter boots, a magical pair of jeans, and a slick, stylish black raincoat. It is a sensible outfit for rainy bluster. The day's downpour has only managed to add strength to his already good looks.

He flashes a smile. "This is amazing. People are all bundled up and are leaping across puddles, sporting wool scarves, mufflers, gloves, and rain hats. I hydroplaned my way to the studio this morning," he clamors, extending his hand to Roy with an intriguing blend of humor and articulation. "Look outside! It is an L.A. afternoon and the impenetrable rain clouds make it look as dark as midnight!"

Roy shakes his hand. "It is war out there!"

Tucker grins. "The gusty off-shore winds have downed power lines and forced a bunch of SUV's off the highways."

"Even the city's inexhaustible film talents cannot alter the weather," chimes Roy.

"No, this kind of weather must be served with popcorn and good company," laughs Tucker. He bends down and gives me a kiss on the cheek. "There will be no tennis, today, Jenna, unless you want to row your way around the court!"

"Oh, that's right! You both are on-and-off tennis players," comments Roy.

"What's it been, Jenna, about eight, nine years?" asks Tucker.

"At least," I answer.

"We'll get to Wimbledon yet," he says.

"I won't hold my breath," ribs Roy.

"Hey, you never know what is in store for you. Fate calls the shots," chuckles Tucker.

"Or Hollywood," jokes Roy.

Tucker's playful character is impressive. His eyes drink in everything around him.

"Care to join us for some dessert?" Roy asks. "I think the weather is giving me a case of chocolate fever!"

"Sure," he says, scooting in next to me.

I pass him a menu.

He pushes it away. "I already know what I want. The Double Decker Chocolate Lovin' Spoonful Surprise!"

"What is that?" I ask.

"It is mounds of cinnamon toast ice cream with just a touch of light milk chocolate mousse. The entire dessert is a hip, cynical façade," he laughs. "It isn't what you think."

"I suppose even ice cream has guises," winks Roy calling over the waitress.

"I'm really not a chocolate lover," Tucker says, "so those who know me freak out when I come here and order this. Hey, Jenna, you should give this dessert a try. You are a chocolate scorner, right?"

I nod. "I already have an unwanted lemon tart coming."

"You're too cute, Jenna," he laughs, elbowing me.

The waitress approaches the table. "Would you like to order?" she asks.

"I'll have The Double Decker Chocolate Lovin' Spoonful Surprise and a steaming cup of hot cocoa for the lady."

I look at him and shake my head.

"Give it a try, Jenna. The entire world loves chocolate."

"Make that two," says Roy. "Cancel my previous order. This one sounds worthy of exploration!"

The waitress scribbles on her order pad and walks away.

"Hey, I hate to tell you, Roy," says Tucker taking off his raincoat and folding it carefully next to him, "tons of people are holed up at Jerico's Coffee Emporium becoming coffee addicts. You will be having a skeleton crew in the executive offices this afternoon. I'm one of the few who are gallant enough to trudge the boulevard back and brave the storm. Remember that when pay increases require your input," he jests. "Of course, beyond my undue loyalty to the studio I was ulterior-motive driven. Given my show-biz pedigree I had to show off my designer raincoat. Pretty darn slick, don't you think?"

Roy gives him a heads up.

"Hey, I'm making it! I've got a reliable car and a cool wardrobe," chimes Tucker.

"Do you have any photo shoots lined up?" scoffs Roy.

"Hey, I am inspired and that is the main thing! I also get a lot of admiring glances," chuckles Tucker.

Roy grins. "Is that tale inspired by your fantasy too?"

Tucker laughs. "Okay, okay. A change of subject is definitely in order." He takes a deep breath as a peel of thunder booms overhead. "So how do you like being natives of rain-soaked L.A., my friends? Makes you not take the sunlit skies for granted."

"I'm getting used to breathing in soggy air!" chortles Roy.

"The West Coast gloats about their weather. Just wait, the next thing you are about to see will be snowy sidewalks!" says Tucker.

Roy grins. "JB will film it with determination in her eyes!"

"You know, I'm originally from Indiana," clamors Tucker. "I could have easily relocated to Florida if I wanted sun and rain."

"Those guys get brutal humidity Tucker," says Roy. "There is no place like Hollywood and sunny Southern California!"

Tucker looks out the window at the downpour. "I'd like to meet the creative genius who coined that phrase together. Yeah, he must have been a struggling Hollywood writer high on hard-boiled fiction!"

"Amen," echoes Roy as we giddily succumb to the good humor encircling the table.

"I'm glad to see this table is not strewn with groaners," laughs Tucker.

Roy looks out the window. "There aren't any shoppers toting their bundles along the boulevard today. Not even the die-hard loyalists are out," he says as the waitress returns with our desserts and my steaming mug of cocoa.

"There are all sorts of blips, beeps, whirs, and pops going on at Jerico's Coffee Emporium," says Tucker, digging into his Lovin' Surprise.

"What do you mean?" asks Roy.

"Well, you know, Jerico's is usually a place where you go to chill. But not today! The place is roaring with phony confessionals and coffee converts! It is absolutely mind-boggling over there. The gossipmongers have set up shop with their astute observations, far-fetched analogies, and sensational stories. Those gossipmongers can be fearsome, let me tell you. Rumors are flying rampant about Oscar nominations. It is otherworldly over there."

"And it is all free of charge," chuckles Roy.

"It is Oscar season and artfully hyped spectacles are full of giddy intentions," professes Tucker. "Bands of newsmongers are trying to make everyone think they are on the inside track. Everyone is primed to applaud at the mere hint of rumor." He runs his fingers through his dark wavy hair. "So, what is the topic of conversation over here?" he asks.

"We are humanizing a subject that is controversial. One that is surrounded by flowers, sentimental notes, and boxes of chocolates," answers Roy, smilingly.

"What is it?" asks Tucker, his green eyes sparkling.

"Passion!"

"Passion!" he exclaims, nearly dropping his fork on the floor. "It sounds like pretty creative stuff going on here! I must say that it beats the blips at Jerico's! How did you broach that subject?"

Roy eyes me. "Do you want to tell him, Jen? It is completely up to you."

"Tell me what?" asks Tucker, furrowing his brows.

"I'm taking a few months off; it is personal."

"Are you okay?"

"Yes." I smile.

"Okay, that's a relief." He pulls me to him. "What is going on? You've got my curiosity zooming."

"Jen is putting a new spin on her life," says Roy, "but I'll leave it up to her if she wants to clue you in."

Tucker looks at me, wide-eyed. "Are you leaving the studio?" he asks, worriedly.

"No." I smile sheepishly. "It is nothing like that."

"There was no degrading demand or invective-filled altercation that catalyzed her decision to do what so many people in life wish they could do," asserts Roy. "But since we are talking, I'd like you to handle Jen's projects in her absence."

"Will do," affirms Tucker. "But what, may I ask, is going on?"

"I'm taking some time off to find passion," I say, softly.

Tucker is astounded and accidentally pushes his silverware off of the table. Bending down he picks it up and places it off to the side. He looks at Roy.

"Her pursuit does raise eyebrows," chortles Roy. "You may notice a certain lunatic absurdity in it. But then again, some people will do anything to be noticed."

Tucker smiles. "Are you out to catapult yourself to fame with the studio's secrets, Jenna? I mean you just don't strike me as someone who is out to get noticed. You actually hit me as someone eager to get home at the end of the day."

"I am on a quest for fire."

A smile hovers over his lips. "This is extraordinary stuff! You are leaving the studio to search for passion? Wow!"

"Just for a few months," I reassert.

"But it is Oscar season, Jen. It is a time of glittering gowns, crooked bow ties, and tantalizing envelopes!"

"I know, but it is just for a few months," I reiterate. "I have to do this now before I lose my nerve."

"I'm concerned about the timing," says Tucker, grimacing. "Still, I think that your quest is truly amazing! I'd love to ditch my watch on life, forward my mail, and live a hammock-swinging lifestyle for even a few weeks! Who wouldn't like to slumber under a few coconut trees?" he asks, chuckling.

"Jenna's idea is really very simple," says Roy. "It is so simple that it doesn't even seem like an idea really."

"Yeah," agrees Tucker. "It seems more like a flicker or a rush. I think it is great to venture out and do something like this. You see, my problem is that I am too caught up in the real world." He sighs. "Tell me about your quest, Jenna. You never mentioned anything like this in our happy-hour conversations or on the court."

"Well, I have been lingering in life. And it was while I was stuck at La Guardia in my recent business trip that I decided it was time to act on my long-held desire to pursue passion. It is time for me to act on my impulse and leave virtue behind."

"It is an immoral age," says Tucker, shrugging.

"You see, I have rarely acted on what I've wanted. I've never even admitted the deep things that I've felt. I've led such a cloistered existence."

"Being stifled is tiring, Jenna. It's exhausting to keep things inside, especially desires. It will always have you imagining something else."

"I suppose I have always tried to delicately proportion things, Tucker."

"Too much rationalization is not good for the mind," jests Roy.

"Well, Jenna, you must simply decide to be bold or withdraw from your quest completely," counsels Tucker.

I nod my head.

"Funny, I never thought you were defined by such impulses," says Tucker.

"I know. I have always pursued life's standard paths."

"Well, do what you must, Jenna, to feed your romantic life."

"My quest for fire has nothing to do with romance, Tucker," I say shaking my head.

"Tucker, she isn't looking for that," affirms Roy. "She is looking purely for passion. Didn't you hear her?"

"Well, that's good. Love sows confusion. But then again, passion is hardly a no-worry paradise," says Tucker.

"Isn't that the truth?" echoes Roy.

Tucker runs his hands through his hair and eyes me with his familiar squint. "You don't yearn for love, even just a little bit, Jenna?"

"No," I answer softly. "I yearn for passion."

"Are you on a cosmic timeout, Jenna?" he asks. "This is heavy stuff! You are in pursuit of life's champion!"

I sink back in the booth. Feeling it hard to breathe, I take a sip of my cocoa.

"You know, to come across a daring, rather original quest like this is phenomenal," says Tucker. "Passion is a world to explore and reveals a person's raw courage."

"No doubt passion dares our soul," interjects Roy.

"For the fabled dreamer passion is teasing, don't you think?" asks Tucker. "It is seductive."

"Yes, but passion is never mistaken. You know it when you have it," states Roy. "Have you ever been impassioned, Tucker?"

"When I sit down to consider my worst moments, I believe I have," jests Tucker playfully. "Seriously though, the heat of passion ignites the fire of the soul. The feeling is unforgettable. I remember being in a taxi, stuck in traffic. Rearranging my long athletic body on the cramped seat, I sighed about how exhausted I was. It was at the end of a travel day in New York City and I looked around at the jammed-in drivers and felt like a trapped sardine. I closed my eyes and within a fraction of a second, I was taken away."

"Taken away?" I ask.

"Yes, by the delicate silk of her gown and twisting her fine hair between my fingers."

"We all have a trunk of scribbled notes," laughs Roy.

"And a footlocker of scandalous confessions," chortles Tucker. "I never forgot her tight body. We flirted from the moment we met. It has been nearly fifteen years, but I can still feel the warmth of her lips pressing my thighs. The fiery nearness of our bodies nearly drove me crazy. Moving in imagined steps, I would dream of taking her at night. My mouth watered at the thought of touching her. And then, at her place, in the background of glowing embers, my kneeling body reached for her." He wipes his brow. "It was thunderous."

"Are you all okay here?" asks the waitress approaching the table. "I'm going on my break now."

Roy quickly eyes her name tag. "So, Nicole, where is your trunk of scribbled notes?"

She smiles. "It is tucked safely away in my obsessive thought patterns."

"See, everyone has a trunk of scribbled notes. It is part of life's mandate," says Roy.

"Do you know what we are talking about?" asks Tucker.

"Why, of course," answers Nicole. "You are talking about passion."

"So," grins Roy, "tell us about passion, Nicole."

She smiles and puts her pencil and pad in her pocket. "Passion is a delicious wilderness. It arrives as a palpable stranger. The vividness of its power is compelling. Its countless minutes are devouring." She pauses. "Passion is a trance spinner and has us staring into the stars of our soul. Its twinkle lures the robotic creature from us and makes us beg for the hot beings that we are. It causes swooning and fabric swirling," she says, smiling.

"And hip wiggling," laughingly interrupts Roy.

Nicole grins as her eyes meet mine. "Temptation's heat owes no explanation. It can make us a fugitive of the truth as well as a dazed dreamer. And sometimes," she says, lowering her voice, "it has us making choices that put us in jeopardy. Our sensibility skids to a halt when we are under its rapturous spell. Once we experience true passion, it is impossible to return to complete normalcy."

"I suppose there is a delicate point to everyone's character when life takes on new meaning," says Tucker.

"No doubt," echoes Nicole.

"Situations occur and we can easily get seduced by our surroundings. Sometimes we just give in to persuasion. When it comes down to it, we are just self-seeking human beings," theorizes Roy.

Nicole smiles at us. "That we are," she says. "If there won't be anything else, I will leave you your check."

"Thanks," says Roy. "And so Tucker, where is your trunk of scribbled notes?"

Tucker smiles. "My trunk of scribbled notes is tucked safely away in my memento-stocked attic, along with my divorce papers." He chuckles.

For an instant I watch the mint-sized marshmallows floating on top of my hot cocoa and lower my head. Inhaling the chocolaty steam, I take a sip, concentrating on its flavor, and wrinkle my nose.

"Passion does not always flame us with feelings that make sense. Sometimes its power sends us into a dazzling world where nothing is simple, and we succumb to wild temptation," says Roy, trying to keep his voice steady.

"Passion arrives as an erotic stranger. Is it any wonder that its aura has us feeling the universe unfold?" Tucker openly asks. "I mean, there is something so greedy about passion. Yet when we are heat-struck, we find we give ourselves so freely. And nothing is as it was." He lowers his voice. "Staring across tangled sheets, we rise with wobbly legs. Messy bed-tangled hair greets dawning eyes still glazed from an evening of rapture." He grins. "And in the curve of purring ears we drop a kiss and whisper hoarsely that it all began with fingers running down bare shoulders." He chuckles. "I need to check my body temperature!"

Roy's face creases into a smile. "I am not a wild man running after women clad in glitzy beaded harem outfits, but I am human and passion is indeed, monstrous. It turns us into fabric-ripping lunatics!" He winks at me teasingly.

Tucker drifts back into the conversation. "Roy, do you know what hot passion is? Hot passion is a lingering kiss and a bedroll for two!"

"Is it? Well, I think hot passion is wild hair and playful linen shirts," chimes Roy. "It is two people licking fire."

"Smoldering glances have ignited centuries of scandal you know," says Tucker. "Watching the sunlight creep in through flapping bedroom shades is the true encore to warm breaths of caress."

"This conversation is starting to sound like mental foreplay," says Roy, winking. "I reiterate. I am not a wild man running after women clad in glitzy beaded harem outfits. But I must admit I am a babe-watcher, and a good one at that!"

"A long-legged woman in silver platform sandals does it for me," says Tucker. "It is an erotically insightful moment when she clops up to me with painted toes. Actually, that is what first attracted me to my ex-wife. It was those dastardly silver platform sandals," he says, shaking his head. "I can still see them glitter."

"When we are impassioned the world is filled with glistening figures," says Roy.

"Yes," echoes Tucker. "We crave so madly that we can hardly breathe. Temptation carries us off to no man's land. No man's land, by the way, is a place where we swim in our own sweat. It is where we are marked only by the rising sun. It is a place only for the adventure minded."

The pace of the conversation quickens, and I am hoping that no one notices my cheeks redden.

Tucker puts his arm around me. "You are blushing, Jenna."

"I was hoping that bad habit of mine would go unnoticed," I say, smiling sheepishly.

"It is hardly a bad habit, Jen," consoles Roy. "It shows that you are bashfully human!"

I look down.

Roy gives me a kiss on the cheek. His lips feel cool on my flushed face. "Allow me to be nakedly brutal. Inside each of us lurks the erotic explorer. Sticking our head out of the hatch of life, we look around and cautiously edge toward our tantalizing presence. Our world tilts and we smooth into the fiery sky."

"Yes," agrees Roy. "Under the fiery sky we no longer sleep inside our life."

"But under a sky of fire, we can instantaneously fall for a mysterious stranger and make a true mockery of ethics," points out Tucker.

"It is hard to read life's riddles, isn't it?" asks Roy.

"Yes, it is," replies Tucker. "It fills us with wary skepticism."

"Well, I can only worry about the madhouse of my mind," admits Roy.

"Meaning?" asks Tucker.

"Meaning, I cannot always do the right thing and be happy. At times I suppose I will be good and at times not so good," he says with a gleam in his eyes.

"So Tucker, what is your account of passion?" asks Roy.

Tucker lets out a deep breath. "Passion invites us to a party full of emotions. Sitting in its heated-throne we behave clumsily and bungle any natural elegance that we might have thought that we had."

"Why is that?" I ask.

"Passion's heat has us in defiance of all fire laws," he chuckles. "What about you, Jenna? What really brings you to your rapturous search?"

"Well, I have been in love but passion is almost entirely unknown to me."

"Passion and love don't always mesh, Jenna. It is all part of romantic disenchantment," says Roy.

"How does one paint Cupid these days?" asks Tucker with amusing intrigue.

"Carefully," chuckles Roy, "but Jenna is not interested in hunting down Cupid. She is on a quest for fire."

"I know my pursuit isn't coming at the most opportune time. But I don't want to remain a stranger to passion."

"Well, indeed your timing is somewhat off," chimes Tucker. "It is hardly a time to mastermind pursuits of your own delight. I know that your quest is important, Jen, but it is also important to understand everyone else's agenda. We must be wary of Oscar strategists."

I wince.

Tucker smiles. "But on the other hand, you can't look back at your life and think you made the wrong choices. You have a connection with yourself, Jenna. We all do. This pursuit of yours has come to life, and you are not going to get past it unless you act upon it. Although I must admit you have set quite an uncommon course at an intricate time, I take the view that chance and timing are equal. But just remember destinies can get tangled. Fairy tales always seem to be plagued with evil spells or wicked witches lurking about."

"But Jenna might catch a glimpse of good fortune," pipes Roy. "It may come out of nowhere and kiss her bare shoulders!"

Rubbing my temples, I lean back into the booth. "Is it wrong to feel playful?" I shyly ask.

Roy grins. "Brushing a kiss against an earlobe, smiling easily at a warm gaze and letting lips lounge in fingers of fire are the glimpses of Heaven that surge the soul, Jenna."

"There is nothing wrong with wanting to be warm and inviting," echoes Tucker.

"Or wanting to feel magical," utters Roy with a smile. "Do you know that a shoulder rub trembles me with anticipation? Yes! It is a fight to keep myself together!"

"I don't want to pretend any longer what my feelings are," I whisper.

Tucker inches closer to me, his breath caressing my face. "Tell us what you are feeling."

"Yes," chimes Roy, leaning in toward me. "You have me quaking with anticipation."

My lips tremble. "I am lounging outside of myself, feeling feelings that are weird and wonderful. I guess I'm trying to listen to what the butterflies in my tummy are trying to say."

Tucker hunches forward. "Those butterflies have roaming hands."

Roy grins. "Humankind has roaming hands."

"Roaming hands drop us back on our pillows with panting breaths," chuckles Tucker.

"They tug at the edges of our mind with their pleasing presence," chimes Roy.

"Roaming hands trail a path of fire that heats the body," whispers Tucker. "Roaming hands cause us to moan into a kiss and gasp for air." He pauses. "The world would be a better place if humankind would just soak in a warm embrace."

Nervously I fidget with my napkin. "Perhaps, I have gone a bit overboard with my morals."

"It sounds as if you are caught between desire and fear or perhaps you are caught between reality and illusion," says Tucker.

"I think I am a tangle of loose ends overpowered by logic," I voice.

"Could be," says Roy stroking his chin.

"But my energy surges when I talk about passion. The wall of emptiness around me crumbles," I say, happily.

"It is astonishing how much of a presence emptiness has," utters Tucker with a far-away look. "It screams softly, mutes the air and makes us feel aweless. The ghost of hollowness wanders over us all."

"No magic wand can make the ghost of hollowness disappear either. It is full of frightening images," chides Roy. "To me it is a bloodthirsty eagle sprouting its wings. Jen, I am unapologetic. I am a complex man who has an insatiable appetite for life. Emptiness is my weakness. It marks my quick ascension as a frightened human being."

"Fear makes us human," says Tucker.

"We are all filled with troubling doubts," clamors Roy.

"I want to thank you both for telling me to jump into life and for being my friends," I say letting out an audible sniffle.

"Jenna, let life brush your ear. No matter how bizarre your pursuit may seem, you must go for it," says Tucker. "Touch life in its entirety, Jenna. May your roaming hands curl in the golden hair of the sun."

I tingle.

"You see, Jenna, too often we live our life in the journey of other people and their conflicting interests, and we forget about our own cravings. You are ready to raise your hemline and detour," says Roy reaching across the table for the check.

Tucker leans toward me. "The world is shrouded in secrecy," he says under his breath. "Be wary of flower-lined lawns and plumed mannequins garbed in trickery's attire. Desperate people make up deception's fabric."

I shiver.

"Okay people, it's time for me to start yakking on the phone," chimes Roy. "Jen, we'll do the paperwork at another time regarding your leave. I'll see you Friday night," he says, looking at the check.

"Yeah, I'll take you, Jenna," chuckles Tucker. "We can duck out early if they run out of food."

"Don't worry! There will be a well-stocked bar and buffet," says Roy.

"Jenna, I'll walk you back to the studio. I've got to get back to work," Tucker says, putting on his coat. "Hey, Roy, don't I owe you twenty bucks?"

"What?" Roy exclaims.

"I owe you twenty bucks, right?"

"Hey man, don't worry about it," says Roy. "I hardly remembered."

"You sure?" asks Tucker.

"Yeah, don't give it a second thought."

I look at Roy and smile.

Tucker grabs my umbrella. "Is this yours, Jenna?"

"Yes," I answer, embarrassed.

"You really should get a new one. The world is full of colorful umbrellas. They are a vibrant display of life's brilliant performances."

I cock my head.

"Life watchers huddle beneath umbrellas," he chuckles.

"And under the hoods of rain coats," scoffs Roy.

Tucker grins. "These are definitely umbrella days, Jenna."

My cheeks redden as I slide out of the booth after him and we duck outside into the trickle of people splashing the boulevard. Shrieking winds blow my hair as I scoot under Tucker's umbrella.

"Man, this is a cold wind," he says, turning up his coat collar. "This is an L.A. blizzard! I'd give anything to see the orange ball of the sun set into the sea."

My teeth chatter as he pulls me close. "Oh look," he points, "there is Troy Robbins, in set design, trudging up the boulevard. I can't stand the guy. He is so animated. Let me give him a taste of his own medicine." Tucker waves his arms wildly. "Hey Troy," he shouts, "wait up! Can you lend me twenty bucks?"

Troy covers his ears as if trying to concentrate but is too far away to hear.

"Will you look at that? He's got an excellent sense of hearing. He's just faking it because he doesn't want to lend me twenty bucks! I'll get it from him though," he chuckles. "Where are you off to?" shouts Tucker.

"I'm headed over to Jerico's to dry out with some hot coffee. I hear the place is gossip-lit!"

"See, I told you he could hear me, Jenna. He's just a cheap wad!"

He grabs my hand. "Remember, Jenna, the whisper of passion is chest-thumping. Wriggling out of reality's grasp is what keeps humankind breathing." He flashes a smile. "Can you make it back to the studio yourself?"

"Yes. I'll be alright."

"Good because I've got to get that twenty!" Winking at me, he takes off along the boulevard to catch up with Troy.

I watch him disappear into his designer raincoat. Soon he becomes nothing more than a black blob fading away in the dark afternoon sky.

Breathing in the moment, a whisk of wind nudges me and I wink my eye to the clouds. "Quite a flame you have there," whispers the wind. My eyelashes flutter. "You must be a dream chaser," it teasingly suggests. A tender kiss of pink blushes my cheeks. "Perhaps, I'll paint my toes tonight," I muse, dancing in the rain.

Temptation knocks on my door
And I answer in clothes that purr.

Chapter 7

The Sensual Genie

As the last remnants of the storm eerily vanish, there is nothing behind but blackness. There is no moon and not a single star hanging out in the heavens. Everything seems desolate and abandoned. Like moths to a flame, beams of headlights pour toward me. I have been driving for hours. Pressing my nose against the glass of life, I am an impassioned enthusiast thirsting for adventure.

They have appeared in a period of upheaval, these thoughts of mine. They are startling, even shocking, at times. In a series of exhibitions they have virtually reinvented my sensibility, and I am a woman changed and redefined. A sizzling rush excites me as anticipation throws yet another log on my fiery breaths. I squeeze the moment. Indeed, these are atypical times. The fuse of passion has been lit, and in a plume of smoke the sensual genie within me appears.

"You rang?" it asks me knowingly.

"Who are you?" I innocently ask.

"Why, I am your sensual genie. I am a conductor of tremendous mystique."

Stilted by earnestness I query, "Are you a wizard?"

"Why? Are you looking for a ticket to happiness?"

"Is that the unthinkable?" I ask.

"Cling to the spirit of your determination and you will find your answer."

"Who are you?" I ask again.

"I vibrate through your riveting body. You know, I am dazzlingly skilled. I am inventive and sexy! I am red satin sheets and lilac-scented bath water. I am candles burning amidst the moans of delightful pleasure. I am a deep gaze and a close whisper. I am a haunting dream and a secret caress. I am thrusting nudity and wet dreams of wild fantasy." The sensual genie draws in a deep breath. "I am ecstasy ravishing your wetness. And there is more."

"Oh wow," I blurt. "More?"

"I am bred for my skills in magic. I cast hot, ecstatic spells that evoke a seducing world. Now, who are you?"

"Well, I am a timid woman with burning ambitions and I am on an enchanting exploration."

"Do tell," says the sensual genie.

"Am I officially insane?"

"No, on the contrary, you are erotically alive!"

"I am erotically alive? Me? I have never considered myself erotic!" I smile for a moment. "You see, I am about to pursue passion. I am taking a leave from my job to do so. I must sound like a woozy grab bag of ideas."

"I don't see you as a carnival spectacle."

"Thank goodness," I say, smiling.

"But I do find you earnest and obscure! Yet it is these qualities that make you an invisible celebrity in the theater of humankind."

"Are you my applauding audience?" I ask.

"You know that I am! My dear, there is always an impulse to free ourselves from endless commitments. It is part of life's lusty ballad! But to do so is quite tricky. Have you laid out the consequences of your pursuit?"

"Yes, to some degree. If I think about it too much, I will lose my nerve to do it. I am filled with an intoxicating feeling of flight, but I am confused. You see, I don't have a vivid understanding of the passionate world."

"Slow down."
"I have utopian visions."
"Slow down."
"I want to be wild."
"Do tell!"
"Sensual genie, please tell me what passion is. I think I need to get things sorted out," I say, wiping a tear from my eye.
The sensual genie smiles tenderly. "It is okay to cry."
"Sometimes, I feel like crying because there is so much emotion in me. Am I a lunatic?"
"No! It is okay to take a walk on your wild side."
"It is?" I ask
"Yes, it is."
"Is it an insanity ride?"
"It can be, but it is part of life's irresistible softness."
I look down. "Tell me about passion," I whisper.
"Passion illuminates a dark night. It is blowing kisses and pleasure dancing. It swirls around you like a phantom caressing the air. And when you are touched by it there is a twang in your heart and a smile on your face."
"Tell me more!"
"Passion is hot glances and licks behind the ear. It is plopping down on the couch and neck smooching!"
"Well, I do believe I am rapturously stirred," I whisper. "I really don't know this world. I haven't ever felt passion before, but it is on my wish list. Actually it is my secret crush," I say, covering my mouth with embarrassment.
"Why not let your secret out?"
"Oh, I could never do that."
"Why?"
"I'm too shy."
"You must not hide from your being."
"I can't help myself. I tend to hold back."
"There is nothing wrong with being fun-loving."

"And rapturous?" I ask.

"And rapturous! Let your lips smolder!"

"How will I really know when I am impassioned?"

"The first thing that goes is your common sense."

"And then?" I ask.

"All notions of time and space disappear."

"Anything else?"

"You are motivated to smile more."

I blush. "Will I really smile more?"

"A smile will just appear on your face for no reason. Life feels good when you are under the spell of fire. You are fun and lighthearted and playful."

"Wow!" I exclaim.

"Passion is billowing curtains and ocean breezes."

"And lace flowing?" I timidly ask.

"Yes! And whispers of soft insistence!"

"And fiery eyes meeting across a crowded room!"

"Yes! And tasting balms," breathes the sensual genie.

"And scented warming oils?" I ask, blushing.

"And orchid crystals! And rose bath petals!"

"And edible body dust," I whisper, my hand covering my mouth.

"You are full of seductive power," says the sensual genie.

"Me?"

"In the predawn, your body is still warm. You are glistening. Your softness illuminates you as you pull the covers up under your chin. You stretch out and curl your toes. You yawn. And then, with tender conscience you start thinking about the world and you realize that you are tired of being sensible."

"You know me well."

"Toiling in your frosty soul you become an accepting human being, thinking that you cannot change. But I have a question for you."

"Yes?"

"Don't you mind being frigid?"

"I want to heat. What is wrong with me?"

"You are tired of living by your own rules."

I sigh. "Is there no escape?"

"Fall back in pleasure. Within you are exceptional finds."

"How do I frolic in enchantment?"

"Undress erotically in my sacred court."

"How do I do that?"

"Feel the lips of life undress you. Let featherlight kisses flush your toes pink! Beckon the sumptuous air to lick the corners of your smile! Greet the smooch behind your knee! Leaning up on the balls of your feet, raise your shoulder, tilt your head, and tingle from the tongue running along the edge of your ear. Only after you undress erotically in my sacred court can you greet the wild beast!"

I gulp. "The wild beast!"

"The wild beast whips up clouds of euphoria."

"I want to know more about the wild beast," I say, tapping my foot impatiently.

"Are your sure?" asks the sensual genie. "The wild beast is magnificently stimulating and utterly exhausting."

"Tell me how I meet the wild beast!"

"For you to meet the wild beast you must first become a sizzling woman."

"Oh, I don't know. I'm afraid to let loose. I am ready to attend passion's feast, but I am so damn shy."

"Pull up a chair for passion, Jenna. Take your apron off and dine!"

I tingle.

"You have become a hurried soul caught up in the concrete jungle. You have spent time where you feel safe. You have a closed in spirit."

"Perhaps at some later time I can hunger."

"You must relax your values today, my dear. Slipping casually out of your morals will enable you to feel your human inferno."

"Today?" I ask. "Isn't that rather sudden?"

"You know, Jenna, at some point you will become a woman who can do nothing more than just fantasize."

"But, I can't just 'poof' myself out of my values."

"You also cannot make love on an ice bed."

"What do I do?"

"Invite your lifeless spirit to a party full of emotions."

"How do I do that?"

"Lift your morals with throw pillows and burning candles. Fall limp in passion's arms and be carried away. Do not try to tame the wild beast within you, Jenna. In you is the heat of an unrelenting sun. Now fall upon my analytic couch and tell me of your intimate confessions."

I gulp. "So, you know I have intimate confessions?"

"Yes. You can express them to me with exhilarating freedom."

I bite my trembling lip. "I don't know. I'm rather shy about them."

"Do you know your dimples show when you do that?" asks the sensual genie.

"I think I've been told that."

"Tell me your intimate confessions."

"I fantasize."

"Do you now? Tell me a few of them."

"Oh goodness, I don't know if I can."

"You can."

"My heart is racing."

"Breathe!"

"I'm so nervous."

"I'm a tender audience."

"Well, I see myself swirling around in a revealing red dress. I feel sexy and very precious."

"Do tell," says the sensual genie. "What does it look like?"

"It is ruffled and very short."

"And the neckline?" asks the sensual genie.

"It is deeply cut and plunging."

"I've had a few of those. Any feathers and flowers attached?"

"Oh no," I say, giggling nervously.

"Oh, well, I've had a few of those too," she chuckles. "Are your shoes skinny and high-heeled?"

"I am barefoot, but my toes are painted. And I am standing very close to the edge of a cliff. I am leaning over and, somehow, my tiny little breasts are plunging out of my neckline! I look down into a sea of blue. It is beautiful and I am trying to take a picture of the ocean. The wind gusts and blows up my skirt. I'm wearing lace."

The sensual genie grins. "Lace is nice."

"There is more," I whisper.

"Do tell," says the sensual genie, cupping an ear.

"I am in bed, lingerie-clad. My heart is racing. I look up and see my image in a mirrored ceiling."

"You are an alluring vision, I take it."

"I am irresistibly attractive."

"Do you look like pin-up imagery?"

"Yes," I whisper blushingly.

"So you look tantalizing?"

"Yes, almost erotic."

"Goodness," exclaims the sensual genie.

My cheeks redden. "I'm good at fantasizing!"

"You can say those words without blushing. No need for your cheeks to redden."

I smile. "My fantasies offer me steamy kisses."

"In your existence you must wrap your hand behind life's neck and capture its lips."

I gulp. "Is it human for one's eyes to hungrily hunt for passion?" I ask.

"It is human to become a fire breather."

"Do I have the courage?"

"You must find the courage."

"I don't know. It just may not exist within me."

"Jenna, your aches must flutter."

"In my fantasies, I soak in palm-oil groves and comb red glowing sand from my hair."

"Are you wearing skinny leggings under flared cloth?"

"I am wearing opaque tights and ankle boots."

"Nice," says the sensual genie.

"In my fantasies, I am jewel tones and jet beads. I am a goddess gown of siren red and a body suit with leather booties. In my fantasies, I am golden shoulder loops and wide-eyed belts. And I am a bubble hem of tantalizing surprise."

"Your fantasies flutter quite a ravishing oasis. Allow reality to do the same."

I drop my voice to a whisper. "In my madness, I descend a long winding staircase of eternal pleasures. Every step becomes more enticing. A slight breeze blows my sheer curtains. Fingers lightly trace my burning lips. A light kiss falls on the small of my back. Goose bumps rise upon my skin. In my fantasies, I close my curtains on a sleepy world."

"Our fantasies are always extraordinary. They tingle away our numbness."

"Why is that?" I ask.

"Fantasizing picks up the pace of life. It is our personal freedom."

"I love my personal freedom."

"Become one with your erotic nature."

"I am afraid of my erotic nature."

"Don't be. It is exotic and beautiful. Let it suckle your skin."

I shiver. "I have another intimate confession. I want to shimmy."

"You what?" asks the sensual genie.

"I want to shimmy. I want to wear a sequined minidress, get on the dance floor and shake my body. And I want people to whistle and think I'm sexy!"

"Oh my word!"

"There is more," I whisper. "I want to blow kisses."

"That is quite thought-provoking, coming from someone who pauses at the barest hesitation."

I blush.

"It sounds as if you are ready to come out of stay-in-cave school."

"Yes. I am."

"But you are a bit ill at ease."

"I am crashing in the clouds."

"Well, you are wrestling with thoughts that are attacking your taboos."

"Will I always crash in the clouds?"

"Maybe," replies the sensual genie.

"Why is that?" I ask.

"As human beings we are forever changing."

"Is that why I keep contradicting myself?"

"Contradiction keeps us interested in what we do."

"Must we always exercise good judgment?"

"Why do you ask?"

"Frantically, I search for lust. I find it and quickly slide up to its ear. Lingering for a few moments, my ragged breaths meet its burning lips. Its lashes tickle my cheekbones. It stares at my bed. I pull back the sizzling sheets. My lacy pillows drop aimlessly onto the floor." I lower my voice. "Lust slides over my shoulders, drawing me close. Inviting against my body, my back arches as its tongue glides easily over my closed eyes. Grinning insanely, I slide its eager hands underneath my shirt and my passionless legend dies."

The sensual genie nods. "It is easy to be lured."

"In my fantasies, I am hotly breathed upon."

"There is anticipation in being ravished."

"My fantasies have me emotionally suspended in my own disbelief. I am immersed in excitement!"

"In your fantasies you don't resist the tug of promiscuity. You allow yourself to feel."

"Sensual genie, please tell me the difference between love and passion."

"Love is created with vision. Passion is created between two people. We make love part of our identity. Passion immerses our identity. Love notices us. We notice passion. Passion awakens us, Jenna. We sleep with love."

"I want to be awakened," I whisper.

"Allow a warm tight arm around your waist."

"Will that open my essence to sensual empowerment?" I ask.

"Well, let us just say that it will invite warm breezes to swirl your body."

I shiver.

"You are in a tug of wills, Jenna. You are creating a world that you really cannot imagine yourself in."

"I am afraid."

"Fear is a coy charmer, my dear. It will tuck you into bed at night and greet you in the morning if you let it."

"It certainly has a way of scaring the daylights out of me."

"Jenna you must embrace your erotic spirit. If you don't, you will remain a seductive mermaid forever. And even the fantasies you claim will be nonexistent."

"I feel absent in my life."

"Well of course! You dismiss yourself so easily."

"I want to smile at warm feelings."

"To smile at warm feelings, you must grapple out of your flannels and stop blowing on your hands to keep them warm. Life is about feeling hot breaths upon your neck. It is about tickles in your ear, kissing dimples and counting the freckles across the nose you have just pecked. Your dream is simple. But you must ease up on your hesitations. You must take a spin above your soul."

"I want to feel a soul-shattering kiss."

"Put your arms around life, Jenna. You are too strict with yourself. I have noticed this for a long time now. You wake up focused. From first light you shuffle to the coffee maker. From then on, every sight and sound is blended into your regimen. You stand before the bathroom mirror, brush your teeth, twist the cap back on the toothpaste, always squeezing the tube in the middle."

"Yes, that's me."

"Then it is off to your hot shower with soap on a rope and your herbal shampoo. After emerging from your soft spray, you reach for your business suit and dry your damp hair. With a quick dust of fragrance you throw on your heels and you are off to the world. Backing out of the driveway you stop, put the car in park and check to see if you have locked the front door. Turning the knob twice you are once again off to join the daily grind. You need to tear off your bra and be kissed by a hero!"

I gulp. "I've got another intimate confession."

The sensual genie purses her lips.

"I want soaring moments."

"Don't we all, my dear?"

I lower my voice. "But I want them to last."

"Oh my," says the sensual genie. "I am a million miles into you."

"I want to illuminate the night with warm cheeks."

The sensual genie gasps. "You are filled with walls of wishes."

"I want stand-out moments."

"Tell me more."

"I want to feel the hot rise of ecstasy."

The sensual genie wipes her brow. “Wouldn’t it be nice if we could bottle the tingle of excitement? Then perhaps, we could dab it behind our ears, rub a bit of it on our wrists, and trickle a few drops of it down our tummy.”

“I would powder my nose with it,” I say, blushing.

The sensual genie grins. “I believe there is rebel in you!”

“How do I get frisky?”

“You must step out of your comfort zone.”

“How do I do that?”

“First stop looking for the glaring holes of logic. You must change your ways. Enjoy an apricot martini under a hairdryer while pampering your hands and feet in a bubbly soak of chocolate sprinkles.”

“I am not one for chocolate.”

The sensual genie groans. “It is not just about white T-shirts and lapel pins. There is more to life than your terrycloth robe and fuzzy bed slippers. Get frisky and you will no longer have to log into your dreams.”

I bite my lip.

“Next you must give attention to your trembling thighs. It will help you confirm some sign of life in your being. Allow the ecstasy in your body to burn. Are you angry at love by the way?”

“No.”

“Well, you do have a brooding eye.”

“I just don’t think it’s all that it’s cracked up to be.”

“You have been loved but you have not allowed yourself to love. You have made love lifeless. Bare your skin! Retreating souls sleep in an icy peace.”

“I have been climbing into a bed of chilly sheets most of my life. How do I heat the sheets?”

“Climb into bed with your sensual spirit.”

“Are you my sensual spirit?” I whisper.

“I am a bed of playful lips covered in rose petals under a quilt on a cold winter day. I am the moans of a warm embrace, the smooch that warms your thighs, the sweet kiss that shivers your breath and the devilish smile that rolls you on your back and cuddles you up in your morning yawn. Really, I am the dreamy glimpse of your essence!"

"Can I explore intimacy with you?" I whisper.

"My job is to watch your steam rise."

"You have quite a rapturous job."

"I wouldn't trade being sensual for the world. Feel the soap bubble against your soft skin from a shimmering bubble bath. Caress the water with your fingertips. Allow your life to be lit by scented oils. And then, in an aura of calm, curve your body in soft affections and let pleasure rock your senses."

I gulp.

"You are a delicate balance of femininity. You are the image of a sensual goddess. Unleash the sensual powers you hold in your hands. The wonders of life are upon you!"

I lick my lips.

"Lean provocatively on life! Kiss the eyes of anticipation! Curtsey to the caress of pleasure! Hiding your feelings has you stuck in the lab of life."

"How do I free myself?"

"Let your fingertips smooth over the lips of the sun."

I gasp. "You mean, feel the lips of the sun? It isn't in me."

The sensual genie's eyes twinkle. "Enchantment is within the real world but to glimpse it you must allow life to touch your soul."

"How do I get lost in the magic?"

"Let a smile play on your lips!"

"What casts enchantment?"

"A spell of enchantment can be a mischievous grin or a polite smile. It can be dark goddess eyes, a piercing gaze and long fluttering lashes. A wink, a nudge, and a tickle can be magical if you are wildly imaginative!" The sensual genie rounds her mouth. A puff of steam radiates from her lips. "Enchantment can be pure thought shrouded in a shadow of silvery mist."

I cock my head.

"To live is to have one foot in fantasy."

"I would like to explore your spirit more deeply," I whisper. "I'd like to hug you tighter."

"I am with you always."

"This has been quite a revealing exchange."

"It has been my pleasure. Now, I need to leave you for a while."

"Leave me? Where are you going?" I ask.

"Your libido is paging you. Will you answer?"

I gulp. "My libido?"

"You will remember this time of discovery. I will be watching you with great curiosity."

And then, rubbing temptation together, the sensual genie vanishes in a blaze of rapturous smoke, and I am carted off elsewhere.

Laughing behind reality's back,
I giggle with pleasure at my
imagination.

Chapter 8

Enter: The Wild Beast

"Usually the office is bursting but today I gave everyone the day off. You are quite an exceptional case, Weyburn. Please have a seat."

I look around at the tastefully furnished office. A round, blonde wooden table dominates a room that hardly reveals any flaws, and I feel almost inferior dressed in my casual fleece attire. Although the space is nicely decorated, I notice there are no distinguishing features, save for the one wall covered with small index-card files, which I eye inquisitively. "I have definitely been drawn away from my daydreams," I think, as I sit down in a curiously anesthetized fashion. Yes, something exciting is slowly making itself known underfoot. Could it be the sensual pleasure of harmony? He sees me looking at the red flowers that elegantly grace his desk.

"Those voluptuous flowers are called 'burning lips,'" he says.

"They are lovely," I voice, crossing my legs.

Reclining in his chair, the wild beast loosens his tie. He props his gray tasseled loafers on the desk. He has a glass of wine in his hand. "I have to learn to wear more comfortable shoes when I'm working," he chuckles. His ginger-colored hair contrasts pleasantly with his charcoal gray business suit and well-tanned skin. His white shirt and red tie somehow further accentuate his confident demeanor. He pushes his wired-rimmed glasses back up on his nose. They slide down again. "I just left a meeting with the Board of Directors. It was an extended ride through steep budget deficits and significant cutbacks. It was not a pleasant experience. In no uncertain terms, I was told to get rid of dead weight."

I gulp.

"It is a hazy day outside today," he says looking through his office window. "The palm trees are etched against the fog." He yawns. "I'm glad it finally stopped raining. I am tired of storm-drenched afternoons. I am lusting for hot sunny days that are bright enough to make me squint. I could live in Seattle if I craved damp weather. Did you notice yesterday how the clouds parted like a stage curtain?"

I shrug.

"You need to watch more for life's vibrancy, Weyburn. In terms of your sprit, you are just breathing dead air. Is it too daunting of a task for you to take a few deep rosy breaths?"

I attempt to say something, but nothing comes out.

The wild beast looks impatiently at his watch. "I want you to know Weyburn, I'm going to be late for my foot soak."

"I'm sorry."

"How do you soothe your tired body?"

I shrug.

"A bubbly whirlpool scattered with rose petals would be an appropriate answer."

"It would?"

"There is no hope for you, Weyburn."

My shoulders sag. "What am I to do?"

"There's only one way to disarm you."

"Tell me, please."

"How about casting a vote for inventiveness over control?"

"What do you mean?"

"Well, for starters you must laugh easily between sips of frothy cappuccino. Do you think you can give that a try?"

I sigh.

"Secondly, you must embark on an accelerated road of flirtation."

I gasp.

"Am I losing you, Weyburn?"

"No, I am still here," I groan.

"Next you must succumb to temptation."

"Temptation?" I ask, wiping my brow.

"It is time for you to hear your reckless voice."

"But what if I don't have the right rhythms or the right climaxes?"

"Insecurity will always occupy a frightening time in your life, but make it brief. Powerful, seductive forces are on your side. You are a sexual creature."

"I am?"

"Stop gasping in amazement, Weyburn. Now, I hear you have been talking about heat quite a bit lately. Being passionate is your ticket into the voluptuous world."

I gulp. "That's where the problem starts."

"Well, we specialize in that here. We are full of electrifying adventure. I do see you as saintly and sensitive. You seem to marvel at the complexity of everything. May I suggest to you some soothing cinnamon candles?"

"I admit there are gaps in my life."

The wild beast holds nothing back. "You are deeply rational. And that alone is a disturbing image. I suggest a fragrant potpourri in your bedroom for starters."

I look down.

"My department is not one of quiet contemplation. We give startling meaning to the notion of special effects.

Some just blend in here, others dazzle the department and others get booted. Of course every department can use fixing. We all have our own savory opinions and self-interests, but apathy is something we will not tolerate." He bangs the desk with his fist. "Personally, I burn hotly, like a fire out of control! But you, Weyburn, are riddled with apathy. Why, you've never shown an interest in any of our festivities. We are out for satisfied silence."

My cheeks flush.

"Weyburn, the sexual elements of life are pronounced here. Are you ready to indulge in some of your own curiosity?"

"Well, one moment I am ready to launch myself free and feel my hot image and then I get scared," I say, rubbing my temples.

The wild beast grins. "It is not your body arguing."

"Yes, I know."

"It is a sensual world of freshly tossed flowers and candle-lit windows."

I swallow hard.

"You are tucked into folds of black clouds, Weyburn. You need to spiral in the world of unhooked loop fasteners and open buttons." The wild beast winks. "Playing with zippers is fun! It is a luminously naked world."

I rub my forehead.

"You have a kind of virgin sensual aloofness about you, Weyburn. I'll bet you would look beautiful drenched in satin."

I tremble.

The wild beast lets out a deep sigh of exasperation and turns business-like. "We have heard about your proposed excursion."

"I am on a quest for fire."

"What brought about your adventuresome streak?"

"A few moments of open-eyed reflection convinced me that I am fantasy-based."

"Yes, well that is all fine and good, but after reviewing your file, I cannot help but feel you are only tempted to indulge in magical thinking."

I frown. "I want more."

"You are all talk. You are astonishingly talented at gibbering nonsense."

"I guess I am afraid to chase my dreams."

"Weyburn, have you ever thought about blowing upon a rose?"

I bite my trembling lip.

"Have you ever thought about heating up cool satin sheets? Aren't you tired of waking up in an empty bed to the boring details of everyday life?"

I sigh.

"This is why you are getting kicked out. You won't allow yourself to feel life's swirling embrace."

"I suppose my boring image is one that I have never been able to shake."

"Well, you are hardly thrilling."

"How do I change?"

"Well, for starters, you can get rid of your organically grown cottons."

"Oh goodness," I moan.

"Look Weyburn, do you have listening ability? There is more to life than the sound of your coffee percolating. You must believe in magical moments."

"What do I do?"

The wild beast frowns. "You are an emotional loafer. So, how can you be wild and crazy in bed?"

I throw my hands up in the air. "I don't know," I wail.

"Consider becoming a rapturous spectacle!"

"Oh wow!" I blurt.

"Stop looking at life with disinterested glances. I believe there is more to you."

"You do?"

"Yes. I see your toes being gently pulled in a mist of fragranced candles. Warm oil drips in between them and you are immersed in the soothing sensation. You put a glass of wine to your lips and I see you gazing in ecstasy for the next three thousand years. Do not resist the primal rumblings that emanate within you. Do you know you have pillowy lips?"

"Me?"

"Yes. I believe you have an eye for folly."

"Well, I do dream of wearing low-slung jeans."

"There is hope for you yet. The problem is you just refuse to take your provocative thinking seriously."

I grimace.

"Weyburn, you need to ferry across the sun!"

I gulp. "I have an intimate confession."

The wild beast opens his arms. "Welcome to my nurturing abode."

"I want to quiver."

"Ah, you want the gift of wild passion," chuckles the wild beast.

"Yes," I whisper.

"You know that passion makes an utterly exhausting companion."

"Yes, I've heard. And I suppose I have come to you at a particularly awkward time in my life."

"Perhaps, I am your destination. Do you think you're sexy?"

"No."

"I can see that. You wince at the description."

"I don't mean to."

"Listen to me Weyburn, your traditional being is a disturbing image. Temptation is not dead," bellows the wild beast. "I'll have you know we overflow with piercing emotion here!"

"Yes, I know."

"You realize, at this rate you will hardly be able to live a hot, lively tale." The wild beast licks his lips. "I'm going to get straight to the bottom line. The moon separates from the Earth here, Weyburn."

"Yes," I say, feeling my stomach tighten.

"I was hesitant to summon you because, in all honesty, you seem to be well beyond hope. We get bleak cases like you here from time to time. Of course we are not always flanked by a chorus line of dancers wearing feathers. We do have our dignity. I personally can be both anxious and mellow. But let me tell you something. As a human being, you are quite dim."

I moan.

"Yes, Weyburn, talk about having nowhere to go but up! At this point I am obliged to inform you that as a hot, impassioned woman you have barely been noticed in life. As a matter of fact, after perusing your file, I don't see any connection whatsoever between you and your libido."

"Well I have emotionally kept my distance. I will admit that."

The wild beast is straight-faced. "This is why you face the nights alone."

I shake my head with despair.

"You can dab your lips with radiance but when it comes down to it, your reflection refuses to join the choir of lighthearted escapade. I am trying to be patient, but frankly, I can't believe how completely out of hand you really are. Why, I don't think you have to think back all that hard to know you have never frequented our department, not even once."

My eyes well up. "I can be intensely shy."

"I've noted that. But you've nearly forgotten us here."

"I guess rolling in ecstasy has just generally been an afterthought."

"Well, we are not sculptured with glue and patience here, you know."

"Yes, I know."

"Passion purrs deep within your slender throat. It rises and falls as you breathe." The wild beast pauses. "Passion is for the fearless, you know."

"Yes. I know," I say, rubbing my temples.

"Do you have a headache?" asks the wild beast.

"Yes. It feels as if someone is striking my head with a sledgehammer."

"Stress will do that, as well as curiosity."

I wince.

"Allow me to get you an aspirin and some water."

"Thank you," I murmur, massaging my temples.

"We pitch paradise here, Weyburn," shouts the wild beast. He hands me an aspirin and a glass of water. "I don't think this is the place for you."

"But I want to shimmy." I say, downing the aspirin.

"You know, often people claim to revisit past lives," chuckles the wild beast. "I'm busy. Let's speed this up. I want to try to get some sleep tonight for a change."

"But I want to be ambitiously recast."

"Emerge from your emptiness, Weyburn."

"I have another intimate confession. I want to feel long, hot, breathless moments."

"So, you want to trade your trembling soul in for the heat of the phantom!"

I blush.

"Are you telling me you are tired of your fall-asleep-on-the-couch dreams?"

"Maybe," I say, still crimson.

"And you want a break from life-as-usual?" The wild beast pauses. "Yes. I know. The tyranny of everyday existence takes over. I've heard it thousands of times. So can we rightfully assume you are on the prowl?"

I let out a quiet sigh.

"I can't hear you. Are you ready to romp or not?"

"Yes," I whisper.

"Weyburn, we have wide-ranging offerings here. Now, we don't sin at every corner, I'll have you know, but we are sexually gifted. We make the past swirl and the present glow. We breathe fire into our future! We are tantalizing and inventive. Passion is quite astonishing. And you have a bright, toothy smile and a sweet, innocent demeanor. We could be a wild combination! Too bad we can't make it work."

A groan escapes my lips.

"Lighten up, Weyburn! Damn, we are radically different from you. You are always looking for signs of life. May I suggest you shut your tired eyes and squint into the light of your soul? My goodness, Weyburn! You have slipped passion into the shrunken pockets of your being. Why not let your dress strap slip off your dainty shoulder as you smooch across a glittery dance floor? Why not become a ruffle-edged, laced-up glint-radiating woman? Have you ever even considered it?"

I wipe my brow.

"Perhaps you should start out by toweling off your body and slipping into a soft negligee."

I let out a deep sigh.

"Do you know keeping your lips kissably soft is what gives life that reassuring grin?"

"I guess I have let myself get caught in the rifts of time."

"You have effectively avoided any madness with lust. It is such a pity. You could be such a promising player! You boil over with possibility!"

"Me?"

"Yes! You! Surprised?"

"I am tossed about by the thought."

"My department is not fixed on frigidness, Weyburn. We slide our hands upon thighs here. We suck in gulps of air with ragged breaths. Do you know you have fluttering eyelashes?"

I bite my lip.

"You are soft with peaceful qualities. We are hot-blooded and our colors are bold. We embrace fantasy. We straddle the sun, Weyburn. I don't see you fitting in here. I'm sorry."

I groan.

"Have you ever considered wearing a slinky, low-cut dress with a neckline to your navel and slit up to your hip?"

"What?" I exclaim, turning red.

"I rest my case."

"I can change."

"I don't think so. You are white cottons and buttoned-up argyle."

"I can change," I repeat.

"Can you be strapless lace and wild mesh?"

I blush.

"We are heat flooded. We may crack an eyelid and peer bleary-eyed at the offending clock-radio alarm, but it is all for good reason."

"Good reason?" I gulp.

"Yes. I don't know anyone in the world that minds rising with a passion-hangover! Nuzzling your face in your lover's belly is a life-altering experience." The wild beast pauses. "You know, a flowing satin robe would do you a world of good."

I swallow hard. "Are you my amoral accomplice?"

"I am not some drooling tiger but I do have an impatient body. I am wild-hearted. I purr ecstatically. Life is a seductive party!"

"How do I get invited?" I ask, softly.

"First, you must feel the rosy glow of your dreams. Can you do that?"

"I don't know," I mumble.

"Weyburn, are you afraid hot sex will make you dreamy-eyed?"

I sigh.

"You are in a class by yourself."

"I am ready to veer off the yawning road of life," I blubber.

"Well, perhaps there is a small ray of hope for you." He hands me a tissue.

I dab at my nose. "I'm longing to meet the wild beast! Can you introduce us?"

"Impossible!"

"Why?" I ask, solemnly.

"You are not ready."

My eyes well up.

"You are a lifeless entity. Your kind is an insult to this department. Why you have shut off your erotic fumes. You, Weyburn, have made yourself a nonbeing."

"How can I feel my human inferno?"

"By not being stingy with your treasures," laughs the wild beast.

"I don't understand. What am I to do?"

"Well, for starters you can stop trying to stomp out your heat."

"And how do I do that?"

"Shake hands with Bravery!"

"What?" I sheepishly ask.

"I need to make a call," he says, leaving the room and I am left hyperventilating in a world I don't belong in.

"You know, I almost got laughed off the phone," says the wild beast, reappearing. "You are quite unique. I'll say that for you. Bravery will be here shortly."

She had been lurking in the doorway. I didn't even know she was there. You could hear a pin drop as she entered the room. Complete with vintage spectacles propped askew on her distinct nose, her hair is pulled on top of her head in a bun. She is hardly rendered glamorous.

The wild beast and Bravery exchange furtive glances as they talk off to the side.

"I'm sorry to summon you this late in the day. Thanks for standing by," says the wild beast in a muffled tone. "I had the feeling I was going to need you."

"Not a problem," assures Bravery. "It sounds like quite an exceptional case you have going on here."

"Yes," says the wild beast. He puts his hand over his mouth in an effort to further muffle his words. I cup my ear.

"It is about craving for life's sultry tale, but that is as far as it goes," he says in a hush. "You know the fear-factor thing. I rarely discuss the specifics of a case outside of my department, but I'm sure you'll agree this case presents exceptional circumstances. However, she does have quite a few pages of imagination to her file. She is not completely hopeless. At least she is not superficial. We would really have a problem then. She really wants to be passionate. I'll leave it up to you."

"Nothing I can't handle," chortles Bravery, making her way toward me.

"So, I hear there is a lot inhabiting your mind these days." She rests her leather briefcase on the desk. "I hear that you are on a quest for fire."

I nod and rise.

"Oh no, please remain seated," she says.

"I'm sorry but I haven't met you before. You are quite unique to my character. Do you come with dangerous ideas?"

She steps back for a moment and curiously studies me. “You didn’t exaggerate about her at all,” she chides under her breath to the wild beast. “She is quite a handful.”

“I told you. It is another timid case of personal uprising. I will leave you two alone to get acquainted.”

Bravery casually leans on the edge of the desk. “So I hear you are ready to feel the Earth tremble.”

I giggle with embarrassment. “Word travels fast.”

“Yes, it does.”

“I’m scared.”

Bravery opens her briefcase and takes out a small spiral notepad and pen. “If there was no fear, I wouldn’t have a job,” she chortles. “I might be able to help you.”

“Really?”

“Yes. I want you to see the world with fresh and fearless eyes. It is my job. Now, I’ve got word that you are interested in firing up your libido.”

“Well, I am on an erotic pursuit.”

“I see. Well, modern life does have its challenges. Do you want to feel as if you are a French film?”

“Goodness no,” I say, blushing. “I am not the type of person to douse in essential oils in a hot tub. I’m too bashful.”

“Well I’m here to shock you out of your complacency. It takes courage to admit fear.”

“I am filled with contradictory notions. They frighten me,” I exclaim.

Bravery is composed. “You can’t allow fear to derail your ambitions.”

“Yes,” I gulp. “But fear feels like my companion.”

“It will every time you grapple with the unfamiliar.”

“You make it all seem so simple.”

“Fear will direct your life if you let it.”

“But how do you stop it from doing so?”

“Think confident thoughts. Become a hot, vibrant woman! Have the courage to straddle the sun!”

I tingle.

Bravery flips open her notepad. "Now then, back to your lusting desires. I understand you want to shimmy."

"Goodness! Isn't anything sacred?"

"Is your face hidden in your fantasies?"

"No." I blush. "I readily show my inner feelings."

"What are you wearing when you shimmy?"

"Silver platform sandals and a fringed miniskirt."

"I see. Now you said you want to be erotically consumed. Can you comment on this?"

"The night closes in upon me. I close my eyes and let the darkness finger the loose strands of my rippling hair. I purr into the indescribable blush of emotion that is devouring me and wonder if I am a lunatic. And then, slowly, I become an impassioned woman ready to strike. Am I crazy?"

"We all go crazy when we kiss fire."

"I have an intimate confession."

Bravery pulls up a chair.

"I want my life to be a tantalizing fairytale."

"You know, with courage in your hip-pocket, the world is one of magical enchantment. It becomes a sensual paradise of quivering bodies, rushing lips and stunned senses. It is a place where panting breaths trail off into the curve of a shoulder."

"Wow," I blurt.

"Life swirls around you with delightful pleasures. But you step steadily back, your fear blocking you. A hint of warming oil touches the air and you inhale a vaporous whiff. Why, it's raining orange blossoms. Full of vibration, you reach for life's awe-filled moments and then disappear into a sky of oversized pillows." Bravery pauses. "Reach for the butterflies," she says, picking up her briefcase. "Life can be potent!"

I gasp. "You are not leaving? I need you."

"I'm with you always."

"Wait! I want to be an enchantress!"

"Breaking your rules will give you a thrill," she says, buzzing for the wild beast. "The world is full of feather ticklers and belly rings. Capture your magic, your mystery! Don't be afraid."

In the shadows of the room, he enters and offers her his hand. They speak of me as if I were not there. Tears well up in my eyes as I nervously wonder what is to come. They whisper softly. Bravery gestures to my vacant expression, and then in a murky veil of illusion she is gone.

The wild beast sits back in his chair and rubs his graying temples. "I have a few remaining questions."

I sit upright and rest my feet firmly on the floor.

"Will you kiss with the heat of passion?"

I wet my lips.

"Will you share your silken bed with burning lips?"

I shiver.

"Will you burst into flames?"

"Where do you come from?" I whisper.

"Why from inside your soul, of course."

Tears drop from my eyes.

The wild beast rises. He takes my hand. "Allow me to awaken you from your slumber. My touch reveals who I am."

"Yes," I moan.

"I am not your sage and soul."

"No," I gasp.

"I am far from it."

"Yes," I pant.

"I am your fire. Within my heated presence, the heat of your soul will rise. Your hair will be pasted on your forehead and your face will be flushed with delight. Soaked in sweat your body will carry enchantment upon its shoulders and quiver from the wetness you daub from your brows."

The wind catches the door to my essence. Whispers against my ear ripple. Lips tease the nape of my neck. I feel a tingle from below. "You are my wild beast," I breathe, curling my fingers into its heat.

"Our breaths have merged," pants the wild beast. "Get ready to ride the sun."

I reach into my closet of
inhibition.
It's another day of timid-ware.

Chapter 9
Frolicking Unicorns

"If stuffed potatoes and chicken wings are tempting, come on in!"

Anxiety powders my nose and flushes my cheeks as my eyes uneasily fix on the jubilant figure walking toward me. I turn and stare intently down the street one last time. My apprehension is overwhelming. Tucker Richmond is nowhere to be found, and for a moment my day flashes before me.

The morning had dawned bright although I was huddled down, waiting for the explosions. I was really jittery and relentlessly scanning the heavens for dark, swelling rain clouds. As a matter of fact I would have given anything for a bunch of thunderheads to barrage the sky and give me a rain-strafed day. But alas, L.A. was back fulfilling its weather commitment of sunny skies, and I was left compiling one hundred feeble excuses why I shouldn't attend Roy and Darcy's anniversary bash. And it was not as if the invitation came out of the blue either. It had been volleying back and forth in my mind for days. Yet it was among the chatter of noontime lunchers when the bombs went off and Tucker leaned over his wonton soup and said he would drive. I covered my ears.

"No need to salt your escape route, Jenna. I know conquering one's elements is not easy."

I nervously grinned. He knew me so well.

"We'll leave whenever you want," he told me, gulping down his iced tea. He spoke convincingly.

I experienced a few outbreaks of terror and then finally relented. "Am I going to carry an indelible memory of regret about this?" I asked him, only half jokingly.

Tucker chuckled. "Jenna, I fear you have relented, not because of a change of mind, but because there is no way out. And of course I am a lovable man, and you are cornered by my eyes. You know, my eyes can convince you of anything!"

I nodded. He was adorable, but more like a brother, although there were times I wondered what he was like in bed.

Smiling he came up from the passenger side, opened the door and loaded me into his SUV. I breathed a weary sigh and we trundled off. The sun was still shining as we became part of the rush hour's dizzying maze.

"I guess this freeway is our hellish fate," he said, shaking his head. "It is hard to find moments of transcendence in traffic! Every car here is in complete violation of any driving code ever decreed. I would love to be a million miles from the nearest SigAlert."

I laughed. "How do small, coral-fringed islands with sandy white beaches and ultra-clear water sound?" I asked.

"Does that dream picture come with brilliantly colored fish and superb snorkeling?" he asked, chuckling. "It is nice that the rain has finally stopped. I hear scores of day hikers converged on the trails in the Santa Monica Mountains. It must have been wonderful not to see gray clouds racing past shrubby hillsides for a change. L.A. has been a place of flash-flood watches, mudslide warnings, and flooded intersections these past few weeks. It was making me weary. You know, no one can drive in the rain in Los Angeles. I think that is a requirement for living here."

I giggled.

"Did you notice that the rain was also often accompanied by thunder and lightning? It was almost as if L.A. was hiding under the cloak of Seattle! The muddy runoff through the streets was a daily occurrence. It's interesting. It really only takes one interruption of the norm and suddenly everything flies off track. I couldn't do my workouts. I couldn't jog. Everything in my life just seemed to turn pathetic because of the weather. I guess we are spoiled living here in sunny Southern California." He paused. "You know, I'm a biking enthusiast, but I never take to the trails because of my daily routine. It seems as though I am always stuck in the city squinting past power lines. It makes me want to read a good book on stress reduction." He wiped his brow. "This freeway is a parking lot. Why, if I didn't know any better it could be a drive-in," he said as I stared at the sea of cars.

"Do you know I am a freeway monger? I can actually tell which drivers are not paying attention? The world is so self-involved. Everyone suffers from insufficient situational awareness. We are at a snail's pace. Time to get off of this freeway," he said as we hit the next exit. We drove for quite a few miles in silence. He appeared to be thinking.

"What a ride this thing called life is," he suddenly said, turning into an affluent residential neighborhood. "How did it go with Roy by the way?"

"Okay," I said, rubbing my stomach.

"The road is a bit twisty. This is the closest you can come to winding country lanes in L.A., Jenna. I love to let loose on them with blitzing vigor. So, tell me about Roy."

"Well, a little over twenty-four hours ago Roy processed the paperwork for my leave."

"Congratulations! Your quest demands respect."

I smiled.

"Roy tends to be generous with his opinions but he is a great guy. So what did he say?"

"He urged me to take my leave immediately."

"Understandable," he said. "They want you back quickly! It's a busy time, Oscar season and all."

"I'm going to come in on the Sunday before I officially return for a meeting with JB."

"Ah! One of those power meetings! I hate those things. I don't like anything long and drawn out. JB knows that. She manages not to include me in too many of them, which of course has raised allegations of favoritism."

I laughed. He was putting me at ease, as usual.

A maze of cars appeared beyond our headlights as Tucker turned onto an unlit gravel road. It seemed as if a few moments passed with no traffic as his black SUV rattled over the rock fragments and pebbles. "We are now riding through a slice of rural Southern California suburbia," said Tucker as we banged up and down along the unpaved road. "Only the residents come around this way." He turned onto a peaceful tree-lined street of rising dust. "This looks like a newly paved road, coming out of nowhere," he said.

"Yes," I remarked, looking out the window.

Tucker flipped on the radio. The smooth sounds of jazz accompanied us as we jounced and lunged a few more seconds of curvy miles. "Jenna, just look at these hilltop homes! Look at their lush front lawns. I could turn them all into fruit orchards."

I giggled.

"Are your ears popping, Jenna? I wonder what the elevation is up here," he said, grinning. "You know, growing up I never knew there were places like this. I didn't come from a tree-lined street with curvy drives." He frowned. "I was raised on a rubble-strewn street. There were no keep off the grass elitists. There were no lawns really to keep off of. It was really a circus-like forum, now that I think about it. We were a bunch of kids running around on instinct. We mercilessly tore our neighborhood apart. I had a great time. Still wished I could have had a bike growing up though," he said, sadly.

I felt a twinge of guilt as I recalled my purple stingray bicycle with the sparkly silver banana seat and streamers hanging from the handlebars.

"I grew up in a generic, lower-middle-class neighborhood full of hard-working, low-wage workers. I never could have dreamed that places like this existed," he said, eyeing the houses on the street. "All I saw growing up were run-down schools and over-flowing sewers. I used to fix my eyes on splintered roof beams. There were quite a few times my brothers and I used to count the stars through holes in the ceiling. You see, growing up I never had my own room. I shared with my three older brothers. We were always jockeying for space." He paused. "For amusement we would stomp in raging gutters and build leaf forts. Can you imagine stomping in raging gutters? But you know, a champ is born anywhere."

I smiled.

"We used to catch rides on the back of buses. You know, as a child you fall into every moment, never balancing risk and caution. You just live to jeopardize everything for a different taste of the world. It is sad that we lose a great deal of that in adulthood. Adulthood is filled with fussy obsessions and myopic tidiness, you know." He yawned. "Not being clothed in designer jeans didn't stop me from living! Besides it wasn't that bad. There were no two-story homes, so I was able to jump out of my bedroom window to attend late-night parties. None of my brothers ever ratted on me. They probably connected to the emotionality of it too!" He chuckled. "It is a funny thing about collective guilt. It has this comic transcendence about it."

"I never snuck out of my bedroom window, but I would have liked to," I said with a gleam in my eye.

"Ah Jenna, I think, even as a kid, you were filled with adult sensibility. I, on the other hand was always filled with child-eyed wonder. I have to tell you that you don't know what you missed! Half the fun was 'the sneak out!' I found out how skillfully directed I was by my renegade days. Yep, in those days I functioned on the far side of reality. Do you know as a kid I had concrete toes? Why, I would walk ankle-deep in freezing mud, my pant legs soaked to the seams. I would scramble among ledges and climb blocks of stone. Something was always happening underfoot. I knew from a young age that there were no buttery-soft landings in life, and I didn't look for them. My skinned knees were quite rewarding!"

I giggled, picturing him with skinned knees.

"You've never let loose, Jenna."

"I guess my sensibility always got in the way."

"We are startling contrasts, Jenna. You try too hard to preserve your integrity. I've always been partial to the monster role," he said jokingly, opening his eyes wide. "You are too civilized. You need to let go of your sensibility."

I guess I am ultimately impelled to do what is correct, proceed with caution and do the right thing."

"In the real world you can't always be a gleaming model of virtue. Don't be afraid of making mistakes."

"What about modern-day conscience?" I asked.

Tucker laughed. "It doesn't exist. Only modern-day brainwashing exists."

"My conscience has the power of influence on me! It prompts me to make decent choices."

"Perhaps, the unknown is your friend," he whispered.

I cocked my head.

"You have heard the words of magic before, right?" he asked, turning down the radio.

I stared out at the homes rising along the street. "Yes." I smiled. "I have been in love."

"Remember when we ditched the nightlife with blaring headaches and headed to my car to hide out from overheard conversations? We sparked some pretty interesting dialogue!"

I sighed. "I want to take some time to reinvent myself, Tucker. Tell me the story of passion and love. Clue me in on the tale of their differences."

Tucker grinned. "Passion slaps you on the back knocking the air out of you! Love twitches the corners of your lips." He squeezed my hand. "Perhaps, it is time for you to meet the woman behind your walls."

I gulped.

"Are you afraid to meet her?" he asked.

"Maybe."

"We are the best of friends, right, Jenna?"

"Yes," I said.

"Then may I tell you how I see her, the woman behind your walls?"

"Yes," I utter.

"She is an ear-nibbler. She has a smooth body. She is uncorrupted and not easily influenced. She is her own person, but a woman who is ready to spawn from her old-fashioned morals. She is ready to turn her fantasies into reality and live a charmed life. She is a seductress."

"Tell me more about her," I whispered.

"Well, she is a tender, honest, and loyal woman with restless nights! She is sweet, kind, and compassionate. She is queen of the soft kiss and she spends long, cold nights with the Ancients wondering if dawn will ever arrive. She is unforgettable and intense, and she hardly knows herself. Actually she is a charming bundle of paradox. She scrutinizes herself with puzzled looks."

I smiled.

"Filled with dark grumblings, she trips over the foot she has in two worlds. Sadness sweeps across her face and pent-up tears spill from her eyes as she realizes she has been a boorish stranger to herself. Of course she has been caught on several occasions sketching out plot lines for fantasies that are themselves growing cold in the grave." He winks. "There is bittersweet consolation here. She has decided to go off the radar of her soul, stumble over her morals and embark on a quest for fire."

"Where are the answers to life's vexing questions?" I asked.

"Those answers are hiding behind a rumpled exterior," he said, smiling. "A wayward soul can find them meandering in the fog." I give him a quizzical look.

"In life you must capture your rapturous spirit. And once you catch it, the next day will not begin as the last one. Just one sip of true passion changes you for eternity. It is all about choked voices and streaming tears. As human beings we are oddly cobbled together," he said and I quirked a brow.

"One night I had sex with a woman in a camper. She was from Seattle. I met her on a flight from Miami. I pulled down the shade on her window seat. We watched the in-flight movie together. When we got to California I had sex with her in her sister's camper. Then we spent the day together and went shopping. I don't even like shopping. But with her, I liked it. I took her to the airport. I was all choked up to see her go. With her, I stepped out of myself. It is impossible to explain. We kissed goodbye. Neither one of us asked for the other's last name. We didn't exchange phone numbers. We didn't want anything to take away from our time together. So, we just said goodbye. I still think of her. I never got so choked up over parting from someone, not even from my ex-wife. Sometimes you have to hop in and out of experiences. Sometimes you just have to get 'smoochy' with life."

I gulped.

"There are no crooked, tilting houses full of warped doors that keep swinging open on this beat," he said coasting to a stop. "No peeling paint for as far as the eye can see. It is wonderfully quaint here," he chuckled, pointing to the sloping roofs dotting the streets.

He pulled off on a quiet cul-de-sac with city views. "Look at that scenery, Jenna. We are not far from the heavens."

"Yes," I said, looking at the sprawl of city lights below. "I feel a beautiful sense of completeness."

"Jenna, the rain has shooed away the smog, and we are high above the world, looking at an eccentric city's skyline view! Listen! There is no roar of passing traffic. This is paradise discovered. I'll bet this view delivers breathless sunsets."

I smiled.

"You know, Jenna, Los Angeles is smothered by concrete. Why, it is a jungle of stained stucco. Yes, the concrete monster is eating up the lush green hillsides and winding, tree-lined roads with asphalt!" He paused. "That is Roy and Darcy's house right over there," he said, pointing to a colonial-style brick house with a sloped roof at the end of the cul-de-sac. "Before we sneak into the limelight as new party arrivals, I'm going to take some pictures of the spectacular view. My ex-wife is into settings. Maybe I can use some of this scenery to ice break my way back to her. You go ahead," he urged, giving me a kiss on the cheek. "We are already late. I'll see you in five minutes."

I sighed.

He touched my face. "Don't be fraught with terror. There are no robots in there with ray guns. Take the master's advice; a party doesn't have to have a foreboding feel to it. Look at it as a short period of time to dust off your social gear and lump yourself into nonsense! Parties have a special pleading about them," he said, starting the car. "You know, there will be the bawdy jokes, the casual points of distraction, and the spicy meatballs! I'm off to make the city pose for me. I think the view was better from the street just before this one," he called as his SUV kicked up dust on the road.

I waved as he pulled away. I never saw him again.

"What about those stuffed potatoes?"

I look at Darcy Saxton. She repeats her question, searching for me in my impenetrable silence. I stare at her long brown hair flowing over her halter-top. She is wearing a short denim pleated skirt and a casual pair of sandals. Flashing me another perfect porcelain smile, she snaps me from reflection and greets me with sunny complacency.

"It appears as if there is ghost light around your feet," she chuckles. A stray breeze flutters her eyes.

"I'm just waiting for Tucker," I say, looking down at my corporate blazer and recalling how he had said there was no time to change. "Tucker went to take some pictures of the scenery and has simply vanished!"

Darcy thumbs her nose in Tucker's direction. "Chalk him up as a frolicking unicorn," she says, chuckling. "A pair of flirty eyes probably has him wrapped in a tattered bedroll somewhere. You know, exotic spells can 'poof' out of nowhere."

"Yes," I reply, desperately scouring the street once again.

"Everything eventually comes around, Jenna. Don't mind him. Sometimes people just do the unexpected! He's a big boy. He'll find his way back even if he is just desperately in search of himself. Roy will take you home if he doesn't show. Now, bring your charming self to the door!"

I smile, detecting she knows I am feeling uncomfortable.

"So, what do you think of our landscaping? We are into the theme of green. We find it quite soothing."

"It is lovely," I say.

"You know, a front garden spins an enchanting mood. It sets the stage before you enter a home. Roy and I have selected foliage plants that paint the freshest ambiance."

"You both are quite skillful," I say.

"We wanted to create a place of lushness, so we focused mainly on tropical greens. Roy absolutely detests plants that are gaudy bloomers. He hates anything showy and pretentious." She winks. "We wanted the garden to feel spacious, yet intimate. Wait until we plant the flowerbed by the swimming pool. It will be tranquility at its finest. We have a great landscape designer. He captures our every whim." She points to the rooftop deck. "Isn't that as airy as you can get? Stand on it and get lost in the fluffy white clouds overhead! I might go crazy and hang down a curtain of foliage over the ledge. I have quite a green thumb. Even as a little girl I was in love with the Earth." She looks into my eyes and smiles.

"You know, living inside a house is like living inside its secrets. This home came with a wraparound porch and a vast array of secret gardens. Roy and I have often wondered about the number of intriguing tales it must hold." She takes my hand. "You are going to have a great time here, Jenna. We are not marked by elbow-to-elbow jostling. There are no jewel-toned gowns and designer tuxedoes here." She feigns a yawn. "You will not pass great banks of paparazzi popping their bulbs. But your angelic face would forever be beautiful in the strobe lights if there were any." She winks. "Join the party, Jenna! Become a face painter and a treasure hunter! Let life charm your goddess eyes!"

Emotion sweeps through me.

"Come on in and schmooze with our handful of invited guests. There is a half-finished pool, an almost-finished stone patio and lots of food and drinks. And that barbecue I mentioned to you earlier is in the making. You'll have to come over when we do our summer steaks!"

A horn honks and I look quickly around. It is not Tucker. Another horn quickly echoes and for a moment I think it strange.

"Release your inner conflicts and peer behind the party curtain," chimes Darcy, catching my puzzled expression. "But I must warn you my house is a jumble of tiny windows, so you won't be able to signal for help once you enter." She grins. "Roy has the fire going and the wine is flowing nonstop."

The aroma of hot pretzels drifts through the open door. "Hollywood tourists are scouring the hills seeking the chance to peek into our intimate gathering, Darcy!"

"Look at Roy, Jenna! He is trapped by his own mystery! He is pacing the front steps red in the face. Did you miss me baby?" she playfully asks.

"Yes," he exclaims. "Everyone is scuffing up our new hardwood floors!" He smiles at me. "Hey, Jenna, the whimsical world awaits you," he says, escorting me through a winding-staircase entrance festooned with sweet-smelling flowers. "You know, we didn't know what the crowd here tonight would be like, but I am pleasantly surprised. The party has a great vibe to it. Conversation is good and flowing."

I step into the hallway.

"Try not to scratch up the new ceramic tile with those high heels," he says, chuckling. "It cost us a bundle. After this party there will be no shoreline restaurant dinners of grilled sea bass for quite a while! Instead we will be dining at some off-season promenade, twirling a plate of calm spaghetti."

I force a smile.

"Allow yourself to be dazzled, Jenna! This is not a bash of noise and brawling. There are no bunny ears or clown noses, but I can assure you there will be lots of wonderful lunacy and perhaps even some body glitter shining the sheets later this evening."

Darcy puts her arm around me. "Your arrival will interrupt cocktail hour just long enough to encourage thoughts of your presence, and then everyone will return to their self-involved conversing. This might not be a rib-tickling evening," she says, lowering her voice, "but I think you'll have a nice time. It is a nice change of pace from the trendy high-pressured Hollywood evenings we've all had to smile through. You'll see. Care for some wine?" she asks.

I nod.

"I'll be right back," she says, disappearing into a stream of cellophane wings and highlight-dappled hair.

I glance around at my surroundings. A wall of windows reflects onto a broad stretch of smooth, imported ivory tile. Its soft illumination descends upon an ornate white marble bench. I walk over and admire it more closely. It appears to be hand-carved. I sit down as the candles in the room flicker.

Soft music provides a mellow backdrop to bursts of laughter. Although the chatting guests appear to be friendly, my irreverent shyness relentlessly yips at my heels. Rising, I scurry to take my rag-doll stance at the wall and gaze at the wood-framed Japanese doors before me. They lead to a dry garden with a stone waterfall and a small gravel river surrounding a Lantern of Peace. It is beautifully ornamental and for a moment all is amazingly still except for the call of the wind chimes. My eyes wander off to the unfinished stone patio. And it is in this innocuous moment that I first feel the thrill of attraction.

Passion signals me.
And I veer off the yawning road
of life.

Chapter 10

Floating on Sultry Air

The sun was setting. I saw him through a dusk-lit double archway. Woozy with infatuation my thinking became immediately shallow as I was swallowed up in initial impressions. Tan and meticulously groomed he was casually clad in tennis shoes, jeans, and a white pullover sweatshirt. I watched him as he offhandedly pushed up his sleeves. His tautly muscled arms and emphatic body language sparkled with the clarity of passion. He was handsome and focused, highly touted and not distracted by my staring. Just one look at him and I could feel goose bumps rise on my flesh. I found him seductive as he took off his sunglasses and used them to sweep back his sun-kissed, collar-length hair. I watched him with fascination. There was energy in just admiring him.

Immersed in his lips, I become a dutiful artisan, sculpting him with breaths of fire. No doubt the smooth slopes of his cheekbones have been sacrificed for wooing. Exhaling slowly, I realize he has awakened every sexual desire within me, and the feeling is unstoppable. I suppose enchantment dawns when we least expect it.

Hesitant to enter his crowd-pleasing space, my darting eyes are in hot pursuit of his every move. Why, I haven't even talked to him yet and I find myself mercilessly vying for his affections. I watch him wondering if he is approachable.

He sits perched on the arm of a chair, laughing, yet demanding the kind of cheers reserved for rock stars and football players. Clearly he is entertaining. He glances in my direction and smiles. I look away. He stands up and his entourage follows him. He gives me a few backward glances, and I give him a few forward glimpses, before he disappears into the thick of the crowd. Entranced, I silently pad off leaving him to the herd of people who flock around him.

A champagne cork pops! I turn around and find myself staring into a turquoise maze of piercing blue eyes. He is soft-spoken.

"I usually make it fly across the room," he says, smiling. "Don't you like the bubbly foam that bursts forth when the cork pops?" He sips the bubbly. "There is a certain sex appeal about champagne. It tempts my appetite." He brushes a stray strand of hair from my eyes.

I hold on to my glass of wine for security. I am surprised he has approached me, and it shows.

"I've startled you," he says, in a gentle tone. "I don't always kick off with the best opening lines. But I suppose I've intruded on quieter moments."

I stare at his smile. It is seductive. Looking at him I can hardly speak. He has attracted me as no one has ever done before. It is quite unimaginable. "I have been admiring you from afar," I say, blushing.

"Have you now? So, it was your eyes dancing upon me!"

"I wasn't the only one with eyes upon you."

"Yours were the eyes that touched me. I could feel your keenly interested presence."

"Well, you were surrounded by a swirling mist of onlookers," I manage to blurt.

"I exude worldliness. I am one of the world's most renowned minds!" His eyes sparkle with amusement. "I am witty, sophisticated, passionate, and I have the ability to pronounce the word monogamy. Are you charmed by my honesty?"

I peer at him, too emotionally incapacitated to do much of anything but muster a pant.

"Oh and one more thing, I have brisk timing."

"You are quite charismatic," I say.

"My spirit of play is alive, that's all."

"There were many eyes on you."

"I noticed none of them. It was your peering face that was magnified!"

"I don't know," I say, shyly. "You seem like a crowd pleaser."

"Yes. I am an endless source of laughter," he says, poking me in the arm and I grin at the goose bumps that follow his touch. "So you've noticed the brilliance of my character. I suppose I do tend to seduce my listeners."

"Oh, yes." I smile, my stomach churning with excitement.

"Are you telling me I am inviting?" He winks. "It is you with the sexy presence. You are irresistible to an infatuation watcher. You have seductive brown eyes and an unassuming glow about you. I like that. And you are quite sensual. I like that too." He smiles and I wonder if I am imagining things.

"Do you know that your eyes flutter angelically when you speak? As a matter of fact you have the mightiest charm of anyone I have met since Darlene Weinbrenner, my third-grade girlfriend!"

I giggle. "Well, I can tell wherever you go you have admirers."

"Well, this is a party and everyone is a small timepiece worth noticing. But aside from being an illuminating rave have I become an object of your affections?"

Shyly, I look down.

He grins. "And since this is a party, everyone here should have a joke on their lips. The wistful sound of laughter is something that should be heard more often. It is a challenge to bring humor to the world at times." He winks. "The world is too serious. It should be chuckle-filled. Perhaps, I should start a laugh-post!"

I giggle. It is about all I can do. I am so mesmerized by him.

"So I take it that you are not a humorless member of society."

"Oh no," I say. "I contend that laughter is life's medicine!"

"Among a few other things," he says, winking.

There is a brief pause when Roy's loud voice is heard. "Make way," he shouts in a falsetto tone. "I am balancing chaos!"

"You are in the line of fire," says my prince taking my hand. Shy about our fingers touching, my body brushes against his, showering me with sparks. Perhaps I am too close to him, I think, and move a bit away.

"I want you breathing beside me," he says, gently pulling me close.

Roy walks toward us with a tray full of cocktails. "We've already run out of wine," he says, shaking his head in disbelief.

"You've thrown a whopper of a party, my good man," says my prince and Roy takes a teetering bow. "Anything can throw me off balance at this point. Now, go grab some eating ware from the bar and indulge in the ultimate scarf-fest."

"I am off to inquire into my mysteries," chuckles my prince. "Perhaps I am chopsticks bound."

"Perhaps you will return with melted butter off your fingers," chortles Roy.

"One of the rewards of life is the element of surprise, but I will return from my quest with curious eyes," chimes my prince.

Roy watches him disappear into the crowd and then lowers his voice. "The hors d'oeuvres are so good, Jenna, everyone thinks we have a caterer," he chuckles. "This is the third appetizer tray to be emptied. We are filled with culinary delights. There are egg rolls, Swedish meatballs with fancy toothpicks, mushroom turnovers, franks in a blanket, and spinach and potato puffs. The tray of green olives stuffed with chicken and mouth-watering ham rolls were the first to go. Everything looks so fancy," he says, "but it is all a façade!"

"We'll try the Swedish meatballs with the fancy toothpicks," says my prince, returning with plates and forks.

"They will melt in your mouth," exclaims Roy. "They are imported!"

"You've done your utmost to impress," says my prince, handing me my plate of appetizers.

"Thanks Dal," yells Roy over his shoulder, as he heads back into the crowd.

So his name is Dal, I muse.

We watch Roy disappear into chaos, and then the source of amazement that so magically caught my attention formally breaks the ice.

"I can flatter myself with a charismatic introduction, but no matter what I say, I will remain, for this evening at least, an unknown entity to you if I don't simply introduce myself. I am Dallas Curtis, at your service." He extends his hand. Shyly, I accept his grasp.

"And your name?" he asks.

"I am Jenna Weyburn."

"Well, Jenna Weyburn, shall we take our plates and go outside for some fresh air?" He puts his arm around me. Lost in a fit of blushes, I walk beside his radiant smile.

"Does fresh air even exist in Los Angeles?" he asks, opening the front door for me.

I take a deep breath. We stroll outside in a way that I have never experienced before. His arm is around me. I feel alive! Walking out to the street, we stare at the city lights.

"It almost looks as if the city is gracefully drifting toward abstraction. Staring at it like this you can almost forget that Los Angeles is a hulky pile of gray concrete."

I nod.

He sits down on the curb and pats the space next to him. I sit down beside him with my plate in my lap and place my glass of wine on the curb.

"Not the fanciest conditions, but I have you beside me, nonetheless. The street suddenly holds prominence now that we are here."

I melt under his gaze.

"You smoke my brand of humor," he says, grinning. "So what do you think about all of this rain we have been experiencing? I was lulled into believing that rain was my destination. Suiting up every day in a slicker and boots became my form of dress up! It was anything but enchanting."

Up close, his shoulders are even broader. I try to smooth my face of emotion but I can't seem to get the butterflies in my tummy to slow down. "The rain was really something," I manage to pant. "All those clouds and gusts were downright intimidating."

"It was rather comical. Only seconds after what looked like the last of the downpours, I kicked off my boots and caught the first bits of the sun. I am sure that the array of businesses owners that I raced out in front of had a pretty good time watching me. They must have looked at me and wondered if it was permanent insanity that was driving me! Nonetheless an audience gathered to watch my spontaneous performance and applauded me for appointing myself as the welcoming luminary to the parting skies. What can I say? I perk up nicely when the sun kisses my face. As a matter of fact, I'd like to touch the sun when it falls upon your delicate chin. Do you know you cutely wear a blush?"

"Do you give all the girls heated cheeks?" I ask.

"Only the girls I like." He taps me on the tip of my nose. "I like you."

"Usually I blush and leave hastily, but a friend of mine from work drove me and has yet to arrive."

"Lucky for me," he says. "I've got you all to myself."

"I love your eyes," I manage to choke out.

"Are you trying to make me blush now?" he asks.

It is a gentle moment. He puts his fingers under my chin and gently raises my face. I wonder if I am dreaming; the moment is so beautiful. He moves closer to me and I feel as if I am curling up to the fiery eye of the sun. I shiver. No doubt these feelings that I have for him will deny me sleep.

"So tell me about Jenna Weyburn," he says, taking a bite of his meatball.

"I'm not too good at talking about myself," I answer, nibbling my spinach puff. "You go first."

"Well, I am sweeping entertainment. I am reliably funny, bristle with wit and am a daunting masterpiece at creating chaos in my life. I am sentimental, emotional, and crave life in its extreme. I am well dressed when the occasion calls for it and classically educated. I have secrets to share. I love to cozy up to an evening of sexy fun and at times feel as if I am plagued by supernatural visitors," he says, chuckling. "Really, I am very ordinary, full of wild innovation and I like to tell stories of magical enchantment."

A red flush spreads across my cheeks.

"I am small town in spirit. I live in a place where there is no rush-hour traffic, where doors are left unlocked, windows are left ajar, and where there is not even the hint of arrogance. As a matter of fact it is a place where you can see people trusting one another, where no one is in a hurry and people ask how you are doing and mean it. It is an odd place. It is called my mind!"

Nodding, I take a romp through his eyes. They are crystal blue and intensely alluring. The wrinkles at their corners have him emphatically defined. His body is temptingly chiseled, and I can only imagine his rhythm to be absolutely magnetic in a slow dance.

"Shall I assume that you cracked Roy and Darcy's invitation list, or are you a well-known party crasher?" he asks.

"I'm hardly a party crasher. I work with Roy at Kenmar Studios. He invited me."

"Ah, Kenmar Studios," he says with a grin. "That's where award-winning movies are made! You must live in high-rise hell," he chuckles, his deep blue eyes shining.

"What?" I ask.

"Everyone in the biz either lives in high-rise hell or in bulky concrete, behind smoked windows, and surrounded by high walls topped with something sharp. They gravitate to rotating lounges high above the city, wearing synthetic threads and flaunting their connectivity to one another. Wowing sporadically, the room spins with deception and phony tirades fringe the roof of every house with an antennae." He shakes his head sadly. "So, are you tweaked with stardom?"

I blush. "No stardom here and I don't live in high-rise hell. I am scared to death of elevators. I assist Jackie Burman. She is the wiz. I am her meet-and-greet woman."

"You are her familiar spirit, I take it."

"I suppose you could say that. So how do you know Roy?" I ask.

"Roy and I met while leaning against a dormitory refrigerator in college. Indulging in the guilty pleasure of wolfing down left over slices of cold pizza for breakfast, we drooled over our morsels and realized we both came from the same hometown. As the story goes, Roy escaped small town madness and fled to 'Hollywood' where he urged me to follow him and wrap my arms around the California sun. And so with a cantina filled with anticipation, I headed out West. We lost contact until the other day when our paths crossed over a pastrami on rye. He invited me here tonight for their anniversary bash. So, I guess I formally made the invite list." He looks into my eyes. "So tell me about the touch of your lips."

I gasp.

"If I were to settle my palms on either side of your face, would they heat?"

I cock my head.

"Or would your lips roll me over onto my back and slip momentarily upon my neck and then kiss my fluttering eyelids?"

I blush, not knowing how to respond.

"Do you know that even when your lips are silent they are the image of a kiss?"

Looking at him in awe, I turn even redder than before.

"Well, let me just say that I look forward to feeling them brush against my ear."

"Who are you?" I whisper.

"I am a human being who listens softly to life. Wrapped in obscurity and encoded with riddles, I am dramatically flawed and occasionally inept. I live for snow glare, love swimming with the sea lions and my face blooms on garden tours. I am self-assembled, carefree, and daring. I'm not one for a coat and tie. I'm provocative and controversial and I do not stagger in inventiveness. I function at my own pace. I am relaxed, amiable, and entertaining. I tap into the well of optimism, dream of faraway places and cherish my altering mind." He pauses. "Can you keep a secret?"

I look at him searchingly.

"I don't want anyone I know to know about this. I don't want anyone ribbing my creativity. Do you really want to know who I am?"

"Yes," I breathe.

"I am scattered plot lines and personal narratives. I am piles of dictionaries and stacks of printed-out scribble. I live in the land of long-shot cinematic hopes and dreams." He lowers his voice. "Although I lack the rumpled up aura of a distinguished author, I am a writer."

I gasp. "I am in awe of writers. They are the backbone of Hollywood."

He smiles. "One day I will have a pile of admiring letters strewn at my feet. I must have fan mail." He squeezes my hand. "I have already made the Hollywood rounds. I have met the assistants of the assistants of the assistants! I just never have met anyone who can make any decisions."

I shake my head. "It is not an easy industry to crack."

"I'll say. Writers do crazy things to get discovered. Did you hear about the desperate soul who parachuted into a movie studio lot last week? I'll tell you, anything to get your script into the hands of the movie gods!"

I nod. His eyes are penetrating.

"Do you know where my book takes place?" he asks.

"Where?" I whisper.

"It takes place in life, Jenna. There is blame, shame, and ridicule as well as willful helplessness."

I nod, captivated.

"Not many people understand humankind. We are human beings and we can't always keep our feelings in logically hidden places. In the average, everyday person, being human is an afterthought. That is what I pen." He chuckles. "Okay, so I am a little on the manic side, but I am lovable. Seriously though, people talk about their feelings in hushed tones. But not me! I am different. You will remember me, Jenna. I have intoxicating powers. I spin magic."

Intrigued, I curl a few strands of my hair around my fingers.

"My first interests were theater and film. Of course that was after football. So it should come as no surprise that I am into storytelling. We always return to our point of origin," he says, smiling. "My novel is the tale of a wayward soul who journeys after the 'gods of life,' who have lost control of humankind. My character is a symbol of darkness and alienation, reminiscent of pure pleasure yet packs moments of raving lunacy. He is a life enthusiast, but holds back and lives in disguise. Remember, I pen life and its masquerade."

I nod.

"You see, my character lives behind a mask in a fearful world of imaginary zombies and fantasy sequences. But know my hero's exaggerated plight as a human being is well translated, for I am a timidly sensitive writer. I speak in volumes about the strength and frailty of the world that surrounds us. And when my fiery pages come to a close, my readers will find out how shockingly human, I have made them!"

"What is the title of your book?" I ask.

"At this point it is nameless! Perhaps you can help me with that, being in the biz and all."

I smile. "I would love to."

"Although I do manage to throw a few inaudible gasps of paradise in my pages I am skeptical of any place that is complete bliss and delight. As I look out on the streets of motorists zipping by every day, I wonder if anyone is even truly searching for paradise anymore. Perhaps, no one believes it exists." He pauses. "Well, shall we go in and hit the dessert tray?"

"I'm not too much for socializing."

"Hey, I'd rather have you all to myself anyway. Would you like me to bring dessert out here for you?"

"That would be great," I say.

"I can only offer you curbside dining. Is that alright?"

I stare at the smooth slopes of his golden cheekbones.

"Get ready to turn into a dessert adventurer," he whispers, softly stroking my face.

"Okay," I clamor.

He smiles. And I breathe the fire of the dragon.

When I look through the
telescope of life,
I see the sketch of my inner
creation.

Chapter 11
Splashdown of the Amorous Creature

"Welcome to Planet Romp."
"Why thank you. It's nice to be here."
"I am Lure. I am mood-lit. I breathe fire."
"Nice to meet you!"
"I will be your temptation while you are here."
"Okay." I blush.
"Here on Planet Romp we speak caressingly of body gliding and sensual mist. We are not a creation of shambling mediocrity. We are sexual creatures. We are body warmers."
"Oh, I see."
"Sexual creatures, by the way, are among the most fearless people on Earth!"
I bite my lip.
"They are in love with life's pleasures."
"Will that type of nostalgia have me lingerie-clad and running after my impassioned notions?"
"You know, life's eternal recipe for elation is to linger in the moment."
"I am shy about being seduced."
"Upon arriving on Planet Romp, most land on the outskirts of their being but you blasted into the heat of your soul."
"I was emotionally abducted."

"Well, we are a rather flirty planet."

"Yes. It seems like everyone has batting eyelashes and sexy accents."

"We are eminently irresistible."

"Yes. Everyone looks bouncy and kind of tight and form-fitting."

"Some of us look like beach bunnies; others are hot bods with corded biceps and sexed-up suits!"

"Yes! Some of you are quite bouncy."

Lure winks. "That is our trademark."

"On my way here, it was the bearded stubble and shirtless chests that caught my eye."

"Well, really everyone's breaths here on Romp are so hot they could blow a windstorm. We are a teasing planet of lip bites. If that doesn't work we will reel you in with falling pants." Lure pauses a moment. "We are definitely not flannel-wearing inhabitants. We don't ignore fiery glances. We give tingles of sure pleasure."

I gulp.

"Now, allow me to search your eyes for signs of life. Hmmm. No signs of life. May I rap upon your soul?"

"Oh yes. By all means, please do."

"Hmmm. Nobody home there, either. You know, your mysteries are colorful. You should allow your truth to enter. The greatest thing about Planet Romp is we are all emotionally nude. There are no impeccably stylized beings here, just sexual heroes. You see, here on Romp we are lustful gazes and sudden kisses! Bedrooms are perfectly pleasant in champagne and charcoal and excessively mirrored. If you don't mind my saying, you are a rather curvy erotic traveler. Would you care to see our playbook? It is quite frolicsome."

"I'm too shy for a playbook."

"We are here to leisurely wrap around life. It is fun to frolic."

"You know, I'm not some panting virgin. I've been around."

"Oh yes. We have the stats on you. You have the potential to warm the sea."

"Me?"

"We would like to tour the secret places of your heart. We want to hear you coo."

"That would be an unforgettable moment." I blush.

"We have heard of your ambitious attempt to find pleasure. Do not lack the nerve to go further. Personal destinies are best if explored. Elope with your emotions!"

"How do I do that?"

"Vanish in the twinkle of your eye. Become a fire-breathing woman carried off by plumes of smoke. Salute the blown kiss! Fall away in the fluttering sensation of eyelids opening and closing against your bare skin. Lose yourself in the soft nips of an earlobe. Planet Romp is a place of intimate nuzzlings. We give out of this world foot massages."

"Oh wow," I blurt.

"We use lavender and rosemary oils."

I tingle.

"We greet the world with featherlight touches. We are descendants of fiery emotion. We dance in our socks!"

I giggle. "Sounds like fun."

"We have a long interest in foreplay. We can drip for hours in sage oil. You know, life can be an erotic courtyard with a rose-colored view."

"How do I join the living?"

"Become an erotic traveler. Offer your voice to your soul! Allow the whiffs of passion to take you into enchanted directions."

"How do I do that?"

"Become human! Become so passionate that your tongue dangles with exhaustion! Allow the fiery image of your soul to materialize."

I gulp.

"Do you want to remain a tiger, crouching?"

"No! I want to burst into flames from the heat of a sudden kiss." I pause. "I have an intimate confession. I am drenched in anticipation. Is that wrong?"

"Allow panting breaths on your belly to take you beyond your limitations. It is alright to scoot a little closer to life."

An esoteric blending of tones fuels me and I tumble deeper into my impassioned stupor. "Who are you?" I ask, looking around.

Lure eases toward my lips. "I am your fiery image."

"My fiery image? Oh wow!"

"Yes. Right now you are a flame folded back. Your borders are edgy. You have taken drastic measures to hold back your secrets. But you can't fool me. I am the stranger within you, watching. You think that you can slip away in the darkness. But you can't. You are torch-lit! You are the holder of the full-body kiss!" Lure's lips brush lightly across the top of my hand. "Cuddle back in candle thrown shadows. Curl your bare toes in light feathery touches. Feel your breath stolen. Melted ice between your thighs is nice."

I gulp. "Should the ice be shaved or cubed?"

"A creative soul searches for the truth behind the illusion."

I cock my head.

"Do you truly crave for life's deepest discovery or are you an enraptured jokester?"

"I want the wet night to swallow me whole. I crave for madness."

"Ah. You want to be licked slowly."

"I want ecstasy to claim my body."

"You want to gleam in the tingling waves of your wetness."

"Yes, but I am guardedly reserved. Perhaps, that is the dark side of womanhood."

"No. That is the dark side of you."

"What do I do?"

"Bundle your fleecy clothes under your arm and beneath a darkened sky descend from your canopy of inhibition. Become a body that rumbles in the distance. Toss yourself a robe of satin. Let it drape across your shoulders. Don't hold it closed. You are the master of your lips."

I nod slowly.

"Passion is alive and well within you. Allow its heat to illuminate your soul."

I light a softly incensed candle and hold it in front of me. Its flame is hot and inviting. Its light darts into my eyes.

"Your fiery whispers can no longer be tucked away within your virtue. Your quest awaits you. Fantasies do come true," Lure whispers. Hypnotized, I step out of my timid-ware.

"The future is seducing. Tilt your head back. Allow your curls of flame to rise. I am Lure. I am the heavenly fire of ecstasy. Are you ready to blast off into the heat of your soul?"

Thundering with emotion, I release the latch of inhibition and the universe becomes an erotic courtyard with a rose-colored view.

My body whispers scandalously,
And I become a maze of curled
flames.

Chapter 12
Speaking the Tongue of Rapture

"What do we remember our lovers for?" he asks, dropping a piece of strawberry cheesecake into my mouth. "Is it the way they arch their back during ecstasy? Perhaps it is the way they dim the lights." He pauses. "How do you blow out your bath-lit candles? Do you purse your lips and blow? Perhaps you just close your eyes. I'd like to see your face in the glittering specks of bath-lit flames."

A blush sweeps my cheeks as his arm moves slowly around my shoulder.

Bathed in the glow of city lights he whispers scandalously in my ear. "Tonight, the universe looks like an erotic courtyard with a rose-colored view."

I shiver.

"Back at the house, Darcy is arranging crackers and funny-colored cheeses on silver dessert trays because they've run out of pastries. But I think there is more to life than padding around in homey domesticity. Quite a bit more possesses my imagination than morning coffee," he says and I cock my head.

"Yes. What do we remember our lovers for? Perhaps it is the way their hair dances in the air after being blown by the hot breaths of our panting body. Perhaps it is how they grasp our hips or the way they stroke our thighs or perhaps it is the way they trace the base of our neck with their tongue." He pauses. "Do you have a fondness for Heaven?" he asks.

Twilight left us long ago, and the light overcast mist has lifted with the descending darkness. The gentle winds of Los Angeles once again tousle his hair. "I think a fondness for Heaven deepens one's sense of interconnectedness," he whispers and I wish I could act upon my impulses.

"The small moon sneaks past us. In just a few seconds it fades to a black dot and then shoots away. Life blows by in slow motion at times." He winks. "You know, without having the pleasure of tasting your skin, I am drawn to the nudity of your smile. I would like to send every inch of you blushing. Do you know I am very attracted to the softness of your pale cheeks? They make me feel as if I am peeking over the edge of the world." He pauses. "I don't want to be a lost soul credentialed as a human being. So, I remain nakedly myself. I hope you don't mind."

A tear trickles down my face and I pray it goes unnoticed.

"It was a classic, picture-postcard day today, wasn't it? The broad blue sky was lightly dusted with white fluffy clouds. Personally, I like to be in temps that are so low my breaths crack in the wind, but L.A. really is quite beautiful." He takes a deep breath. "Too bad everyone here is looking to snatch the top-spot."

"I don't want to be famous," I say.

"I do! I would settle for being a reel of discarded bloopers," he says, grinning. "Hey, I'm perfect for Hollywood! I can channel adversity. I can pace back and forth with hunched shoulders. I can pump my arms aggressively, click my fingers and hug on cue when my name is announced. I can be the perfect storm of celebrity. Just light some fumes under some of those Hollywood bigwigs you work for and I will gladly deep kiss anyone on my way up to the stage."

I smile.

"It seems like sincerity has little relevance in today's world. I believe there must have been glimpses in time when it could easily be tasted upon one's lips. Now it jumps out of the window with fright!" He shakes his head. "Sometimes I want to just slip my arms around deception, nestle its cheek against my shoulder and say, 'Let go of the world. If you weren't here anymore, we could all be human!'" He pauses. "Forgive me. I get carried away at times." He idly taps my nose. "Do you know Roy and Darcy have a moonlit balcony that overlooks romantic ideas?" He pauses. "Do you know moonlit balconies can make people famous? They incorporate a range of discoveries. Come on! Let's catch the stars." He takes my hand as we walk past the shrouded trees.

"Look at Roy and Darcy's front garden in the starlight. It is very different from their garden by day. At night, moonshine is tangled in the hedges and the crickets sing unseen. All creatures in life have their own standard of fame," he says, winking.

"We have been greeting new arrivals and perching them on stools around our kitchen island because we've run out of chairs," shouts Darcy walking toward us.

"You have both honed in on the magic potion for party harmony," says Dal greeting her.

Darcy winks. "Well it looks like you have stumbled upon a bit of magic yourself."

"I heard the wind and just turned my head," Dal says.

I turn a sparkling gaze on him and break the flirty moment. "Darcy, I am enamored by your front garden."

"Uprooting a handful of stubborn wildflowers was the real trick," she chimes.

"I like your old-fashioned porch. It really feels well built."

"Thanks Jenna, but appearances are deceiving," she says, escorting us into the house. "The rains have been unkind to us. We need a new roof and other repairs. The rainwater seems to have damaged quite a few of our wood frames and porous concrete. Roy has made the house look better than it really is."

"I have many talents," interjects Roy, joining the conversation. "I can distort reality!"

"This is all so unexpected," pipes Darcy, glancing at the crowd. "We were getting the tray of exotic cheeses together when guests started arriving. This is L.A. No one shows up early." She pauses. "It has turned into quite a chatty party. This bash is knee-deep in nonsense! If you'd both like to seek some quietude, step out on our balcony. The moon is full and mystical."

Dal wraps his arm around my shoulder. "Jenna, in my next life I will be a celestial navigator," he says as we stroll outside. "The stars are full of life tonight. I do believe the universe is full of clever fun! You know, I grew up in a little house in a town that I swear was on the outer edge of the galaxy. It was a place where my dreams marched away to infinity. I spent a lot of my time selfishly stargazing. It was my escape. When the snow lay heavily on the ground, I would slip away from the house and follow the star's icy gleams. A backward glance at one's childhood is usually at a sense of distance, but I can still feel the crisp clarity of the winter sky." He shivers. "Have you ever lain on your back in the snow?"

"I have never seen the snow."

"You are a snow virgin?" he asks and I blush wildly.

He smiles warmly. "I can still remember my fingers curling in my mittens, my eyes stinging with cold as I lay in my little space so deep with silence. In my muffled solitude somehow I was free." He stops for a moment. "Do you know you have melting brown eyes?"

I shrug.

"Even though I haven't been caught in the fangs of a blustery winter for quite sometime now, I still yearn for the cold. Thinking about it warms me. Do you know that there is nothing more magical than a snow rub?"

I tingle.

"If you don't mind my asking, what is your point of fire?"

"What?" I exclaim.

"What makes you infinitely hot? For me it is my writing." He winks.

He is filled with sweet emotion. "You have the instincts of a great author," I say. "May the world see your name rolled atop the credits as a great writer!"

He grins. "Wearing my tuxedo unbuttoned at the neck, I drink my scotch in a corner, looking sad. Hordes of press scurry past me, and for a moment I am lost in a posse of black ties. Excuse me! I shout after them. I have emerged from my limo drop off. I am ready to be noticed! Shall I pose nonchalantly on your red carpet ride?" His mouth crinkles at the edges. "I am ready to laugh uproariously. Just give me the cue! I promise I will sweep your viewers off their feet!" He pauses. "Jenna, if we conceal who we are, we only create illusions of false ease."

I nod.

"So, what have you learned about yourself, browsing your life?" he asks me and I bashfully turn from his eyes. "Perhaps you are shy in my presence because you find me interesting," he whispers.

The stars hang high in the velvety black sky. Their soft light is almost golden. I watch the gentle wind tousle his hair. He has an unmistakable profile against the moonlight. I take in a deep breath. The air is sensual.

He stares into the night. "Yes. What do we remember our lovers for? Is it their smile, their hairstyle, their dimples? Is it the way they nudged our lips with their tongue? Perhaps it is the way they licked our closed eyes. Perhaps it is the way we devoured the soft flesh of their neck. Maybe it is the way we sent moans to their parted lips or maybe it was the way we nibbled their ear lobes sitting on old rickety chairs." He lowers his voice. "I have many cravings. Would you like me to share with you something I deeply lust for?"

"Yes," I whisper.

"I lust to feel the force of heat it takes for an iceberg to melt," he says and I gasp.

"And there is more. I long to view Arctic wildlife from a small inflatable raft and meet villagers and hear the legends of their elders. Icebergs and their beautiful images are scenery unrivaled anywhere on this Earth. Take me on an Arctic cruise and I will happily bundle up in layers of clothes and be lost in my binoculars." He looks searchingly at me. "I am not a fixture of the city. Are you?"

"What do you mean?" I ask.

"Would you drift with me on my little blow-up raft and watch modern life fade?" he asks and I blush at the thought.

"You see, when I was a kid my parents represented rational thinking. I went insane from it so I created my own private space. Sometimes my world was dark and medieval. Other times my wild imagination was one of magic and sorcery. And sometimes I would dare descend into hell as a legendary hero slaying the mythical monsters of my made-up lands. Snatching evil from the world of fearsome castles wasn't easy! Do you ever dream?" he asks.

I bite my trembling lip.

"Wander the night-time sky with me! Cup your hands and wait for the stars to fall!"

His voice is soft. I fall back in his arms.

"Look, the heavens are glittery," he whispers. His words sink into my ear. "The moon and stars are just unreal tonight! They look as if they are clinging to the hills above L.A. You see those two bright stars up there? There is chemistry between them. Their twinkles are seduction by moonlight. Jenna, the galaxy has existed forever. But the Earth and sky don't play by the same rules. Each has different talents. One day the Earth and sky will meet. There is a world and time beyond this one," he says, cupping his hands. "I firmly believe that and it is one of pure pleasure."

I tingle.

"What is the figure of pure pleasure? Is it walking barefoot through summer grass? Perhaps it is holding someone tightly with your eyes. Perhaps it is rose petals tickling your ears." He winks. "Maybe it is just feeling a kiss that is above a whisper."

The heat of his face brushes up against mine.

"Tonight is a fabled remnant in my life, Jenna. If there are indeed other times, other worlds and other galaxies, I am happy I am here in this moment of time with you."

I smile shyly.

"You have fiery lips," he whispers. "May I kiss them?" he asks.

I close my eyes. His lips descend upon mine. I wave farewell to the tiger, crouching.

The heat of my being
Rages on a chariot of fire.

Chapter 13

Snow-Women Melt, Don't They?

"I want to have an affair."

"Don't be ridiculous. You are lost in the hypnosis of infatuation."

"No, I'm not!"

"Yes, you are."

"I am not!"

"Don't argue with me. I'm your conscience."

"What is wrong with wanting to live a little and have some fun? I'm ready for some extra-curricular nonsense."

"You are not cut out for it."

"I'm not cut out for living?"

"No. You are not cut out for fun."

"Oh great, that's good to know."

"I'm just telling you the way that it is."

"I have a question."

"Shoot."

"Why do you make it a practice to grab and seize my moments?"

"Well, I'm your conscience, remember? I need to set you straight. Besides you are tasseled together with deep emotions."

"What does that mean?"

"It means you don't take anything lightly."

"You are ruining my moments with your depressing predictability."

"I don't mean to. I've just captured you vividly. That's all."

"Well, I'm not the world's emotional heavyweight that you think I am."

"Perhaps not, but you are definitely a contender!"

"Conscience, I have an intimate confession. I have a restless mind."

"Uh-huh."

"I don't think you are taking me as seriously as you should," I whisper. "I dream of fiery nights of reckless lovemaking."

"I know that. And I also know that you have never been able to pull it off. Skipping down memory lane, may I remind you that you are a relationship woman?"

"Don't remind me."

"Everything has always had to be just right with you."

"I've had exaggerated expectations."

"Well, you have moral requirements."

"True."

"You've done it the right way."

"Yep, and it is hard to imagine any duller sex than I've had."

"Oh my word!"

"Well, it's the truth, Conscience. My sexual orientations have hardly been a knockout."

"And now in just a few hours, one man's splendor has erotically riled you!"

"Yes. There is something rarefied about him. Nearly every inch of me is splashed with intrigue!"

"What?"

"He doesn't talk of ordinary things."

"Uh-huh."

"Want to hear something cute?"

"Oh brother!"

"He kissed me lightly atop my forehead and asked me to spend the morning with him."

"Uh-huh."

"Well, immediately I bundled up in my timid-ware. I mean, you know I'm not that type of girl."

"Well, I should hope not."

"'Spend the morning with me,' he said. I gave him a dispiriting look. And then do you know what he said?"

"I haven't the foggiest."

"'How do I convince you of my good intentions? Shall I send you a convoy of roses? I'm not asking you to venture into the sheets. I only want you to greet the dawn with me.'" I sigh. "He is articulate and polite and he has knockout blue eyes. And there is more, Conscience."

"Oh please."

"'I'll pick you up at 5 a.m.,' he said. 'We'll watch the fishermen with their dotted hats, standing waist-deep in the water, patiently casting their lines.'"

"He is casting some pretty good lines, himself."

"I have an intimate confession, Conscience. I'd like to walk barefoot into the dawn and have him blow on the back of my neck."

"You have drooling lips."

"Give me a few moments, Conscience. I'm just enjoying being alive."

"You're hopeless. No question about it."

"Do you want to know what else he said?"

"Do I have a choice?"

"'The dawn is greatly anticipated. I can't wait to see its light upon your face.'" Shyly I bite my lip. "I hope I never cool down, Conscience."

"Get yourself together."

"'Sit with me, goggle-eyed on the shimmering beach and drift in the salty green waters. See the sun streaking the heavens orange and gold. We'll wait for the dawn curled up with sand in our toes,' he said."

"Stop fanning your gullible eyes."

"I just look at him and my skin radiates this warm sensual glow. He fills me with unknown anticipation. When I first saw him, ecstasy filled my body."

"Get hold of yourself! Consider the consequences."

"I'm tired of doing that. It has gotten me nowhere."

"Look, you are just caught in the dicey triangle of intrigue, infatuation, and lust. That's all."

"That's right! He has me peering into life. I am seeing it for the first time."

"It is life as he sees it."

"He is passionate about it. I like the view."

"He is passionate about storytelling."

"What is wrong with having a bold imagination?"

"Calm down. You are infatuated."

"My breath flutters!"

"You are out of control."

"He makes me smile so much my face hurts."

"You are making me sick."

"There is nothing wrong with exploring ideas."

"He wants to get his work from the inkwell to the big screen. You are his vehicle."

"I don't think so. He just dreams big with playful energy."

"You are lost in tongue-tangling kisses."

"There is nothing wrong with feeling hot friction."

"Open your eyes."

"In just a few hours he has driven the dungeon chill from my bones."

"Find out the hard way."

"I'm peeking into life."

"Try to hold your hips in place."

"What is so wrong with wanting to frolic? What is so wrong with wanting to lounge on a nude beach?"

"Oh wow! Do you have to undress completely?"

"Well, that's the idea, Conscience. Others do it, you know. It is rather popular."

"You couldn't pull it off. You would be swathed in towels."

"Well others do it."

"Yes, but you are different. You will sleep restlessly and awake in embarrassment."

"I know. That is my problem. I have a cowering body. I have never been able to comfortably waltz around Planet Nude. If I were a piece of furniture, I would be a vinyl-covered table, with my legs covered."

"Look! You are fragile and delicate."

"I want to wear a black, lacy bra."

"You are flat chested."

"I have an intimate confession. In high school, I used to stuff my bra with wads of tissue."

"So, that's how you looked puffier!"

I grimace. "You know, they have these nudity spas. I want to skinny-dip."

"Where have I gone wrong?"

"There is more, Conscience."

"I don't think I can take much more."

"Are you hurling me one of your steely glares?"

"Maybe."

"I want to skinny-dip with him. I want his hair to feel like cold silk in my hands."

"Allow me a moment to redouble my shudders. Okay, go on. And by the way, I am hurling you a steely glare."

"I want a sexually octane-fueled life, Conscience. I want to feel my desires."

"Not in the cards."

"Okay. I'm discarding any attempt at cordial conversation."

"You don't have to be sarcastic. You can't get rid of me, you know."

"Yeah, that's for sure. I just would like it if you'd be more on my side though."

"It's difficult to praise you for your ecstatic insight."

"Now you are being insulting. Look Conscience, he is going to be here in less than two hours. I need to get some sleep."

"I'm not stopping you."

"Yes, you are. You are always hammering in my head and then you mire me in hopelessness."

"I don't mean to. I'm just trying to make sense of your innermost thoughts. We are an inseparable combination, you know."

I groan. "I know."

I roll over and my lacy pillows drop to the floor. I'm too tired to pick them up. The keeper of the realm of dreams is just about to take my hand when I hear a voice.

"Turn on the lights."

I sit up and rub my eyes.

"Whom do you plan on having an affair on?"

"What?" I yawn.

"Whom do you plan on having an affair on?"

"My morals," I say leaning over and pulling the cord on my lamp.

"And just whom do you plan on having an affair with? The gentleman you just met tonight?"

"Yes. He has a rapturous smile."

"Give him an ecstatic ovation and move on. He will have you jumping through hoops."

"I can't listen to you anymore. You are infringing on my happy time."

"Go ahead! Shut the door on my guidance and criticism. You'll be back."

"You always try to destroy my fun."

"I'm sorry for the intrusion. I'm your conscience remember? I'm just trying to help."

"Are you telling me he is a glaring miscalculation?"

"I'm telling you there are larger issues."

"I only want a tentative courtship."

"You don't take anything lightly."

I eye the clock on my nightstand and know it is futile to try to sleep. A hot bath sounds soothing. Draping my blanket around my shoulders, I get out of bed and head to the bathroom. I pass by my hall mirror. I look like a tousled spectacle. Quickly I move beyond its realm. Perched on the edge of the tub, I watch the bath fill with suds of lavender and toss in a few rose petals. I light some incensed candles around the tub. Their glow illuminates the water as the scent of jasmine burns.

The blanket draped around my shoulders falls to the floor as I step out of my flannel pajamas. Slowly, I lower myself in puffs of steamy air and let the warm water hug my body. It is heavenly. I close my eyes and for a few moments I lose touch with reality.

"Hey!"

Startled, I look around.

"Yes! You! The one up to your chin in sudsy water!"

"Oh god," I groan.

"Are you still party indulging?"

"Not you, again! Don't you ever sleep?"

"I usually doze, surrounded by the comforting murmur of silent voices, but being your conscience is a twenty-four hour job. Your elations are rather boisterous. You still haven't descended from the social heavens I see."

"What? I left the party long ago."

"No, you didn't. You are still partying."

"I'm just recalling the warm sound of his voice."

"You are doing much more than that. You are fantasizing about his irresistible body-moving rhythms."

I blush. "Can't you grant me some personal space?"

"Please don't look at this as an intrusion, but rather as a pointed moment. As your conscience, I am not easily distracted, but I must say you have captured my wandering attention."

"Leave me alone! Can't you see I am soaking in bliss?"

"See! You are still partying. You have left the canned music and lip-synching behind, but you are still soaring in the social heavens with your erotic suitor. You can't fool me."

"Conscience you are hardly a sympathetic character. I am growing tired of your criticism. A rapturous sexual relationship on my horizon is the rush I am looking for."

"Rumors are you want to let loose."

"I'm approaching truth, that's all."

"I see."

"I want to add a little fun to my rather grim and unimaginable life."

"He is a sentiment invader. Perhaps you should go elsewhere for your discovery."

"Not a chance. I want to feel his warm lips on the back of my neck."

"At first glance he is straightforward, warm, and engaging. But just wait. He has a hidden agenda. He is deliciously deceptive."

"Maybe you didn't hear me! I want to feel his warm lips on the back of my neck."

"I heard you. You wish to frolic in venues of risk."

"Why try to destroy my rush?"

"It is stopping you from cherishing your mind."

"I am in no mood to sacrifice this hot intensity that I am feeling for sensibility. It is hardly time to move on from him."

"You just want to stroll through your panting breaths."

"Look, there were no awkward silences."

"Uh-huh."

"Well, that is a big thing. Usually my stomach rumbles and I hear the anxious shrieks of life. You see, from the beginning, our encounter was amorous. I was tingling just at the mere sight of him. You don't understand. We locked eyes. It was intense. He gave me a lift home. I was at ease, for once."

"Uh-huh. You are rambling."

I sigh. "He stroked my face and told me I have a sexy presence. It was paradise. I don't want to control this rush I am feeling. I am in a warm and fuzzy place, Conscience, and I am fascinated."

"He will have you trapped in cycles of lust."

"Is he going to have me communicating with the dead too?"

"You are not taking me seriously. He will give you frazzled moments. He has a talent for turning expressive gesture into powerful body language."

"I don't want to speculate on his motives. He has stirred new life in me."

"Yes, I know. His human credentials are impeccable."

"I just want to live my life."

"Have you looked closely at this tangle?"

"I am tired of bundling up in my timid-ware."

"Oh, so he tells you that you have a sexy presence and you are ready to shimmy seductively."

"I like the way he words things."

"Oh brother, he has really wooed you. He is getting under your skin. His words have you half-vanished."

"Whatever. All I know is he is pleasantly shaking me up! How on earth will I ever sleep again?"

"Do you know how many lives are ruined by affairs? No matter how much you lie to yourself about them, affairs come with false expectations and end with dashed hopes. Unspoken loves don't remain a secret."

"Affairs are never dull, though."

"No. But they are not necessarily well worth your time."

"I'm tired of everything being well worth my time. I want to live a little."

"I'm your Conscience. I'm just letting you know that affairs can create an air of almost constant foreboding."

"Then affairs are like you, Conscience!"

"Uh-huh. You will learn the hard way."

"Your problem, Conscience, is that you are trying to make me a nose-twitching bunny. And I want to be a sniffing hound."

"I'm just trying to turn on a light bulb for you."

"Conscience, I tend to turn away from ridicule."

"Uh-huh."

"You don't understand. When I first saw him, his face flashed expressively. I was filled with such heat it made me gasp. It was unbelievable. I've never felt such electricity before. He speaks to me in a whisper. It is so erotic."

"He whispers to you so you will lean in forward to hear him. It is a trap."

"What?"

"Maybe he's paid to play."

"And maybe you should stop trying to topple my peak moments."

"You, my dear, are flinging yourself head on into the shocking, inexcusable complexity of being a feeling human being."

"What can I say? My boring self has come alive."

"He is trouble making."

"No, he isn't. You are."

"Don't be absurd. I am your conscience. I am on your side."

"Look, I am human. I am a bizarre concoction of strength and weakness, achievement and failure. I am sorry if you consider what I am saying an act of madness, but I am ready to explore my possibilities."

"What has come over you?"

"Life has come over me! I have become a purring woman!"

"I see. Allow me a moment to breathe."

"Sure, Conscience! Take all the time that you need."

"You must make good use of your insight and wit."

"I am tired of being composed of lectures, seminars and case studies. I have sensations and desires. I'm trying to escape self-imposed limitations. Doesn't that mean anything?"

"You are what you are."

"I don't like what I am. I want to be adventuresome."

"Well, currently, you are embarrassingly dopey and desperately infatuated."

"I am tired of your never-ending finger wagging. Your staggering lectures and booming growls are tiring."

"Well, I just can't imagine you stayed up late last night drinking wine and now you are up early this morning racing to see the dawn."

"I'm not racing. I'm soaking in bliss, remember? And I had a few sips of wine."

"Whatever! What has come over you?"

"Conscience, sometimes I don't think we cohabitate the same universe. Sometimes I think you have a mean-streak."

"Well, I must admit, at times I stare and blink at your imagination."

"Thanks a lot."

"You are far away from being a fairytale creature, my dear. As a matter of fact your soul is at risk."

"Conscience, I have a question. Will I ever be able to live with zero guilt?"

"Not on my watch."

"Keep going, Conscience. You are topping my list of enemies."

"He is delightfully deceptive and you have a questing mind."

"What in the world does that mean?"

"Don't ask me questions. You are the one with the answers."

"You confuse the hell out of me."

"Just what is hidden under your self-possession?"

"His extraordinary smile!"

"He is life's dreamy sleeping potion."

"What is so wrong with letting his hand linger on my cheek?"

"His lips twist and so do his fingers."

"At least I don't stiffen under his touch."

"Uh-huh."

"He makes me gasp many times. He is witty, seductive, and enchanting. And he has phenomenal looks. He gave me a lift home. Did I mention that already?"

"I've lost track. Your enthusiasm is crowding my ears."

"Well, he drove with my hand in his. It was like riding in a rapturous coach, Conscience. It was magical."

"You are hopeless. You know that."

"I am not hopeless. I'm just filled with wild emotion. That's all."

"No, you are hopeless."

"I leaned my body into his when we were slow dancing, but I don't think he noticed," I say, blushing. "But I noticed! He tipped my head sideways and ran his fingers down the length of my neck. And then my face tilted toward the floor. He put his finger under my chin. He lifted my lips to his. His breath was warm on my face."

"Uh-huh."

"Well, I hope I never kick this rush. Life feels deliciously dangerous."

"Oh, so now you are a thrill seeker?"

"I'm just highly praising him for his wit."

"Give me a break. He has provocative ideas. He is mentally toxic. He will have you kicking and screaming."

"He is brilliant on life!"

"He is a glimpse of hell."

"Conscience, is it your ambition to make me crazy?"

"I'm your conscience. It's my job to make mental notes."

"Well, I'm tired of your civilizing themes. I want to feel the sensuality of my soul."

"Your thoughts are disturbing."

"I want to skirt around in a slinky, curve-hugging red cocktail dress."

"You know, you are becoming a horror image."

"I can't always wear the weight of the world on elegant shoulders. There is an erotic beauty to living life."

"He is a horror."

"And you, Conscience, are amazingly dispassionate."

"I can't pay homage to your tantalizing thoughts."

"Don't careen through them with leaden feet."

"What do you want from me? I'm your conscience."

"Have the capacity for surprise."

"I don't like surprises."

"Conscience, I've got an intimate confession," I whisper, and all is quiet in my head. "He has dynamited my soul."

"You are hopeless."

"I've caught the glint in my eyes, Conscience. I am no longer lifeless."

"You are hopeless, utterly hopeless."

"Well then, being hopeless feels damn good."

"He is destroying."

"And you, Conscience, have swallowed up my minutes again."

Rising out of the bathtub, I make a grab for my hooded, pink terry-cloth robe and bundle myself up. It is a generous fit and my arms are immediately lost in its elbow length oversized sleeves. I clutch it to my chest like a blanket of security. My robe has always been a warm place for my body to snuggle.

The air in the bathroom is warm and still. I blow some anxious breaths on the mirror and watch them steam. I am nervous as hell. The chicken in me wants to move slowly. Perhaps meeting for lunch in a crowded restaurant would be good for starters. But a date at dawn! I've never done anything like this before. What does one wear to the dawn? I have no idea and for a few moments I want nothing more than to be swallowed up by my terry cloth robe.

Deciding on a pair of baggy gray shorts, I pull my favorite gray sweatshirt over my head. Just thinking of him, I feel a warm rush of affection, and the wetness in my panties kind of catches me by surprise. No doubt I am starry-eyed and still under the spell of his glimpses. Closing my eyes, I feel his warm lips. He is close to me now and speaking softly.

A few raps on the door are startling, and my heart feels as if it is leaping from my chest. Tying my sneakers, I glance at the clock. Goodness! He is about a half-hour early! "Just a minute," I call out, twisting my hair into a ponytail. I dab on some peach lip-gloss and smack my lips together. Praying I look presentable, I draw in a nervous breath and open the door.

On the edge of existence,
I step out of the margins of life.

Chapter 14

The Sensual Rebel

"It is just us and the birds," he says, sweeping me up in his arms.

It is the wee moments before dawn and he has arrived as a perfect human being! Perhaps I am exaggerating just a bit. But I have become an escalating rush of exploding sensation and I am utterly drunk on his charm. There is no way I can cradle my feelings any longer. Acting on impulse, I kiss him!

"Morning energy is ambitious," he says, twining his fingers in my ponytail. "Why you are pink-cheeked," he whispers and my soul turns bright as a rose.

Dressed in casual shorts and a sweatshirt, he is zipped up with impeccable charm. I pant at his body. His legs are wonderful all the way down to the island flaps under his feet. Although our kiss is close lipped, it is hardly robbed of passion and my buzz for him begins early.

"These are my play clothes," he says, winking and I lunge for my second blush of the day.

He casts his eyes on me. "Do you hear the insects rustling in the grass? Those wiggly little bugs are up early." He grins. "I have been up listening to them and to the leaves falling since I left you. I couldn't sleep. There is a lot going on while your body is safe in bed." A smile plays on his lips. "You have an enticing spirit," he whispers, and my body vibrates like approaching thunder.

"Do you know when you wear your hair pulled straight back it highlights your exotic cheek-bones? I like the hanging strands of hair by your face. You are adorable. And by the way I like your baggy shorts and sweatshirt attire. I like your legs."

I look down shyly. "They are skinny."

"They are sexy," he says. "Do you know that you cutely wear a blush?"

I shake my head in flattered disbelief. I can't believe he digs my legs!

"No encrusted rhinestones?" he asks, fingering my sweatshirt. "It seems like everyone in this city is fascinated by shiny objects. Are you sure you are from L.A.?"

I smile.

"I like that you are quietly designed. You know, sometimes I feel as if I am stuck at the intersection of weird and weirder living in L.A. I mean I love the gorgeous weather, swaying palms, and dazzling sunsets but it seems as if everyone is out to translate their character into clothing. People scout stores and meet with designers here. L.A. is a Mecca for fashion pilgrims. Who is your wardrobe stylist?" he asks, helping me into his SUV. I look at him closely. His eyes are leading-man blue.

"I mean this is L.A.! Doesn't everyone have a wardrobe stylist?" he playfully asks.

"I don't," I say, sinking into his car's soft leather upholstery.

"You mean to tell me you are not one of those clothes-hunting beauties that crunch at the mall scouting out their dream gown?"

I shake my head no.

"You mean you are fashion impaired like me? Personally I would rather bundle up in a blanket and snooze through the trends. Yes. Give me an ill-fitting cap and I will hide my face in the endless stream of fashion seekers haunting the Earth."

I smile, hoping he doesn't drive fast.

"People should focus on their character, not their clothing but it is all about image. The desire for the latest thing is very alluring. It is just amazing to watch people dart in and out of shiny boutiques in these gargantuan malls and skirt out with their trinkets of treasures. I am not an impeccably tailored guy by any means. Actually, I am casually dismissed by society as an unglamorous man in my jeans and tennis shoes. I don't need to live stylishly nor do I have to eat in the best restaurants. Give me French-styled buildings and Old Quarter streets and I'll do just fine. Do you need a red carpet dress?" he asks, climbing into the driver's seat.

"No," I giggle as he fastens my seatbelt.

"Are you telling me you don't spend your weekends strolling with packages?"

I nod.

"Good! You are a woman who doesn't need to make the best dressed list." He turns on the ignition and I pray for a smooth take off. It is and I am good to go.

"I don't need to go on a buying spree. I would rather stretch out in a lounge chair and read the newspaper. I am not out for the avant-garde shopping adventure nor am I out for the supreme bargain experience either. Just change into a bikini and get into a hot tub with me," he chuckles. "L.A. is a tabloid-grabbing town. Hey, can you roll around in jeans and a sweatshirt and no makeup?" he asks, grinning.

I blush. I can't take my eyes off of him.

"There should be no traffic on the freeways at this hour but it is L.A., and the spunkiness of this city always has you guessing. You know, there is no dissembling the spirit of this place, and I love it, quirks and all. But I do have these fantasies of car-less days." he says, grinning. His smile makes me all fuzzy inside.

"Do you know that I am passionately driven when I am involved in a cause? With the fever of a deviant and the curiosity of a child, I go after what I believe in. Do you know why? Because, I am a rebel! You see, I am a person who exhibits great independence in thought and action. I openly reveal my fantasies and the critical establishment scowls for I have stretched the boundaries of comprehension." He yawns. "I have no problem exploring my ideas, but I have such a large collection of interests, it is shocking. I am artsy, hip, and tech-savvy. Plus, I am hardly a stranger to nature. You see, it is my customary playfulness that is the key to my character. I am against gridlocked highways, scowling faces, and diesel-scented air. And, did I mention to you that I think society should be bare-shouldered?"

I giggle.

"One day I must consider what my legacy will be, for there is a lot to this tanned contemplator."

Intently, I watch his mouth with dreamy eyes. His lips are sexy when he speaks.

"One of the main things in our society that really frustrates me is the lack of respect for relationships. Infidelity troubles me," he says. "We need to examine why so many of us are willing to make a commitment and then freely engage amorously around town. Infidelity's scoundrels think they can stumble through a few apologies and all will be forgiven. I am not one to give candy kisses to those aimlessly floating in unfaithfulness."

My lips tremble. "Are you my imagination?" I whisper.

"I have a haughty disdain for emotion masquerading," he says, cranking open the window. "Feelings should be expressed. One needs to know where one stands. I certainly don't need to sit forlornly in my flawed eccentrics next to a potted palm in some upscale restaurant wondering what is going through someone's mind. I think whether it be sitting in a wraparound booth over a plate of fries or pouring coffee from a thermos at an outdoor cafe, feelings should be conveyed. Would you like for me to share some more of my human credentials?"

My heart flutters.

"Well let's see," he says, broadly grinning. "I own a good handshake, am jargon-spouting, and punctuate my ramblings with long digressions. I have a true desire for sexual love and romantic attention, am insightful, believe in impulsiveness, decry inaccuracies, and have a touch of defiance to my soul. I beset a distinct sense of style, never question my choices, fearlessly attack life with unyielding intensity, am rooted in stick and ball games, and have yearned for most of my life to pursue stardom. Did I mention that I am sun dependent? L.A. will do that to you," he says as I breathe in the touch of his hand.

"I am a wine enthusiast, a rule-breaker, and when I don't want to talk about something I slide into a mumble! On my flight to reality, I have made it my policy to abandon sensible scandal and go after things in life that make my eyes spin. Strictly speaking, I am an engaging man who keeps moving forward. Perhaps all this stems from the fact that when I was a boy I had big dreams of being a high-booted rock star. Air-smashing my guitar all over the world, my fantasy was to crash through the amplifiers on stage to a cheering crowd." He chuckles. "Perhaps that fantasy was a temptation that shouldn't have been resisted. Perhaps I am the voice of laughter. Care to hear more?" he asks and I nod emphatically.

"I am choked by the language of myths and fairytales and have long been fascinated with medieval times. I have made countless failed attempts to like science fiction, none taking hold of me as of yet, and autobiographies can make me go into exile. I am bored by most dinner conversation, struggle with the manipulation of slimy insincerity and am hardly impressed with the magic of politics. When I travel I don't head to see sparkling mega shopping malls or high-rise hotels either. I would much rather see goats being herded through dusty unpaved roads and milked for the passerby requesting a drink than to bump up and down in a battered cab gawking at raved about hot-spots."

A coy grin tucks at his face. "Jenna, I must be forthright and tell you, I have never dispensed a title, crowned a king, chosen a general or appointed a minister. I've never transformed a movement, conquered a country or even welcomed a dignitary. I've never been invited to join the moon expedition or monitor solar explosions. I leap quickly from idea to idea, draw on the psychology of unmistakable curiosity, and am a person bottom-lined with pointed observations who jets between grace, tact, and sheer folly. Unplug him you say! Not a chance! I spin out of control with self-analysis! Truly you can tell that there is quite a lot of amazing stuff going on in my head. And there is more," he whispers.

"I am courageously carved but a work in progress. I shrug off controversy, am not poll-obsessed, and have a desperate need to be above mediocrity. In other words I am not content to be pushed aside without a fight, so if you are thinking of getting rid of me I warn you that it won't be easy! Besides, I am enchanted with the freckles that cross your nose," he says, pecking my cheek.

"I make it a point to read my fortune cookie scrolls, am an ambassador of the truth, an outlaw of the norm, and I've been known to be menacing. I am an avid reader, enjoy a stroll in the drizzle, and live to run barefoot through life. I am filled with jump-in-the-car spontaneity, crave to race the wind, and I am eager to blow the strands of your hair across your finely featured face. I am full of imagination, am out to achieve greatness, was raised to respect the Earth, and I don't feel that truthfulness should be a last gasp." He places a small kiss on my lips.

"Last but not least, I love the thrill of seeing a new film in a crowded multiplex, or maybe I just like making my way past spilled popcorn and posters of Hollywood fluff. I don't know. I do try to live unencumbered and enjoy a comfortable lifestyle and one day, aside from my writing, I would like to be recognized for my noodle-bar jesting." He pauses. "Oh and one more thing that you might want to know, I am an absurdist."

I squeeze his hand. "Tell me more about Dallas Curtis, the writer!"

"I am garbed in black lights. I have been unhappily tabulating titles for my novel. Nothing fits. You see, in my pages I explore life and love, passion and humility, truth and illusion. My work is a fearless piece of flesh and soul, not designed to be flipped open only to be closed and slid back onto a shelf somewhere to collect dust. You see, the title of my book must not only be thought provoking, it must be pulse pounding. Life inhabits my pages, Jenna, yet I am stuck in stale thought. I need something to bring me back from the literary dead." He puts his finger to his lips. "Do you want to hear a secret?"

"Yes," I whisper.

"I write my pages in a paper-strewn lair accompanied by wastebaskets filled to the brim with discarded ideas. And there is more."

"Oh no!" I jest, my hands covering my mouth.

"Yes! Much more! Mechanical pencils dart gaily over long yellow scratch pads with never ending jottings as piles of specially ordered dictionaries, encyclopedias, and thesaurus' are scarred for life by the tip of my vivacious red pen. I search the contents of their soul, hunting for the suspected culprits of my mind. It is no ordinary engagement." He winks. "Staring into thin air, I dig my heels into my eccentricity. Half-empty mugs of cold coffee accompany my infinite musings as my humble cloth sits perched upon my infamous folding chair, waiting for just the right mental rousing. And then, with frustration ransacking my mind, an idea comes forth and gives me goose bumps! Dispelling the silence, I make an impulsive lunge for my whirring computer, which has patiently waited for me off in the corner. Manically, I punch at its keys. And there, I remain in obsessive fragmentation hungrily creating." He pauses. "Will you be my rolling crowd?" He lowers his voice. "Will you be my ardent listener?"

I tingle.

"Will you serve assorted chocolate fondue in martini glasses as I scrawl my name across the title page of my sold out stock?"

"Yes," I nod.

"Will you offer crackers and fresh fruit to those standing in line to buy my book?"

"Yes!" I exclaim.

"Will you create chic-memorabilia so I will be remembered gallantly?"

"I will even arrange your newspaper-clippings," I blurt.

"Will they festoon your walls?"

"My house will be covered with your exuberant literary reputation!"

"You're going to give me an ego-stroke!" he jests.

With flushed cheeks, I look into his smoldering eyes wondering if he has a clue to my thoughts.

"Fishermen casting their empty vines in dotted hats and baggy yellow slickers await us," he says, a smile playing upon his lips. He steps on the gas. "What is wrong with a cloudless sky making front-page news once in awhile?" he asks.

I shrug.

"I think a picture of a fearless setting sun would make for an excellent headline grabber. The uniqueness of it making the front page would buzz the boulevard for sure! But alas as readers we are herded into columns of gossip and scandal. Perhaps the culture of bust-line enhancements and baggy-eye surgeries should give way to a beautiful sunset once in awhile. But then again who has the time to read about something so natural?"

I nod, wondering what it feels like to run my hand down his cheek.

"Even on the boob tube what would be so wrong with substituting blistering sexuality for treetops blowing in a soft summer breeze? Although I don't know if sales would flourish selling a hamburger to the backdrop of a bunch of palms swaying, unless they were topless of course." He grins. "As you know, I am a rebel. I briskly trot through life unaware of the notion of truce. You see, to a rebel everything represents direction. Every step is a start and every step is a finish line. I pursue my own interests and take off after my own bliss. I act on impulse. So for the moment free yourself from the responsibility of thought and allow me to chauffer your mind! Fasten your seat belt and allow my rapturous coach to glide you through the elusive streets of L.A."

Picking up speed, we soar past palm-lined lawns. I glimpse his profile. He is sexy even while driving.

"Let's explore L.A.'s personality and surprises! Sit back, ardent listener and let the elusive city of alternate reality captivate your imagination with its charming personality. And allow me, to point out the abundance of fresh flowers and trellis greenery the city has to offer as well as its ability to exceed your expectations of fun! Behold! L.A. is a dynamic city with a passion for the good life! It guarantees you wild nights and assures traffic jams at sunrise."

I giggle.

"L.A. is a city of behind-the-scenes secrets that eludes definition. It is a place of hot spots, suburban sprawl, and relentless momentum! Its chic metropolis of fine destination hotels, terraced balconies, and outrageous billboards are enticing! Beware! It has a passionate relationship with bright sunshine and its casual ambiance will motivate you with rebelliousness. Yes! The city's tempting presence stands unchallenged and guarantees to keep its inhabitants starry-eyed to their dying day," he says and I clutch my sides with laughter.

"Lay your eyes on sets of curvy romantic streets with vivid colors and cloud-clumped skies! The outrageous happens in our back lots. Behind a studio's walls are heat sealers, laminators, frost guns, and metallic faces. Walls of ash and wild explosions of confetti burst around glittering icons reading scripts and formulating characters in their head. Astonishing achievements create an energy that take us far away, ardent listener. At times it is fantastic beyond belief. Behind a studio's walls is swoon-screen storytelling at its finest." He gives me a wink and the mystery within me deepens.

"Behold an actor's lingering qualities of climbing waste bins and skirting volcanic ash, just to mention a few heroics in the name of talent! Yes. Humankind will eternally be on a journey of perfection, galvanized by Hollywood's imagination." He pauses. "Everyone wants to be a part of Hollywood's glitter and glory, including me! I am a star! Tomorrow I will outfit surveys and be plastered all over the country's box offices! People will rush from the snack bar to see me on film. Soon, I will become a household name and be on cereal boxes! You know, I would give anything for my pages to hit the big screen," he says and I shiver.

"L.A. is an enchanting city. Its charisma cascades over your shoulders. You can't help but fall under its spell. I mean where else in the world can you jostle madly for a parking spot at any hour of the day! Yes, ardent listener, L.A. is the center of the universe. Behind its sunshine and swaying palms are impressive traffic jams and long lines guaranteed to turn you into a wriggling mass of vulnerability." He lifts a brow.

"L.A. is full of tasty discoveries. While defying your emotions you live them here in the City of the Angels. Look behind your image and you may even endure a slew of endorsement contracts! Yes. You, too, can truly catch a glimpse of yourself in L.A. The promise of your profile awaits you in the entertainment capital of the world! But beware my ardent listener! L.A. is loaded with atmosphere. Delight in its ingenuity but beware of the city's flirtation. Its charm lies in its bizarre extremes."

The passing streetlights radiate softly upon his face, their flickering yellow halos gleaming a powerful aura. I stare out of the window. The twinkling lights of a few cars whoosh by. A car signals to another and gets my attention for a moment, but then my mind is back eyeing his tantalizing profile. I angle my head back on the headrest and close my eyes.

"Are you tired?" he asks.

"No. I am just experiencing happiness," I say, shyly.

He pulls off to the side of the road and gives me a playful kiss. "When I first saw you I wanted to feel you sweat. I thought you were a sensual rebel. But I don't think so now. There is even more to you. You are a magic box. What will emerge when I lift your lid?"

I blush.

"The impending dawn brings lovely temptation," he whispers.

Softly he brushes his lips against mine. I uncross my legs and the erotic warrior within me awakens.

The dawn winks at me
And I blush the sky.

Chapter 15

The Erotic Warrior

Edged in black lace, I emerge, a solitary speck of flame caressed by folds of plumed ruffles. Locks of braided hair duck in and out of my shadow, delicately falling upon my rising hem. In shimmering candlelight a tantalizing woman begins to breathe and then vanishes into thin air.

A scowling face awakens me. "Oh, so now you are an erotic warrior?"

"I'm just on the path to totality, that's all."

"I see. You are out for a happy collision."

"I am tired of just staring intensely at life."

"Uh-huh. You are sick of stepping in and out of your character as your schedule permits. You want to be an earth-charger."

"Conscience, I am not in the mood for your weighty presence. I just want to give off some heat, that's all."

"Are those jungle drums I hear or are those tantalizing breaths ringing in my ears?"

"Conscience, you are hardly charming."

"You know, you have ignited a world so magical as to be almost unbelievable except in its superhuman storytelling. Where are the magic potions and cauldrons of enticing brew? I feel as if I am immersed in a fable. I can't take too much more of your erotic spear-hurling."

"Get lost, Conscience. I'm tired of reporting for moral duty."

"What is the color of your passion?" Dal asks and I wonder if I have made my imagination real. Shaking my head, I respond. "What is the color of my passion? Oh my goodness, I don't know."

"Mine is fire engine red. It is the color of raw energy. I am not an impersonation of a human being," he chortles. "I am a feeling soul! You see, I am not into starched shirts or the trappings of luxury. I am not a shiny boy in a sharp suit. I don't stand on a platform of strategy trying to conquer the world. I find my finest consolation in simplicity and can spend hours looking into the petals of a rose."

"I've never taken the time to do anything like that."

"You've been a career driven woman for too long."

"Well I am taking some time for myself."

"People don't take time for themselves anymore."

"I'm dealing with warring emotions regarding it."

"Why is that?" he asks, knitting his brows.

"It is Oscar season and a tricky time."

"Well life is full of groaning moments. They are the backbone of our dreams!"

"I suppose so," I say half-heartedly.

"Chocolates in a gauzy bag cannot always top the pillows of our cushy bed. Life is a tug of war." He twines a finger in my hair. "Sometimes life demands from us a few leaps of logic," he says and I give him a small nod.

"Don a sarong and let me lead you to a sauna where the steam is thicker than fog. Dripping wet we will turn the world into a torch-lit hula show!" He brushes a gentle kiss across my lips. "Sometimes we just need to make time to kiss the sunlight," he whispers. "Sometimes we just need to take some time off to be human." He looks into my eyes. "Do you know what I see when I look at you? I see an erotic warrior," he says and I gasp.

"Well, we had better step on it if we are going to catch the dawn breaking over the ocean. Are you ready to dare the speed limit?"

"Yes!" I exclaim.

"How does it feel racing to catch a bit of nature instead of running to catch a power meeting?"

"It feels great. I feel so carefree, like flowers!"

"You are feeling human!" He winks. "How is your tummy doing?"

"I've cast my tummy to the wind," I shout.

"You will only hear a whisper of squealing," he says, easing down on the gas. He smiles. "Do you know Heaven blows softly when we are enchanted?"

I glance at him sideways wondering what he must feel like when his head hits the pillow. In a room bathed in just the barest of light, I snuggle close to his breaths and let my fingers roam through his tousled hair.

"Do you know sometimes I tuck the moon back in the evening sky? I can stand outdoors gaping at the heavens until the night sky vanishes and dawn rockets the wind. Cold, my neck stiff from looking up, I watch the world wake up unnoticed."

I cock my head.

"The light in the pre-dawn morning is soft and perfect. The shadows it casts are tender. I am a light-headed elixir of anticipation when the sun rises. With a secret smile on my face, I watch the early morning rise. Smiling at the touch of coolness, I shiver as the morning breeze blows my hair from my neck. It is awesome when the first rays of morning hit things. I feel like I should sit there with a box of popcorn and rise with ovations. You see, the dawn doesn't fake confusion or endlessly wag its finger at you to prove you wrong."

I give him a soft nod.

"There is nothing like watching the sun climb slowly. I remember when I first became dawn-obsessed. Unmercifully swamped with a gnarly hangover, I dragged my stumbling body out of bed to open my bedroom window. The light moved softly as I parted my curtains. In complete serenity with the morning's gentleness, I grabbed my lawn chair and set it down on the dew-laden grass. Kicking back in the faintness, my pounding headache vanished in the sleep chirps floating down from the trees."

I sneak a peek at him. He is gorgeous. I can't keep my eyes off of him. Exiting the highway, life blurs by.

"I love the beach," he chimes. "I've spent many hours breathing in salty air and listening to the surf. I much more prefer laying in the sand with a newspaper over my face than sitting at a busy outdoor café, drinking coffee, and observing the tattooed hipsters flocking the boulevard. The beach is naturally laid back. I miss my lifeguard days."

"You were a lifeguard? I used to have a huge crush on you guys."

"Are you telling me you used to ogle us lifesavers?" he asks and I blush wildly. "I can see you curling up in the warm sand giving us guys the once over behind your dark elusive shades. Were you one of the girls bringing us pops?"

I giggle. "So were you a lifeguard full of harrowing rescues?"

"Well, while I was posed for daring rescues I must admit that I was endlessly sidetracked with bikini distractions." He pauses. "I'd like to see you in a bikini."

"I'll bet you looked cool with sunscreen spread across your nose," I blurt.

"I'll bet you looked cute scrunching your toes in the sand," he chuckles. "I miss those days of loafing in the warm sun! Where on Earth did those days go?"

Driving safely out of first date tensions the mood in the car is heavenly. He slips on some tunes. Soft jazz fills my ears. I put my head back. Life is good.

"Hey! Don't fall asleep on me!" he says. "I fear soon I will see your bobbing head!"

I giggle. "I think that you are amazing!"

"Well I think you are sexy."

"I've never had a lifeguard call me sexy!" I say, blushing.

Beams of oncoming headlamps break up the morning darkness and whiz past us at breakneck speed. He honks the horn and there is a honk back. He shakes his head. "We are a rush-rush society but I must admit I love feeling the rush of speed as I zip past my fellow spectators ambling along in their jumbo haulers. Their faces of horror are beyond humorous." He lowers his voice. "What language of the Earth do you speak?"

I cock my head.

"Perhaps, your dialect is restrained or perhaps it bursts with sexuality and is enticing! Perhaps, your tongue busily dreams about its possibilities!" He chuckles. "Have you ever been softly nibbled upon while wandering through shady glades, rippling streams, and towering pines?"

I stare at him, wide-eyed.

"Well, we must go hiking. Next to loafing in the sun, hiking is a favorite of mine. Just because you are immersed in box office grosses, production costs, and celebrity rhetoric doesn't mean you have to bog yourself down in concrete. Nature has exceptional talents but few people heed the invitation of its lips. They are too busy concentrating on picking up their midsized cars at the airport and becoming weary tourists."

"What is a weary tourist?" I ask.

"The weary tourist follows his dotted maps searching for picturesque villages to drive through. Snapping the world with flash, he makes up stories to go along with his photos when really all he needs to do is spend a day hiking. Nature is inspiring. There is nothing like spending the morning walking along a looping trail surrounded by wildflowers. There is something very stirring yet tranquil about it. The humming of insects and the sound of the birds evokes sheer magic to your ears. It is great not to hear car horns blasting! You just wander at your own pace. It is so much better than driving in your rent-a-car through some dreary seaside resort. You cannot drive through serenity, Jenna. You have to leave your footprints in it; only then can true experiences multiply."

I nod, captivated.

"Nature is not some clever forgery. It has no image blending or voice-overs. It has no control switch and experiences no technical difficulties. And do you know something? It is not guacamole influenced like I am. You make a good guacamole and I am yours forever. Nature takes no bribes."

"You're truly amazing," I utter.

"Do you know in life I am barely noticeable, but in my windswept imagination, I am marvelously alive?" He cradles my fingers in his lips.

"Well, I think you are amazing."

A twinkle comes to his eye. "I'd like to stroll with you and watch the sunset streak the sky."

"Will you hold my hand?" I ask.

"I will do more than that. I will hold your soul."

I gasp.

"Jenna, stop sweeping the flames of your essence aside. Let your breath become the wind! There is the beach," he happily points. "Roll down your window and hear the waves deep kiss the beach."

I tingle.

"You don't see sun-bleached hair, hot boards, and baggy clothes at this hour on the strand. But the surfers will arrive soon on sun-flecked swells. They are just recuperating from their beer-drenched parties," he says parking the car.

He stares into the distance. "You can have your sunburst windows and your master closets. You can sing away in your whirlpool tub and spend eternity fingering your stained wood cabinets and granite countertops. Hurl after me warped window frames, cracked glass panels, and endless walls of peeling paint. I'll gladly embrace it. Just don't take the rising sun from my eyes!"

A tear wets my cheek.

"Let's warm the break of day," he says getting out of the car. I follow the heat of his body. Closing my eyes, I settle my cheek comfortably to his. The candle in my soul flickers. I lick my lips. No doubt, this is sensual heaven.

"The early morning beach lays dark with night waters," he whispers as I cast my eyes over the foaming sea. "The dark is mysterious. I wonder what cavorts off shore at this hour of the morning. There is life out there," he says stroking my hair.

"A tumultuous underwater world of fascinating reefs and erotic caves beckon us with inviting clues. Are they trying to tell us that tantalizing nights of discovery await us? Will it be exploration by torchlight or will our fire give us our mystery? Waving kelp beds eye us wearily. They are afraid of human pollution and rightly so. My mind delights as to what other creatures may lurk in a world where we are but drops in the haze."

I shiver.

"I believe in crashed spaceships secreted away in locked hangars and secluded cities at the mercy of aliens and their hidden agendas. And, I believe green pointy eared creatures watch me everyday thinking I am nothing more than a worthless faceless ignoramus!" He cups his ear. "Am I loony or do you hear the hyper rush engines of spaceships off in the distance?" He winks. "Too much sanity is not good for the soul, you know."

We stand together, body against body staring into the darkness. "We are far away from tabloid hell," he whispers. "And look, Jenna, no assigned seating," he says, feigning to scour the beach. "Where are the retractable camper shells, pop up covers, and Euro tail lights? Where are the sleek roof racks mounted on top of the wide load minivans? Where are the truck toppers? I don't see any. Where are the hot rod enthusiasts with their spinning wheels and deuce coupes? I guess they are still slumbering in their garages," he chuckles.

"Jenna, where are the sizzling body fanciers with their curved sunglasses and bottle bleached hair? Are they with the spiked tipped sun worshipers with tanned abdomens hiding behind their sleek polarized shades? Where are the wardrobe trailers, the celebrity hordes, and their quizzical glances? You can be sure they are launching a tornado of tabloid coverage somewhere. And where are the rolling spectacles?"

"What?" I giggle.

"You know the stretch limos, big black SUVs, and curious media! Are they all bottlenecked somewhere illuminated by the press? The early morning dunes are still and yawning," he says, staring out at the beach. "But the quietness will soon change and the dawn-strand will become a sun soaked bikini world of lounge chairs, brightly colored umbrellas, bouncing beach balls, and coolers filled with shaved ice glitter and soggy potato chips. Yes. Very shortly all this will become a laid back zone of yellow sun, body dunking, and a parking lot to burn the bottom of your bare feet on." He pauses. "Would you like to hear an intimate confession?"

I cup my ear.

"I get a glint in my eye when I am embraced by rock cliffs," he whispers. "I'm a sun-lit rock climbing bum! I am one of those white-knuckled, tan-faced outdoor enthusiasts whose fingers act as groping claws! I don't suppose you have ever gone rock climbing?" he knowingly asks.

I frown. "I've never even worn a backpack."

"Have you ever been around any tumble brush at all in your life? How about when you were a kid? Perhaps your parents snuck in a camping trip and you just don't remember."

"My parents have never been camping either."

"You mean it's generational?"

"I'm afraid so."

"Lugging coolers of food from our car camped abode, my family and I mosquito-swatted our way through our yearly bush-whacked expedition of summer fun. Heaving our backpacks onto our shoulders, we sought the wisdom of nature in our sleeping bags. Curling up into the nocturnal animals we imagined, natures' breaths zoomed us into the first rays of soft sunlight where we snapped up creatures we couldn't see." He shakes his head. "I have another intimate confession. A falling leaf touched my shoulder on one of my expeditions of fun and it was the first time I glimpsed my emotions."

I cradle his words.

Softly he tugs at my fingers. "Hey, have you ever paddled among the dolphins? It is extraordinary! However imperfect you are, the dolphins are always forgiving."

"Tell me their magical nature," I beg.

"The first time I swam with them I drew in nervous breaths. I didn't want them to be frightened away by my imperfection. Snorkeling out with my mask and fins, a lone dolphin swam in front of me. He eyed me, twirled around and spun in the water. I hollered ecstatically at him and he chattered back excitedly. He was so playful. We made eye contact. The next thing I knew I was snuggled up by silvery flashes! Being with the dolphins truly put me in a sea of celebrity. When you swim among them you know you are swimming among friends." He pauses. "Have you ever been sailing?" he asks.

I shake my head from side to side.

"Sailing makes me feel alive! Feeling your hair tousled in every direction, you forget about the maddening details of life. You are just out there defining your identity," he says, and I become an enchantress locked in a sensual spell.

"People spend oodles on pampering massages. In their polished world, they make appointments to be soothed and energized. Laying back for hours in their salt scrub soufflés, they pay extra for small steaming sacks of herbs and cloth-wrapped lemongrass leaves to be placed on their stress-eaten body. When in reality one can naturally be nourished by the ocean breeze! It is far more soothing than a wellness center of mummified goop," he chuckles.

"Tropical ambiances of lit palms have replaced gawking at a beach of pelicans and seagulls. Why put forth the effort? It is easier to bite on crispy crab wontons and scour down drinks with little parasols by the pool. People get a phony sense of relaxation by taking quick dunks and snoozing in their restored bungalows. They think that is communicating with nature! I guess charming arched windows with views of golf courses is a serenity package. As you can see society's prissiness gets me in the mood to grump." He pauses. "Have you ever been whale watching?"

"No," I answer, embarrassed.

"It is the only thing that comes close to swimming with the dolphins. Some people wallow in old memories, while others laud an imagined future. Me, I don't do either. I simply revel in experience." He eyes me playfully.

"Bobbing on the waves, breathing in diesel fumes, I stood at the front of our rickety boat with my fellow excursionists, scouring the white caps for whales. Not finding any, we cast our binoculars to the wind when a puff of smoke rose from the sea and for a moment there was no longer an Earth or sky. The world turned into a maze of foam. Hundreds of whales surrounded our boat. Shouting like a kid, I leaned over and pet them ecstatically as they slapped the water with their fins. Spray flew in my face! It was like a warm caress, utterly breathtaking!"

I bite my lip.

"Jenna, I sit in the office of the sun and travel the shadows of the Earth and in the curvy darkness of a star-lit night I smolder in the pulse of the wind. You know, all that truly exists is the fire of the dragon," he whispers and I blink my eyes open.

Leaning against the hood of his car, I stare off toward the water. A gentle breeze blows through my hair as I breathe in perfumed notes of salt and beach.

The wind caresses my cheeks. "Just lean in and lick its lips, Jenna," he says, his breath warm on my face. "Let the wind snuggle under your chin and caress your closed eyes. Let it tickle your ear and turn you into a blushing rose." A shiver runs down my spine.

He twines his fingers in my hair. "Are you ready to wiggle your toes in the sand?" he asks. His words end in a glisten.

Barefoot, I walk into the dawn. He blows on the back of my neck. I pinch life! It is real.

Stoking the fire of ecstasy,
I fan the flames of my intimate
confessions.

Chapter 16

Life Puckers Its Lips

"In the beginning, there was darkness followed by fire. Temptation roamed the Earth. There was an emphasis on life and heat." He lingers at the water's edge. "Enticement draped each rising sun. Tantalizing winds howled and the flames of seduction leaped high. In the beginning, fever swept the land. Rapture blazed the heavens and drops of sweat thundered down upon humankind." He looks at me longingly.

"In the beginning, there was stillness. Life was rendered inanimate. There was no power to move. And then, there was gesture! Animalism captured the clouds, the stars twinkled suggestively, and humankinds' passionate breaths caught the force of the wind." He lowers his voice.

"In the beginning, there were fantastic enchantments and moonlit adorations. Charm swinging fantasies lauded mystical effects and seduction rocked the sea. In the beginning, humankind turned away from enticement. There was fluster and shame. But then, lust creased humanity's brow and Creation was no longer itself."

I wet my lips.

"In the beginning, batting lashes spirited the eye, lingering kisses pursed the air, and the magic of engagement began. Fingers entwined. Tongues touched. And pleasure danced upon questing lips." I stare at him, his words burning forth.

"In the beginning, there was a glimpse of movement. Muscles flexed. Hot breaths fluttered the sun and flirtation dimpled the air!" He grins. "In the beginning, magic souls steamed the night and enchanted spirits rubbed the sleep from their eyes." He smiles. "In the beginning, lips were gentle and lasting and humanity's softness submerged in the warmth of the blaze." He beams me a smile.

"In the beginning, lust swept downward. Roaming hands leaned into tight embraces and humankind clawed its way out of the darkness. Yes. It all began strangely enough, the abnormality, the strangeness, the abandonment of sanity."

He lowers his voice. "On tantalizing air, they came. The gods of fire! Licking their lips restlessly, shocked by their own audacity, they came. Engulfed in blazing breaths, humankind awoke from its hollow bed and under a blanket of stars melted into the heat of the Earth."

I gape at him, wide-eyed.

"We are civilized now with gleaming floors, soaring ceilings, and décor accented stairways. Don your dark glasses! We've come a long way in our transparency." He smiles. "Humankind has forgotten how to cup its ear to the wind, Jenna. It is too caught up listening to the clanging of its shirt buttons whirling in the dryer."

Fabulous and enticing he drops next to me on the sand. I draw in hot breaths. It is inconceivable how I existed before knowing him. It is almost bewildering. Eagerly, I hang on to his utterances.

"Deep inside of us are stirrings," he whispers.

"Stirrings?" I query.

"Yes. We yearn. We crave."

I gulp. "What do we yearn for?"

"For fire," he says and my body shakes.

His lips curve into a tantalizing smile. “Do you crave adventure? I mean do you yearn to explore the exotic?”

“I don’t know,” I answer.

He speaks with a twinkle in his eye. “Do you know what I long to be? I long to be an erotic traveler.”

I gulp. “An erotic traveler?”

“Yes. You see, an erotic traveler is quite different from your ordinary, slow-talking, loud-speaking tourist. He doesn’t travel the world in funny printed shirts, fanny packs, and wraparound sunglasses, with eighteen cameras around his neck. The erotic traveler is powerfully engaging. He tours the fire of his soul.”

I gasp.

“Speaking hotly to his essence, the erotic traveler is on a thrill-seeking excursion for blow-away climaxes. You know, the world is a sexual inferno,” he whispers. “Tossing out his suitcase of old values, the erotic traveler enjoys the wind in his face and the sun lingering on his lips.” He pauses. “Excuse me, but is your mouth spun in silk?” he asks and my cheeks take in the blush of a million flamingos.

“Look into my eyes without hiding. Are you voyeuristic? You see, the world is a magical place when you override the critical voice in your head. Life is an aura of mystery. I dare anyone to rob me of my enchantment.” He runs his fingers through my hair. “When you are seduced you want nothing in this world but just to breathe. Life is a lantern-lit tour of erotic passageways,” he says and I let out a wooing sigh.

“I want to sunbathe with both of us immersed in hot streaming cocoa butter,” he whispers and I nearly swoon. “So tell me, do you wear daringly low cut evening gowns?” He smiles. “Everyone has fantasies. It’s party of living.”

I stare at him, my willowy body exploding.

The sunlight has fallen across his face. My arms curl around his body. Slipping beyond my brink, I take a deep breath and paint his tantalizing shadow in the back of my lustful mind.

"Have you ever noticed how naked skin glistens? It is so shiny it stirs the wind." He pauses. "Do you know I am drawn to you?"

"You are?" I timidly ask.

"Yes, like an unleashed cyclone!" He winks. "Do you know you are etched in flame?"

I tingle.

"I can be a wonderful sex partner. Excuse me, but is the air shaking or is it just me?"

"The air is shaking," I whisper.

"The pleasure of touch is hypnotic, Jenna. I look at you and feel the muscles melt under my palms. If I should rub the base of your neck and warmly caress your shoulders, would you run from me?"

"I, I don't know," I stammer.

"If I should place my hands upon your lips to quiet your mind, would you flee or would you allow my body to be your sexual oasis?"

I draw in a deep breath.

"If I were to tumble onto you, my fingers bounding for ecstasy, would you allow me to strip you of your sanity or would you just allow the clouds of sensuality to float on by?" He lightly strokes my hand. "I am up for an intimacy-fest. What about you? You know, it only takes one interruption to fly wildly off course in life and suddenly you are willing to give whatever is asked of you. It is called temptation," he says and I try to stifle my gasp.

"Do you dare feel your secrets?" he asks. "I want to hold you in a bed of soft pillows. I'm in the mood for seduction." His lips curve into a smile.

"Don't tell me you are the founder of discipline. You know, Jenna, you can spend a lifetime peddling your morals, but it is hardly the utopian spell." He pauses. "I wonder about you. I wonder if your eyes will close when you touch me. Do you know you have an exotic mysticism about you? I think you are full of sexual prowl," he says and I wonder what kissing him deeply is like.

"Sometimes you have to hang your morals in the breeze and let them blow away." His glittering eyes tighten. "How much longer can I be polite with you?"

My lips quiver.

"So, where are you when the wild night sounds?" he whispers. "Are you garbed in leather, satin or lace? Perhaps, you are a maze of crisscrossing zippers or translucent layers of flowing chiffon. Perhaps, you are dressed in nothing at all." He pauses. "Look! The ocean is caressing the sun!"

I raise my eyes.

"Do you believe in the tales of magic?" he asks.

I shiver.

"If I could send a wish out to the tide I would wish that I may feel your hands upon my face." His voice whispers seductively. Trembling I put my hands on his cheeks, my fingers lingering upon his lips. "It is an intimate moment when soul meets soul," he murmurs softly and my body curves into his words.

"I have faith in magic," he says, his gaze penetrating my eyes. "The wind is in your hair. How lucky it is to caress you. I am but a man and I must follow the rules of courtesy. But know I've not been given life to be a mannequin. It is destroying to be emotionally vacant." His lips curve. "Do you know what I am? I am pressed kisses on your bare shoulders and tender lips on your sore calves. Why, I am the heated flow that comes when the night falls suddenly," he whispers and I am lost in his waiting hands.

"I'd like to see you in loosely draped clothing. Do you like candle-lit baths? What about lavender-scented massages?" He fingers my lips. "I want you to peek teasingly at me from under a pile of blankets. Under a million blankets, I want you to moan beneath my lips."

A blush creeps up my cheeks.

"So what weapons will you use when we are nude? Will it be your fingernails digging into my shivering spine or your tongue drenching my hips? Perhaps it will just be your belly spooned against my back." He smiles. "I want to get to know you intimately. I am full of surprising touches," he says. His eyes are warm with invitation.

"I don't want to be a lost soul credentialed as a human being, Jenna. Therefore, I remain nakedly myself." He takes a deep breath. "So, have you mastered your sexual energy?"

My eyes tear.

"I've offended you. I'm sorry."

"No," I whisper. "I have an intimate confession."

He leans in closely to me.

"I am out of synch with Eden."

Gently, he squeezes my hand. "I'll bet you are precious when you sleep." I rest my head on his shoulder.

"Life is a candle-lit enclave," he whispers. "Come with me. Come with me and be forever drawn to the lips of the sun."

Timidly I fly off of hesitancy's wings. An intimate otherworldliness engulfs me. All is sensual.

I take up a slow, soft rhythm
With the fire dancing in my soul.

Chapter 17
Provocatively Human

Damp-haired and barefoot I return from my bath. He sinks to his knees. In the dark his smooth cheeks are soft hued. Gripping his shoulders, I fuse my body to his. Holding his head breathlessly against my throat his lips turn to fire on my neck. He lifts his gaze. My tongue darts out to greet him.

It is 4 a.m. Somewhere between arousal and sleep, he has caught me. An amorous sweetness awakens me and I peer inside my human window. "Oh look! Intimacy's raindrops are falling!" I shift in my spot. The view is electrifying and momentarily makes me lightheaded. Pressing my nose up to the pane of my soul, I watch with anticipation. "Who are you?" I whisper, glued to the image.

"Why, I am your passionate self."

"Really?" I ask, wide-eyed.

"Yes, really!"

"You are no longer a tantalizing promise just out of reach?"

"No."

"Wow!" I exclaim.

"You are layered with vibrancy. Be fearless! Have the courage to embody your moment. I am your passionate self! I am here! I have arrived!"

Emotional ushers stand in a mist of red roses, proudly brandishing my sensual spirit. I shiver and tap the glass of my soul. It shudders. I take a few deep breaths. His fingers lightly dance on my skin. He smiles. I watch the crinkles tug at the corners of his mouth. His eyes lock into mine. We rub noses. And in a mist of red roses, I become provocatively human.

Enamored, I stretch out, my toes pointing over the edge of my feet. A tiny smile plays over my lips but a tap on my shoulder quickly makes me aware of my surroundings. "Hey you, with the infatuated eyes, he will haunt your dreams."

I groan.

"Don't get too comfortable, old friend."

"I feel your usual composed eyebrow, Conscience."

"You know, I was determined to let you go on, but I just couldn't."

"Conscience, you can't snatch the charm from his eyes."

"What?"

"You always seem to tune in during my enchantment."

"I'm just trying to stop you from colliding with your emotions."

"Well, I am under siege and it is hard to argue with my feelings. You know passion harks back to the first day of time."

"I see."

"I can't distance my thoughts from him. His breath is warm on my cheek. He licks my neck and the blood pulses in my ears." I grin. "Conscience, I do believe that I am sexually fueled!"

"You know, it's creepy, yet almost compelling, to watch you cope with your inner demons."

"The trouble with you, Conscience, is the whole world is a moral issue. You need to submerge in your ego."

"And just what exactly is he, may I ask?"

"He is scrawling comments and amusing opinions. He is a teasing light and a half-smile that catches my eye all day."

"Want to know what I think?"

"Not really, Conscience, but you can't seem to keep anything from me, so go on."

"He is a jungle cat stealthily seeking its prey."

"Since I've met him it is hard to carry on as usual. I am crammed to the gills with sensation. You wouldn't understand, Conscience. I feel sexual."

"You need to get yourself together. You are a bleak image."

"I am a bleak image because I want to curl up with him on a swing chair and softly moan upon his velvet kisses?"

"You lack emotional maturity."

"I want to rise and lift my mask, Conscience. I am a sexual woman!"

"You will end up as nothing more than an abandoned carnival ride."

"I am tired of imagining what life should be."

"He is not the air of authenticity you are looking for. He wears sly shoes and is guaranteed to cause you grief."

I sigh. "His fingers linger upon my skin. He is full of intensity."

"He has a knack for telling his stories with extraordinary zest."

"You know, before I even spoke with him, I was seduced."

"Why don't you lower your glimmering eyes and see the truth?"

"He brings out my stashed away feelings."

"Okay, so you find him vaguely amusing."

"He is wildly confident."

"He is hot-tempered and arrogant."

"You are halfway right. He is hot."

"You exist in a sweet-smelling, bird-twittering world."

"My emotions are blowing across my quaking skin. Please don't mess this up for me, Conscience."

"You are imaginatively engaged."

"Conscience, you certainly don't practice compassion. Can't you see that I am tired of the watered-down version of my life?"

"Weaving emotion is his craft."

"Stuff it, Conscience. I'm feeling alive!"

"The next thing you are going to tell me is that he carries the power of the extraordinary."

"Well, something wonderful is happening."

"Uh-huh."

"He is sexy."

"He is nothing more than an escapist fantasy coming to life."

"He is a man of distinction."

"You are dazzled by him."

"Yes, Conscience, I am!"

"Well then, Hollywood's hocus-pocus comes in handy, doesn't it?"

"Conscience, you are a seizer of life."

"I'm merely trying to point out that he is pretentiously soulful and full of meaningless chatter."

"I'll have you know, he has philosophical value."

"Like the plague."

"His tender expressions brighten my eyes."

"He will have you on a collision course of emotion."

"There is a mystical air about him."

"Your walls are crumbling."

"Well, that is a good thing, Conscience."

"You think so? He will have you shaking like a leaf."

"I will feel a void if he leaves."

"He is full of ridiculous rant, and so are you. You don't know what you are thinking."

"Maybe not, but I know what I am feeling."

"It is truly amazing."

"What is, Conscience? I sense you are smirking."

"Despite his nifty special effects, he has managed to pass for human."

"Oh, so you think he has created a shady portrait?"

"Definitely!"

"He sees the world through inviting eyes."

"Go on."

"He peers beneath the surface of humanity and marvels at contradictions. He is wonderful and funny."

"Oh yes! He is comic perfection."

"Do you know, Conscience, even when I am just giggling with him, it's erotic?"

"He is diluting your essence."

"Maybe so, but his whispering tenderness is wonderful."

"You have an amused expression on your face."

"The wind whistles through the trees when I am with him."

"Give me a break."

"It is the truth."

"Uh-huh."

"You see, Conscience, he senses the rhythms of life."

"Does he sense them through whispers and gasps?"

"He lavishes life with licks and nips."

"Uh-huh."

"Golden light pours through him."

"He sounds like pure flame."

"He has turned me into a vibration of flesh."

"Uh-huh."

"There is more, Conscience. I want to wear see-through tops with strappy backs and feel the brush of his palm upon my fevered skin. I want to get lost in his fiery caress."

"You have become quite immoral."

I blush. “Intimacy’s raindrops are falling.”

“Who incorporates your narration?”

“Keep going, Conscience.”

“Get the starlight out of your eyes!”

“Now you are getting ornery.”

“And while you are at it get rid of the glowing blush of roses upon your cheeks. It is really getting on my nerves.”

“Why, Conscience?”

“He is drawing you in emotionally, and you can’t see it. He is hauntingly articulated.”

“I’ve fallen into a nice bit of misdirection. Let me be.”

“He is a mind-bending illusion.”

“You have an emotional connection to pessimism, Conscience.”

“It is my unapologetic shadow.”

“Conscience, have you ever read the story of trust?”

“Yes. It is not the story of his spirit.”

“Conscience, I am tired of clinging to my values.”

“You are filled with crowded voices.”

“I’m trying to stifle conformity.”

“You are full of internal contradiction.”

“I have a desire to escape my life.”

“You are on a thrill-seeking excursion.”

“I was kissing his ear and whispering.”

“You’ve fallen under his spell.”

“I am full of pounding rhythms.”

“You are a collision of emotion.”

“You need to lighten up, Conscience, or I’m not going to talk to you anymore.”

“Your fantasies are getting way out of hand.”

“I no longer have soundless lips.”

“He is filled with ruinous allure.”

“He has a distinctive touch.”

“You cannot resist his power.”

“He finds me enchanting.”

"Hot! Sexy! And sultry! I believe those are the words he used."

"Yes, those are the words," I say, beaming.

"His song really got to you."

"Excuse me, Conscience, but I'm watching life differently right now."

"I see."

"He lowered his face into the curve of my neck."

"His acting is flawless."

"I ran my fingers through his rumpled hair."

"He will loot you emotionally."

"I want to crush my body into his."

"You are in the hands of a storyteller."

"He has rendered me breathless."

"You are not listening to me."

"I want to lean back in his arms and tingle."

"You want to conjure up your own rules of etiquette."

"Conscience, you are nothing more than a behind the scenes intruder."

"He will raise your anxiety level, guaranteed."

"He is a man who reminds me that there is more to the world than the mundane."

"He is a high-wire act."

"He has mysterious charms."

"I'm telling you that there is menace under his skin."

"It is sexy when soul meets soul."

"Keep your life in perspective."

"Conscience, I want him."

"Oh brother!"

"I crave for the unfamiliar."

"And so you think he is worth the detour?"

"Yes, well worth the detour."

"Go outrun your demons. I'll be here when you are wallowing in self-pity."

"You are grounded in reality, Conscience."

"You need to be emotionally mature."

"Why do I have to be emotionally mature? Why can't I be a whirlwind of desire?"

"What do you want to do, run after sex in upstairs bedrooms?"

"I detect you are scowling, Conscience."

"Take a deep, long breath and listen to me. He is amoral. He has seized you emotionally. What is wrong with you?"

"I'm happy."

"I see."

"Analyzing life too much is an obstacle."

"I see."

"His face was warm against my cheek."

"Uh-huh."

"He pushed back the loose strands of my hair. His lips brushed the inside of my wrist." I smile. "He is a sizzling connection to existence."

"It sounds like he percolates time."

"I detect you are scowling again."

"Yes. I am."

"Why?"

"His evil ponderings are doomed to succeed."

"Conscience, you paint him as if he is some kind of never-will-die villain."

"Go on."

"He interacts through magic eyes."

"Now you're getting corny."

"My skin tingles at just the thought of his lips traveling down my throat."

"I don't think I can take much more of this."

"Must I always glance out of the passenger window of life?"

"He will have you in the throes of despair. He is a terrific performance."

"Conscience, he takes emotions seriously and that is what makes him exceptional. He is wildly inventive and genuine."

"He is keeping his actions crisply paced."

"I have a question for you, Conscience."

"Yes?"

"What reveals humanity?"

"Humanity is revealed in softness."

"He is not a study of evil images."

"He has contagious charm."

"Ah, so he does."

"Remember, you're happiest when your values are in line."

"Having a good time, Conscience, is not a bad thing."

"You are flirting with the unknown."

"I feel like prattling with the whatever."

"You will be plagued by nightmares."

"Give me a break."

"May I remind you that he will have you trapped in cycles of lust?"

"You know, Conscience, I would be happier if you were out of my life."

"We are a rocky love affair."

"Uh-huh."

"You can't get rid of me."

"Uh-huh."

"Remember, I am your lingering presence."

"And what am I?"

"You are a fragmented soul."

"I am tired of being dreary and predictable."

"You can't bear the pain and rage of conflict."

"I also can no longer be a boring woman."

"What is it that you want to be?"

"I want to be magical and indescribable."

"Is that what he is?"

"Yes, and he is more!"

"You paint him as if he were some sort of golden mosaic."

"He is fascinating and adventuresome."

"He is glib and manipulative."

"He speaks sweetly."

"His talk is deadly."

"Conscience, I want to bounce before the easel of life and feel the brushstrokes of my soul. I want to be paint-splattered with sensation! Do you know I have only felt the edges of my body?"

"Did you take a mind-expanding pill this morning? Do you know what you are in for?"

"Yes. I'm in search of the human touch."

"You definitely are induced by something."

"I am induced by fascination."

"You are walking down the road of self-destruction."

"I am walking out of the castle of paradox."

"I see."

"You know, Conscience, you are certainly not a place to lay my head."

"I can't help my cynicism. You are on an offbeat destination."

"I want to discover the unusual."

"You are full of strange noises."

"Conscience, I am allowing passion to pique my interests. I am knocking on the door of my soul."

"Will your banging ever cease?"

"Not until I find what I am looking for."

"And that is?"

"Passion!"

"Venturing off the beaten track of life may not go smoothly. Your eyes may widen and your face may hold expressions of bewilderment."

"I want to slide lingeringly down his body."

"You want to 'poof' out of your values."

"No, I just want to let loose."

"Uh-huh."

"A rosy glow shines from my head to my toes since I have met him. What can I say? I am feeling human!"

"You are flirting with danger."

"His eyes are extraordinarily blue."

"He is too clear-eyed for sentimentality."

"I'm not looking for a wedding cake."

"You are traditionalism."

"I don't want any rules of etiquette in my life anymore. I just want to live. What is so bad about just living? Other people do it. Why can't I?"

"What has come over you?"

"I have been smiled at, Conscience."

"You are plunging into a vanishing soul."

"I want to feel his kisses land between the dimples in the small of my back."

"You are off your rocker."

"You are pushing my buttons."

"No doubt, you are gripped in lunacy."

"I am not coming back to my senses."

"I see."

"Was that a chuckle I just heard, Conscience?"

"No, that was your imagination."

"His body moves me."

"You are tumbling over the edge of your life."

"My body craves for release when he runs his fingers through my hair."

"You are out of control."

"When he whispers in my ear, I tingle."

"He has a falsetto voice and an automated smile."

"He has handed me the thrill of pleasure."

"Uh-huh. He's nothing short of magical."

"I won't allow you to sabotage these sensations."

"Evil shows up in human form."

"I am yells and screams and hums and whistles."

"Disrobe yourself of illusion. Listen for stifled laughter."

"Inhibition is slipping off my shoulders. The flame in my eyes is growing brighter."

"You are bats."

"I want to prance in mesh."

"You need to go to a place where folks weave baskets and stare at peeling paint."

"Some of the best things in life are things you've never thought of."

"You are nuts."

"That's the best compliment you've given me."

"You belong in a loony bin. Have you considered taking up chicken-raising?"

"I'm tired of being frigid."

"It's the card you've been dealt."

"Conscience, you need to take a few breaths of mystical enchantment."

"Uh-huh."

"You don't understand. He kissed me softly."

"Where are your high standards?"

"I have slipped off virtue's boots."

"So, you've got naked toes."

"Snow-women can melt, Conscience."

"Not you."

"My lips have turned to fire."

"You've burned your moral scorecard."

"Conscience?"

"Yes?"

"You're fired."

Holding a magnifying glass up
to my fantasies,
I see the woman I truly am.

Chapter 18

The Lords of Seduction

I pull my stuffed quilt under my chin and rub its silky edging between my fingers. Its warmth takes me back to when I was a thumb-sucking little girl. Giggling to myself, I remember how I used to live under a cocoon of covers. Silently I would dive under their velvety warmth, tip my head back, and glare at the dark! In my tiny bed-space oasis, I was hidden. Kindergarten couldn't find me there. Lying nose to nose with endless moments, I remained until my fuzzy pajama arms stuck out above the covers and felt for safety. With a lump in my throat I burrow deeper into my quilt. Those days are gone I softly reminisce, as I drift off into a sweet slumber.

Something light caresses my lips. "What is that?" I muse, wrinkling my nose. "It tickles."

"It is a feather caught on your whisper."

I blush.

"You appear wanting."

"Me?" I ask, staring into the darkness.

"Yes! You are sprawled wantonly across the bed."

"Ah, so I am. What is that noise?" I ask, covering my ears. "It sounds like engines revving."

"Go see for yourself."

I jump out of bed and move across the stillness of my room to my bay window. Parting my curtains, I lean my forehead against the cool glass and take some deep breaths to calm myself. With my nose pressed hard against the window, I crane my neck to look out to both sides of the street. My breathing gets heavier as my eyes frantically search for something, anything. I crank open the window and listen. All is silent except for the sound of leafy trees blowing in the breeze. I stand there unable to move, my mind racing. "Where on Earth is the noise of revving engines coming from?" I muse.

With my heart leaping against my ribs, I take one last look outside. There is nothing out there except some very early traffic whizzing by. I make my way back to the edge of my bed and close my eyes. There is an inkling of something watching, perhaps even lurking, but I can't put my finger on it.

"We understand that you are awaiting discovery."

Hearing voices again, I look around, my heart racing.

"What? Who are you?"

"We understand that you want to ignite your life!"

I cover my ears. "What is that noise?"

"That is the engine of your soul, revving."

"Wow," I blurt. "It sounds like a motocross!"

"You see, you have ferocious revving ability." They wink. "You are roaring thunder."

"Who are you?" I ask, feeling a kiss in the middle of my back.

"We are nibbles on your neck, teeth on your earlobe, and fingers of sensual caress. Why we are the tangle of arms that you make hot passionate love in. We are the eyes that make your legs grow weak. We are the lips that unclasp your bra that casually falls to your feet. We are the flow between your legs." They wink. "So, are you ready to become a panting woman?"

"Who are you?" I whisper.

"We are the Lords of Seduction. We are from the sexual world, and we have come to take you away."

I gulp.

Clad in blue jeans, leather jackets, and a flaunting sensual attitude, they are immensely appealing with their slicked-back hair, a massive affair of seduction. They rub their jean-clad thighs against my flannel body as they sit next to me at the edge of the bed. Their presence is addicting.

"What is your occupation?" I ask.

"We sweep excitement across the Earth! We are tingle inducers."

"Are you passion's descendants?" I whisper.

The voices laugh. "We are more than that! We are body glitter and massage oils. We are warming lotions and pleasure feathers. We are sparks of erotic electricity! Close your eyes and ignite!"

"Oh my god," I gasp, staring at them in astonishment. "Do you have a plan to take on the world?"

"Yes. Our agenda is to bring sensual luster to those who are desperate to breathe. We are the deep kiss that awakens sleeping lips."

I gasp.

"We are crooning tender love songs and low growls of sexual pleasure. We are sweat-soaked and full of emotional voltage! Few embody the genuine charm of seduction that we do. We are immeasurable sensitivity. Although we don't waltz around with willow-wands casting magical spells, we carry the distinct aroma of sexual bliss." They smile. "We are the scent of roses."

I extend my arm.

"We don't shake hands. We breathe fire."

I shiver. "What are you doing here?"

"We are here to spice up your soul."

"I don't belong in your world."

"You don't want to live with frustration flapping around your legs, do you?" Their hands dangle between my knees.

"Tell me more," I say, trembling.

"We are spine tinglers. Allow us to trace your curves in a mouth-watering path under your lacy hem. We will make tension leave your body, guaranteed."

"How?" I ask.

"We have hot roaming hands."

"Wow! Will I moan as your tongue crawls aimlessly up my arm?"

"We will make your mind scream."

I lick my lips.

"Take long, exquisite breaths. Share your desires. Allow us to lure you for eternity."

"I want to wear lacy rose-colored panties," I say, breathing deeply.

"You should. Your presence emits a sexy beast."

I tingle.

"I want to kiss so passionately that my face heats and then I want to burst into a thousand shivers."

"You have shiny lips."

"Really!" I exclaim.

"Yes! Now, we have an inquiry of you. Will you struggle to keep yourself under control?"

I shiver.

"Why do you hide your charms?"

"I am dueling with my inner self."

"Do you dream of escaping to a better life?"

"Yes, of course."

"We detect you are full of contradiction."

"I am shy."

"Allow your body to explode with adventure. Drop yourself into the sun."

"I want to sail on the vessel of passion. Where do I board?"

"That ship docks in your soul."

I look down. "Perhaps I am an eccentric visionary."

"Allow life to whisper lightly in your ear."

Tears pour down my cheeks. "Who are you?"

"We are the Lords of Seduction. Intimate, passionate, and erotically unforgettable, we defy logic. We blur reality. Of course we may draw smirks and darts from our frigid critics, but remember they are not more powerful than smoldering sex." They smile invitingly. "We are here to rescue you from your stillness. Come with us. Just wet your lips and off we'll go."

I tingle. A slight curve of a smile appears on my face. "Did someone just blow in my ear?"

"That is the art of seduction giving you a shout."

"I felt the heat loud and clear!"

"We noticed a grin sneak across your face."

"I thought my silly grin would go unnoticed."

"We notice everything."

I lower my voice. "I have fantasies."

"We make fantasies come true."

"How?"

"Follow the twinkle in your eye. Come with us. Taste our magic."

"I crave."

"You are our type of girl. We will fulfill your longings. We can make the wistful twilight linger. In our arms, you can clutch the rainbow you are seeking."

"I want to be kissed along my jaw line. I think that would make me squeal."

"Would kissing your closed eyes inspire a magical sense of wonder too?"

"Yes. It would steal my breath away. But there is more."

"Talk to us."

"I want to be transformed into a creature of pleasure.

On a bed of throw pillows, in front of burning logs, the inside of my thighs are traced with steamy lips. The outer rim of my ear is licked. Mad with sensual kisses my skin prickles as I blink through the mess of hair that has fallen in my eyes. Sizzling pecks dust my chin, soft caresses blush my cheeks as I transform into a creature responding in uncontrollable ways. Making my way to my sparkling eyes, I stop at the change in my voice. I am purring. I tilt my head. Looking at myself curiously, I shyly smile. The sun is waiting to pounce."

"Everything is in your power. There is nothing wrong with temptation."

"I want to be filled with flowers and sit in a pool of moonlight and let the wind reveal my candidness."

"You are tired of existing. You are ready to live."

"What is the difference?"

"Existing is thumbing through the book of life, emerging and saying you have lived. Living goes far beyond that. Living is gripping pillows and curling toes. Living is when you crush your breasts against his ribcage and the intense darkness is more than something curious. Existing is a quiet, unimaginative place where fluffed up pillows are stacked neatly at the end of the bed. It is where breaths are cool and caught easily. It is a place where your blank expression is hidden for all time in the mundane clutches of the missionary position."

"I have an intimate confession," I whisper.

The Lords of Seduction lick their lips.

"In a sea of sunlight, I am nude, except for a strand of pearls. My shroud hoisted, a sensual liveliness inherently kittenish, emerges and I transcend into a wildcat. Slipping on my high heels to bed, I catch my hot breaths in the half slip draping my body. Seated by my morals, my face is unknown to me. A string bikini blows off in the distance on a beach of topless sunbathing. I have fantasies."

"We make fantasies come true."

"I just felt a hip bump into me."

The Lords of Seduction wink. "Become daring. Stop at the mood fountain of life. Become a person of hot interruption."

I tremble.

"Tell us, what do you see after the lights darken? Do you splinter into stunning authenticity? Are you ardently unforgettable? Do you ache for definition?" The Lords of Seduction grin. "Your skin feels incredibly soft," they say, caressing my face.

I shiver. "Did someone just blow me a kiss?"

They smile. "Are you an emotional enthusiast?"

"I want to run wild," I whisper.

"To do so you must lift yourself out of your slumber. Come with us. We are not stern-looking border agents carefully examining your passport to eroticism. We welcome you into our world. Taste our magic!"

"You are a world of mystery but are you also a world of illusion?"

"You must discover our secrets for yourself."

"This can't be happening," I utter.

"But it is. Come with us. Disrobe enchantment!"

"I want to linger in life with my bellybutton exposed. I want to feel the comfort of silk glancing my way. I want to be lost in the sound of my animated spirit."

The Lords of Seduction grin. "We have an intimate confession for you."

I stare at them wild-eyed.

"We want to see you in a skimpy tunic top."

A lump forms in my throat.

"Is button-up your normal garb?"

"I suppose I am a knee-length and sweater girl. You see, I am bashful."

"We think you are mysterious. Come with us."

"There is more. I want to be a sultry woman in a nightgown, lounging."

"Allow yourself to become radiant in an instant."

"What do I do?"

"Allow yourself to be kissed by fire."

"Have I entered the land of fable?" I whisper.

"Let a soft warm tongue touch you softly."

I tremble.

"Meet your erotic soul. Become one of us. We are the brave and the curious. We go beyond our wildest dreams. Foolish, you may say!" The Lords of Seduction lower their lips to my neck. "We are vibrant, provocative and hot."

"Your voices are smoky. You are burning my ears!"

"Physical madness can be soothing. It is time for you to meet the titillating hunter."

"Who is that?" I ask, feeling my skin warm.

"The titillating hunter explodes your being. Its sworn duty is to turn the universe into flowing lace. Smoldering the globe into erotic flames, the titillating hunter is celebrated all over the world. Tantalized by flirty chiffon, hypnotized by black silk, the titillating hunter sees creation as a burst of shredded ruffles and floor-sweeping gowns."

"What about bubble skirts and black crushed cotton?" I whisper, "And slouchy suede and squiggly embroidery?"

The Lords of Seduction hungrily rub their hands together. "We would love to see you sensually puckered and sewn. Shed your sleepy bone corset. Slip into a glossy red cocktail dress and come with us! It is a gleaming world of billowy sleeves!"

I sigh. "The titillating hunter searches for the impossible."

"The titillating hunter is a blessed form of madness. Don't blink away your tantalizing thoughts. Circle the world in a tiny satin skirt."

"My tantalizing thoughts are my enchanting fiction."

"Tantalizing thoughts can become reality."

"They can't," I say.

"They can. We are the Lords of Seduction. The erotic world is insanely charming. Join us."

"It is not available to me. I am too sane and controlled."

"Allow us into the secrets unfolding within you."

"I have never played fast and loose."

"You have never toasted life with a kiss. Our fingers trace your careful path. Your bed is nicely made and incredibly neat. Are your sheets ever ruffled?"

I sigh softly. "This is my first bout with revolutionary genius and I am wobbling dangerously."

"We are seduced by ripples of silk and incense at dusk. We seductively menace the world. Come with us."

"How do I do that?"

"Steal a kiss whenever possible!"

"Oh my god!"

"Become skin tingled! Unfasten your life. Discover the ecstasy of a whisper."

I tremble.

"Open your ears to the hiss of a zipper and the sound of buttons popping."

"Yes," I whisper.

"Whisking away on impulse is hypnotic. Allow your voice to become a purring caress."

"I'm scared."

"Allow us to puff away the strands of hair that keep flopping in your face. It is okay to tease. Stop your note taking and sprawl upon us on scarlet cushions."

"I can't."

"It is a sumptuous world."

"How do I arrive?"

"Give yourself a shot of magical thinking."

A tear drops down my cheek.

The Lords of Seduction are kind. "Allow us to awaken your soul."

"This is a joke. I am being seduced by dream ears."

The Lords of Seduction raise their hands. "We don't joke about temptation. We want to lick your belly," they say with a devilish grin. "Come with us. Take in inviting breaths."

I tingle.

"We are filled with fiery hugs. Come with us."

I turn my head away.

"We are not a dungeon of horror."

"I'm scared. I fear what I will become."

"What is so wrong with becoming a fire-breathing woman? Free your mind and body. Come with us."

"I have never fancied myself as a player."

"Wrap yourself in easy moments."

Warm lips kiss the back of my neck. Strong arms encircle my waist as roaming hands pick up my flannel pajama top and caress my bare stomach. "We are seducing you," chime the Lords of Seduction. They run their fingers up and down my pajama-clad legs. "Join us and become amorous."

I shiver. "Did someone just peck my neck?"

"Let us nudge you into excitement."

My panties moisten.

"In our arms you will touch the wind of your soul."

I gulp.

"Now, tell us who you are."

"I am a woman who wants to disappear behind the villains of play."

"You are a woman attempting promiscuity. You are nestled between fantasy and reality. You must let go. Delicate feather touches are the soft knock on your soul you have been waiting for."

"I am timid."

"You are living a lifeless existence. How will you ever feel intimacy's raindrops fall?"

I wipe my eyes.

"Life is seductive gestures and suggestive glances. It is tantalizing postures and charming flirtation. Live like it is the last night on Earth. Smooch with breaths of fire."

I stare at the Lords of Seduction. "I don't know why I am looking at you in this way," I pant. "I cannot seem to turn away."

"Don't try to understand the mystery. Smooching can be delightful! We will give you a searing kiss before taking you off to our bedroom."

"I am overcome by burning energy." I squeal.

"Come with us! Feel your shivers!"

"I am overwhelmed with intensity."

"We are forming a sweaty liaison with you."

"I am brimming with heat. Am I a lioness?"

"Tantalizing surprises await you."

"I am scared. I don't believe I have a compatible spirit."

"You have only half-imagined yourself. It is time for you to really sound. Come with us. We are pure sensation."

"Perhaps a wilder self will have me in ill-suited shoes."

"Slip off your ebony slippers. Come with us. Step into the ring of fire. Become an erotic traveler. Find your silky voice. Feel your fingernails sensually glide down craving skin. Hear voices cry out in ecstasy from your touch. Your willingness will take you by surprise."

I blush.

"Do you know who we really are?"

"You are the Lords of Seduction."

"We are the pulse of life."

"Oh wow," I blurt.

"While the world looks away, we smile. While the world looks away, we wink. We don't let anything stop us from venturing out on the tantalizing turf of life."

"Am I imagining your presence? I feel as if I'm absolutely ablaze!"

"We move between past and present, reality and imagination."

"Are you glittering icons?"

The Lords of Seduction laugh.

"Your hot breaths are sinking into my sweat-slicked skin."

"We are here to entrance you, entice you and take you on the sensual romp of your life. Of course we will allow you to stop many times for large gasps of precious air."

"Are you going to take me away from all I know? Will I be in a place that will possess my mind, body, and soul?"

"Oh yes," they naughtily grin. "We are going to take you to a place beyond your fantasies. We are going to take you to the wild beast within."

"I can barely breathe," I say.

"Now, are you available for quiet encounters?"

I swallow hard.

"Do you have willing lips?"

I shake.

"Is your body intense and commanding?"

"I want it to be," I whisper.

"Allow us into your world with the art of seduction. Close your eyes. Feel the luscious touch of our flesh."

"Is this really happening?"

They touch my cheek. "This is as real as it gets."

I shiver.

"Life is alluring gestures, suggestive glances, and flirty grins. Now, let us try this again. Become an erotic traveler."

"I want to be a dripping adventurer," I pant.

"You are no longer apprehensive?"

I smile mischievously. "My image is fading. Is that the hiss of zippers I hear?"

The Lords of Seduction grin. "You have intimately awakened."

I tingle. "There is something magnetic happening."

"You are peeking into the heat of your soul. You are purring erotically."

I gulp.

The Lords of Seduction crook their fingers at me. "Come with us. We wish for never-ending moments. Remember, we are from the sexual world."

"Yes," I echo, trance-like, extending my arms toward them. "I am no longer hesitant, but eager."

"Let your sexual energy flow. Lure us to your bed."

"Yes," I repeat hypnotically. "I am burning."

"Your body is thundering."

"Yes," I breathe.

"Fall into temptation. We are a world inhabited by erotic warriors. We are the quick glance that you give to that winking eye. We are the hot streak that crosses the sun. Come with us and feel your panting soul."

Glowing in the dark they move toward me, their heated breaths blazing the air. "Your essence clings to your dreams," they whisper. "Allow enchantment to open your eyes."

And in this instant a rushing sensation overcomes me. Unable to resist the madness, my body ignites! The invasion is sensual, irresistible, and welcome. "I am ready to discover my magic," I whisper.

Trailing sweet kisses down the side of my neck, the Lords of Seduction smack their lips together and I am gone.

Slanting my mouth over life's lips,
I break into a wolfish grin.

Chapter 19
Blushing in Lace

"Last night I had a dream that you were clad only in a fig leaf. I removed it with my teeth and licked your body all over. You were so enticing and natural in the flesh. You really shouldn't wear clothes," he says.

Shyly I look down at my strawberry margarita.

"You are bashful. Will you be like that in my arms?"

I am pink-cheeked and cannot reply.

"I love making you blush," he says. "One day I will whisper softly to your pillow." He lowers his voice. "Do you dare feel your secrets?" he asks.

I give him a meek smile.

"I'm sorry. I guess my mind tends to run away with me, but I am completely immersed in all that you are. As a matter of fact if I were any hotter for you, I would self-combust. What are your thoughts?" he asks.

"Excuse me while I enter Nirvana," I say and we kiss over a smoldering appetizer of firefly shrimp.

"When we were at the beach do you know how much I wanted to smear your body with wet sand? Since then, I've had endless fantasies of you running bare in the sun. And there is more. I drop a grape between your rosy lips. You loosen your fingers. The siren of pleasure goes off." He pauses. "Do you know you have a ravenous mouth?

Know that in my fantasies, I capture your lips and grab that grape with my tongue."

"One more slice of paradise please," I pant.

"My obsessively compulsive behavior is beyond my own recognition. Was 6 a.m. this morning too early to call to ask you to lunch at my favorite haunt? I thought you would be up anyway thinking about my seductiveness," he says, winking. "Do you know that in a swoop you have managed to occupy my thoughts and I am sleep deprived because of two nights of endless arousing sensation? I keep feeling your tongue tingling the night."

I stir my margarita. It is difficult to pretend that this is a normal conversation.

He grins. "I think when we are naked you will make love to me with the fury of an angel." Shyly, I turn away from him. He touches my cheek softly with the back of his hand.

Sensing my bashfulness, he changes the subject. "This is a unique establishment," he remarks, admiring the striking rose window. "It is a modern-day spin-off of a sixties beatnik café, but it is really an anything-goes eatery dedicated to the art of sizzle. Everything in this place is full of fire. The burn, the sweat, and the euphoria that follows dipping a single tortilla chip into its howling chipotle salsa is pure insanity. It can raise the dead! But the ambiance is festive, and the quirky dishes make you want to linger. Still, there is nothing fancy here, but I am not into fancy. I would eat off of paper plates and settle for a glass of rainwater just to be in your presence."

"Is this place full of distinctive faces?" I ask, glancing around.

"This place has people sitting outside on the edge of planters waiting for a table. That is how popular it is. And it is full of every kind of species imaginable, but I have a theory. People lunch here to scheme their way up the social ladder and camouflage their limitations. But not me!

I like to relax on the veranda, scan the boulevard, count the pros and cons in my life, and text message my friends."

I smile adoringly at him. He is so damn cool!

"Come on, let's go outside for a little more atmosphere and sip some cool ones under the shade until our gutsy salsa and taste-bud scorchers arrive." He grabs our margaritas and we move amid the lunchtime chatter. "It is noisy here even when it is half-empty," he calls to me over his shoulder. "After four, this place reverberates with thumping dance music."

He chooses our seats carefully and guides me to a small table under a green tarp that provides relief from the afternoon sun. "The rains have definitely scrubbed the sky blue," he says, pulling a chair for me. He sets down our drinks. "The light dusting of clouds makes it one of those classic picture postcard days."

He seats me as if I am a queen. He is dignified and gentlemanly. He reaches across the table and touches the tips of my fingers. I turn to face him more fully. Trembling, I curl my fingers around his. He smiles. "Do you know when I look at you I am a highly spirited blend of spectacular inventiveness?" he says, scooting his chair up closer to mine. "I am a cathedral of feeling for when I am whooshed to the heavens I want to know that in my life I was nothing more than utterly human."

"I think you are emotionally admirable," I blurt.

"I'm just a gung-ho expressionist and I find you unbelievably sexy. To divulge the truth, you have this amorous shimmer about you." He pauses. "I feel as if I am a hormone-charged sinister serpent that is poised in the lush grass waiting for you with passionate venom."

I twine a few strands of hair around my fingers. He smiles. "I love your innocence. You are a tantalizing slice of life that one day soon I will nibble upon. You excite me in unavoidable ways."

We are rambling in a warm L.A. afternoon when a hot burst of emotion pours through me. "So this is what it's like to feel human," I muse.

"Do you know that your dimples talk to me? I think they've got ideas," he says and my tummy flutters.

"Dimples are hot. I don't know what it is about them. Perhaps, it is the way they deepen one's cheeks." He winks. "Dimples reveal secrets. They are not like push-up bras. Dimples are natural. They are a riot of curls that you can admire a hundred times and forever remember the smile that brought them on. I can tease out the hint of your dimples," he says, winking. "Do you know you cutely wear a blush? I suppose I've probably said this before but your hushed tones are a turn on." He pauses. "But there is a part of you that is hiding. It doesn't pass me by unnoticed. It makes me wonder if you know the feel of silk upon your bare skin."

I look down.

"You see, I have just teased out a dusting of curls in your cheeks. What truly calls you to your soul?" he whispers. "Are you a day-tripper flourishing through life or are you a wanderer who loiters at the window of your essence?"

My lips tremble.

"I look around humankind. Do you know what I see? I see gold-rimmed reading glasses and glass displays of fabled croissants. I see soup to go and cups of coffee on plates boasting of outstanding puff paste. I peer into life, Jenna, and do you know what blinks back at me? Automated smiles! Yes. They wish me luck, catch my movement in the hallway and are the mass of hair I follow crunching autumn leaves. They loiter, glisten with temper, shift their eyes, and scurry behind counters wishing me a nice day. No one takes the time in life to watch the steam rise, but I do. I peer into humankind and watch people living their own fiction." He pauses. "I asked you to meet me here today to encounter reality. What crafts your soul?"

I cock my head.

"Sometimes I feel as if I am a mad scientist leading an expedition into the heart of honesty. Perhaps when one is exposed to honesty, chaos breaks loose. I don't know. But no doubt it is a great shock moment. I would like to write about truthfulness one day, but I fear it would be another monster-on-the-loose thriller." He chuckles. "Life might even be charming if it wasn't so bizarre. You know, there are days when I wish I was a watering can in some old nursery. Tilted at an angle, water pouring out of my spout, I am a life preserver wetting the petunias of the world!" He shakes his head. "And those petunias of the world think I am falling rain. You see, the masquerade never stops," he chuckles and I stare at him, entranced.

"Do people even talk about their morals and ethics? I wonder. Do people even have any morals and ethics? I think not. Where is the simplicity of earthy values, Jenna? Curious, we stroll up to humankind. Immediately we are taken in by its inviting presence. Listening intently, we are astonished to learn that humanity has buried itself in camouflage for the sake of profit." He chuckles and points to a group of people scuttling the boulevard.

"My god, Jenna, look at the urban spectacles with their featureless uniformity. They need to get home to their pruned hedges and bedded flowers. You see, on the beloved boulevard minds wander and human beings follow their own logic. They have it all figured out," he mutters.

"Look at the people and their stylish flairs. They are all stuffed with colorful stories and fictional identities. You know, a white-linen dinner is fine at the Hotel Façade with its elegant setting of tall framed windows and floating sorbet. But I would cast aside its delicate entrees of pickled peppers, awarded wines and spectator awards for a gentle getaway of bird watching. Now those are true moments of luxury." He winks. "Don't tell me that you have never been bird watching?" he asks.

I frown.

"Don't be hard on yourself. The majority of the population is just not lured to watching a smattering of warblers get rained on." He raises a brow. "I suppose spa treatments and prime tee times are far more alluring."

He leans back in his chair. Gazing the boulevard, his eyes gleam. "Give us your puffed, your strapped, your trimmed! Give us your laced, your flannelled, your ruffled! Give us your tattered, your patched, your faded! We will take them all here on the boulevard!"

I look at him, my eyes wide and wondering.

"Shredded into strands of fabric they come, the sun-drenched posse, denying the rumors they've spread. Taking their bows, they offer their wares shamelessly. Howling, growling, and rumbling, they hiss down the boulevard, pouncing on every store they see, their hypocritical virtue boldly fanning the air. Goodness Jenna, sometimes I think that we are all just slivers of slate floors, granite countertops, and candy-apple-red front doors." He pauses to listen to the blaring of car horns. "L.A. is smothered by noisome traffic. I say the legislators make it mandatory to set a rose on the armrest of all motorized vehicles," he says and I applaud him with my eyes.

"Glimpse humankind with me, Jenna! Let's peer into the yearning, the curious, and the sexually rebellious!"

A man ambles up to our table. "Excuse me, my good sir; your sleek patent-leather hair is quite dashing," says Dal. "Why I can see the tracks left in it by the teeth of your comb." The man quirks his brow. "Well, I do converge on the swanky grounds of razzle-dazzle, but I am just as comfortable in a tin-roofed mountain hut with wind screaming through the cracks in the walls." Dal nods. "I take it that the truth is inaccessible to you." "Ah, the politics of identity," quips the man, strolling off.

"Jenna, sometimes I feel as if my destination is a tongue-clucking world of hustle and bustle. Time-hungry lives wait impatiently in line for their fast food. A few styrofoam boxes and they are on their way melting into the concrete jungle's smokescreen of torrential facade. And then after their day of phony triumphs comes to a close they head home as lunatics saluting their trickery. Why must it be that way?" he asks, scanning the boulevard.

"Forgive me sir," he calls to a disheveled man. "Are you easily tangled in disarray? You look as if you've just emerged from a series of cabs." "Well, I am a bit ruffled," replies the gentleman, raking his hands through his tousled hair. "So you are a madman?" Dal asks. "Oh just when I get panned by my critics! Now, if you'll excuse me, I'm off to a catfish buffet." "Carry on with your confusion," says Dal, clapping a friendly hand on the man's shoulder.

"Pardon me madam, but do you have a moment to let us into your bustling atmosphere?" A woman caked in makeup stops by us and looks at her watch. "I have a few moments," she chortles. Dal gazes upon her. "I notice your lips are decorated in deep shades of gold." "I am quite ornamental," she says, winking. "But have you ever journeyed into frankness or are you hindered by the language of honesty?" Dal asks. "Well, I have hung my enlarged image on the billboard of exaggeration and then made a moral beeline for redemption. But I have heard that the truth can leave you breathless," she says, scurrying off.

A gentleman with a sharply knotted tie catches Dal's eye. "Excuse me sir, do you hug cans of beer after work?" "Well, I do have a need for compassion," replies the man. "Yes. But are you charming enough to overcome your predictability?" inquires Dal. "I have time to attend lunch pretenses and flaunt phony traces of my character if that's what you mean," he replies, sauntering off.

Dal cups his ear. "Are those your fancy wheels I hear purring at the curb?" A dapper dressed fellow jaunting by us stops momentarily. "Why yes," replies the gentleman, "but I do manage to brake for insight." "So can we presume you are morally bankrupt?" asks Dal. The gentleman furrows his brows. "I don't crumble under the crushing burden of expectation. Now, if you'll excuse me, I am in my usual rush. I'm meeting someone at the corner of Have and Have Not Street and I'm running late as usual." Dal chuckles. "I know that street well. Go back to your jet shower and the crystal chandelier in your bathroom!" "We are a frontier corrupted by black gold," says the man, vanishing in a maze of shop demons.

A tall woman with ice-blonde hair blowing in the breeze sleepwalks by. "May I commend you? You are having an excellent hair day!" says Dal. The woman gives him a coy smile. "Forgive me! I am still counting the bubbles in last night's champagne." "Are you into making sweeping entrances in life?" Dal asks. "No. I just burst with sexuality, that's all," she clamors, flouncing away.

"Jenna, look at the redhead flickering the boulevard." "I can offer you the world," he cries. "Yes, but can you offer me the finest in la-di-da? Luxury is my style. Surprise me with diamonds," she chimes. "Does that come with an unflagging commitment?" Dal scoffs. "Just stroll the night with me and be exceptional. That's all I ask. I am full of human frailty," she says, padding off.

"Jenna, life simply wants us to crack a smile. But we can't. We are in the clutch of value creators and it makes me wonder if we are too modern-day to be authentic. You see, everyone is in search of the luxury getaway. Stay overnight in our courtyard configurations. Come delight in our scrumptious buffets. Cozy up to our fire pits! Ooze in our mudpacks and saunas! Get me out of urban hell, Jenna! Wrap me around a fireplace lodge with the sweet smell of pine. You know, even when I am grandfatherly and gray-haired, I will grab my motorcycle and chase after the sun."

Picturing him hunched on a bike, the wind gliding through his hair, I flash him a smile.

"The rosy future of deserts and mountains are forever in moments of crisis. How much longer can they be skillfully maneuvered out of the way? It has become part of the life chain to search for the ultimate makeover. Let's go to the manicured parks on the bluff! Let's go sit down on the over-stuffed sofas scattered intimately in the marble lobby! For a mere credit card swipe you can indulge in mind and body rejuvenation. Care to hop into the hot tub, Jenna? All luxury resorts furnish soft robes to wear and knobby sandals!" He pauses. "Throw popcorn at my words, Jenna, but do you know what I want to be one day?"

"A recognized writer," I reply.

"Yes, but I want to be more. I want to be a hobo with a bedroll on my back and roam." He winks. "Absurdities make up life. Now, let's watch the costumed creatures cavort the boulevard."

A lady adorned with diamonds walks toward our table. "You are quite pleasing in appearance," says Dal. "Do your sunglasses hide moist eyes?" "I've just experienced an accidental finger touch. It was quite moving," replies the woman, skulking away. Dal grins. "Keep clinging to your small moments," he calls after her.

A woman with orange-spiked hair strolls by us idly paging through a leaflet. "Excuse me madam, are you startled by the intensity of being human?" Dal asks. "Well, I am studded with moments," she replies. "Oh, so you flinch with emotion?" Dal inquires. "Well, I do walk around with an air of pleading, but I fear that makes me vulnerable so I put on my mask." "Being honest is a potent weapon," chortles Dal. "I wouldn't know," chimes the woman teetering off.

"Jenna, did I tell you I read faces?"

"No." I giggle.

A long-lashed lady with dangling earrings averts his gaze. "Excuse me madam, are you a documentary watcher? You might conclude I just asked something harsh. I only want to know if you've picked up your values this morning." The woman grins. "I am into fad diets, but who is flawless these days?" she asks, giving him a long-lashed blink. "Perhaps some mood enhancers may be in order," says Dal. The woman shrugs and walks away.

A man in his late fifties, of average height and build strolls by licking an ice cream cone. "Pardon me sir, are you a navel gazer?" Dal asks. "I am not glass enclosed," replies the man, dabbing his mouth with a napkin. "I am hardly a provocative tale of obsession. I just have a bit of play to me, that's all. You know, there is nothing wrong with good old-fashioned sin," he says, skittering off.

A thirty-something man stops by our table to light a cigarette. Dal concentrates on his pose. "You have probing eyes. Are you feeling lost and disconnected?" he asks. "Well, I am in another world right now. I have just crashed with my lover. My eyes are still piercing but they display fear." He flicks his cigarette. "I want to be held. I am a feeling human being. Must I suffer because of this?" he asks, wiping his eyes. "In life you must practice your survival skills," says Dal. "In the end it is the only thing that warms the Earth." The man sobs. "Yes, but for now, I no longer fit in the common world." Dal stands up and pats the man on the back. "Perhaps you will master your existence someday." "That is my fluttering wish," replies the man, "but for now I wallow in uncertainty. Have a nice day," he says, weeping away. Dal shakes his head. "His emotions will soon hurt his wallet."

Three women in five-inch heels tower by in violet-tinged shades. “Will you ladies be slam dancing this weekend?” Dal asks. They shrug their shoulders. “We are not sure. This weekend, we may be jumping on tables and bellowing anarchy!” “But can you signal your authentic feelings?” asks Dal. “We can smile on demand at any time, day or night,” they say, waving good-bye.

“Now there’s a woman who cries out for the spotlight!” “Pardon me, madam,” Dal calls to a lady clad in green. “Are you mint-fragranced?” he asks. “Why yes,” she beams. “I spent all morning complementing my fragrances to my apparel.” “You’ve done a fine job,” Dal says as she wiggles by. “I’ll bet she is dressed in lime-colored undies. Of course, lacy rose-colored panties are my favorite,” he whispers and in his eyes my soul is trapped.

“Are you growing tired of my rambling?” he asks.

“No, not at all,” I reply.

“Are you sure? No need to sit in this open-air café being polite.” He tousles my hair. “You know, Jenna, women crisscrossing the boulevard with their long flowing hair or flirting with long-legged babes no longer surges my interest. I am no longer lured by ladies batting their eyes at me and breaking the style barrier with their charming theatrics. Isn’t it unfortunate that glitz will never go out of style?”

Some surgically buffed women pant by before I can reply and I wonder if they will catch his eye. Subtly, they look in his direction. “Perhaps it is a staggering revelation that there is a lot more to life than wrapping lotion and conditioning creams,” he calls to them. They shake their head in disagreement. “You are beautifully packaged ladies. Go home! Prance and preen! Make your entrance down your grand curved staircases. Smile as your guests unfurl their linen napkins. Drink your expensive fermented grape juice. I can tell you ladies are sprinkled with disastrous dinner parties all year long."

I can't help but let out a giggle.

"Jenna, this town is full of people ducking to avoid synthetic shrubbery as their chauffeur treks through mud puddles on artificial grass. I'd like to stop their limos and scream for them to put a pair of cut-off jeans on and bang along some unpaved roads once in a while. It just makes me want to shout, 'Go grab a ragged T-shirt and live a little!'" He pauses. "People and their fussy obsessions! It's all about myopic tidiness. One must look beyond one's plate of mushroom pasta and seasonal fruits. Life is out there. It angers me that society seems to be full of cocktail-party wisdom more than anything else. I mean, people are starving to death in this to-go world of ours. We need to stop cradling civilization and let the Earth streak our soul!"

Gently he touches my face. My eyes encircle his body.

"Jenna, take a look at the animated being approaching us. Now, there's a woman of antique reproduction. Her softly painted brows and delicate blushing had to cost her a bundle." "My but you look like you should be decorated with rosettes and pink ribbon," he calls to her. She shakes her curly auburn hair. "You will make your manufacturer famous someday. Where is your heart-shaped hat?" he calls after her. "You see, Jenna, I never know when to stop. Underneath it all I'll bet she wears a full cotton and lace slip with matching pantaloons and cream lace tights," he scoffs, and I laugh so hard I ache.

"Hey shopping-bag-laden woman," he cackles to a lady virtually spilling out of her low-buttoned top. "Are you a people person?" he asks. "I will give courtesy to your whisper," she replies. "Are you flanked by curved metal benches?" he asks. "The city is full of them. What about setting your lovely behind down in a patch of green?" "I do embellish a fair amount of hip-wiggling," she replies. "The playful fox is humankinds' most daring invention," Dal chuckles. "Don't I know it," she says, wiggling away.

"Pardon me lady of natural food, is that tofu cheese wrapped in a whole wheat tortilla you're devouring?" "Why yes," answers a woman in snug cut-off jeans. "I've been on the run all day." "Those are sexy curved sandals you're wearing," says Dal. "Why thank you," she chimes, pushing up her random holed sleeves. "They slip off easily after dark," she says, confidently striding the boulevard.

"Pardon me madam," Dal calls to a woman with hair extensions. "Are you addressing me?" she asks. "Yes! Are you brushing back large strands of artificial hair?" The woman grins. "Eons ago I was human." Her eyes flash. "But now I travel incognito. You see, I pack my mask wherever I go." She pauses. "Does one ordinarily associate being human with sweetness? I wonder," she says, waving good-bye.

"Excuse the intrusion," Dal calls to a woman walking briskly, "but are you fleeing the ruins of your life?" "No," she calls back over her shoulder. "I meditate. I gather around life and coo."

A tall bearded fellow, slightly thick around the middle, edges his way toward us. "Pardon me sir, are you focused on anything else but quarter-end results?" inquires Dal. The man strokes his whiskers. "Is it that obvious? I have been stoically rubbing the sleep from my eyes for years." "Oh, so you realize you are robotic?" asks Dal. "Oh yes," chortles the man, pointing to his gray hair. "I have mechanically noted the power grid ever since I got my head stuck between the bars of life." "What is your solution?" asks Dal. The man flashes a teeth-whitening grin. "I don't allow something like authenticity to impair my performance," he says, walking away.

"Hey you with the curtain-call smile, are you honest with the world? I mean if I were to rap upon your soul, would you be quietly masked?" A woman with locks of wavy curls lowers her eyes. "Can we say your defining moment is a soft-drop-shoulder coat or are you still trying to assemble your identity?" Dal asks. "I sink when plagued with questions," she replies, slinking away. "That is why there are forced smiles on painted faces," Dal calls to her.

"Excuse me," chimes Dal to a man with thinning brown hair, "are you a seat crasher?" The man laughs. "I am full of odd credits." Dal grins. "Ah, so you have been caught touting credibility out of one side of your mouth?" The man snickers. "I do provide solace to dark times. It's the nagging air of unreality that I find haunting."

A small, prissy woman dressed in a neat crisp manner stops by our table to dig in her handbag. Dal grins. "Should I ask her if she is a lunatic in bed?" he whispers and my cheeks pinken. "Is the local department store coaching you on how to dress?" he asks. "I'll have you know that I was once a bespectacled librarian sort with short stringy hair! Now I am cosmetically improved," she says, strutting off.

A group of tourists with their cameras clicking stop by our table. Dal nods to them. They run off. The leader of the group dressed in a polo shirt and khaki shorts lags behind. "They are mistrustful of strangers," he says. "Excuse their lack of greeting." Dal winks. "Perhaps my glittering feather-cape and alien eyes are not photogenic." "I think they are just under the influence of bewilderment and curiosity," replies the man. "Ah, they are vibrating from the special effects of being human," chuckles Dal.

"Jenna, exotic brochures of tourist traps don't make my heart flutter. Offer me an expedition hundreds of years into the past. Let me experience what triggered evolution and then whisk me into the future and let me find out if life ever gets on track. Those are the little hands of gold I am looking for," he says and I nod.

A buttoned-up corporate woman walks stoically by, her image appearing as a corporate drone. "Your powdered appearance infers that you have worked hard at your composed day. May I suggest to you madam that you consider an image makeover? I apologize for the pessimism of my comment." The woman puts her hand to her head. "Are you with a local news station? I didn't have a chance to get my hair French-braided today. I just took off for a latte." Dal grins. "No, it is just one imperfect human being to another." "Oh okay," she says. "I am a self-described perfectionist." He winks. "So tell me lady of perfection, do you choose between frivolous thrills or deep meaning?" "Well, I do try to consider the facts before I jump into the sauna of love," says the woman, her eyes fluttering. Dal, winks. "Too bad, impulsiveness can be such a fiery correspondent."

A thin man in a pastel suit, a hat jauntily perched on his head, holding a flute dances toward us. Dal waves him over and his half-shy smile fades to a defiant stare. "Deception is the biggest show on Earth. We are all basking in the echoes of a ruined world," says the man. "We are all stuffed with fantasy-filled dreams and half-heard whispers," says Dal. "It is the theatrics in life that has humankind shaking its head."

I look at him with awe-filled eyes.

"Jenna, I stare into life everyday and pull my soul a little closer to my skin. You see, I am not here to journey through facts and study what people are babbling about. What is the significance of statistics? They only cast doubt on the reality of the problem. I am suspicious of excuses," he says, and I feel as if I am in a magical place in time.

"The fierce howl of humankind sprang upon me, and I closed society's doors behind me a long time ago. Society's highest priorities no longer played into my ears. The inaudible whispers of living beings made me tune into the subtler whispers of nature where clouds of covered thoughts no longer roll on the edges of my mind." He winks. "Humankind, you are covered in emblems! Take your plush-covered chairs and cartoon thoughts and pour me a glass of dignity! Pour upon the Earth some truth and humanity will no longer wipe away glacier-like tears." He pauses in thought. "Give us your worn, your ragged, your ripped. Give us your strapless, your pleats, your pinched. Give us your wools, your knits, your cottons. We'll take them all here on the boulevard!"

Our eyes lock.

"It's easy to admire the apparent Jenna, but what you see isn't always what it is."

I cock my head.

"Is that cashmere?" he calls to a big-breasted woman dressed in a thin, black woolen sweater and jeans. "No affiliation," she says, smiling. "It is really just old yarn. It is what's underneath that is new." "Looking good," says Dal and she blows him a kiss.

"So Jenna, are you a make believer in your spare time?" He winks. "I have a lustful nature. I establish a playful connection with life. Now, if you'll excuse me, I'm off to hunt down our waiter and inquire about our order of chaos," he says walking into the eatery.

"Well, aren't you Miss Hilarity!"

"Oh no, not you," I groan. "Not here."

"When are you coming home?"

"Never," I respond. "I am my own fear factory and I'm tired of it. By the way Conscience, I fired you, remember?"

"I'm here, informally. I'm just watching you in amazement."

"Well in case you haven't noticed, I no longer feel like an old bedtime story. I've come to life! I feel so carefree, like flowers."

"Your existence with him is fragile."

"He is loaded with late-night appeal."

"He is thunderous and apocalyptic."

"May I remind you Conscience, that you've been dismissed?"

His touch on my shoulder brings me back from my thoughts. "The boulevard is full of tantalizing forces, but do you know what truly is an erotic spirit? The tumbleweed," he says, a smile gracing his lips. "Scurrying across the boulevard, a tumbleweed crosses our table and its image instantly takes us to the dusty road of a desolate ghost town. Out of nowhere, we see saloon doors hanging on one hinge and abandoned cemeteries sinking in the forsaken dust. But don't let the tumbleweed fool you. It only masquerades that image. In reality, the tumbleweed is a rainbow chaser with a vise-like grip on life."

He chuckles. "You see, the tumbleweed has set its erotic spirit free. Tearing itself away from the other scraggly brush, a strange mixture of excitement flutters inside of it and its round sticker bushes tumble sensually with the wind. And when the time comes that its bushes are suffocated by brush it will leave its lonesome secret only to the howling gusts. And humankind will never know the tumbleweed as a jewel of movement whose intimate confession was to harness the wind."

He kisses my ear. "I have a secret for the howling gusts," he whispers. "I can watch the rise and fall of the ocean for days. Yes. Give me a wind-battered folding chair and I will pull up a seat to the tide."

Stilled in his kiss, I smile, for I have an intimate confession of my own, a secret that will never cross my lips. I am for the first time edged in seductive-ware and I know he will have me blushing in lace all night.

Authenticity opens the door
To those who invite
enchantment.

Chapter 20
Pardon My Animalism

On an early evening, with thunderclouds hanging menacingly low across the Los Angeles sky, he asked me to meet him at his beach house in Malibu. In an oasis on the edge of the sea, I walk up his winding cobblestone gateway. It is like a path to inclusion as I stop to listen to the sloshing of waves upon rock. In a sea-salty mist I watch his abode gracefully cascade down the hillside toward the surf and endlessly dissolve in lacy flounces of tide. In a ring of haze Nirvana-like riffs engulf me, and I am lost in curls of sculpted waves. I close my eyes and hold out my hands to the amorous winds. If I didn't know any better, this might indeed be Heaven.

In a nighttime canvas of dotted streetlights I climb the stairs and timidly ring the bell. Butterflies momentarily authenticate me as I anxiously wait for him to answer the door.

"Come in and get lost in hungry nestlings," he says, rapturously receiving my uneasy brown eyes. "Did you notice that my sloping front yard flourishes with Lady Slipper orchids, your favorites? How is that for having something in common?"

He is well coiffed and soft spoken. "Let your feelings flow," he says. "Trust me. This night will not become a fading montage."

His words tilt my head. Nobody knows what I am going through, nobody but me and the ghosts of fear.

"Look out at the tide! It is filled with wonder." He puts a finger to my lips. "Can you keep a secret?"

I nod.

"Do you know, ever since I was a small boy the ocean calmed me?" His fingers stroke up the side of my face. A cold breeze blows in from the surf. He reaches out and catches my hair in his hands.

"Watching the tide can make me fall silent with my mouth slightly open for hours," he says, lifting my lips to his. "The surf has an imposing presence. Can you hear its exotic rhythms?"

I close my eyes. His lips brush lightly upon my neck. I gasp. He has sprayed the crook of his arm with cologne. Enamored, I take his hand. His fingers softly pinch the inside of my palm. A thousand butterflies greet me.

"Welcome to my humble abode. Bid hello to my clustered window garden, dense with fresh flower arrangements, hanging baskets and trailing vines. Plants and flowers create a world that is so freeing. You know, they hold the key to heated devotion. Even more, they conjure an enchanted realm. I trade in my idle time to be in their presence. They make me a starry-eyed wanderer." He smiles. "I can stare at the light of the moon for hours from this window. A good body snuggle while doing so would explode my breath for sure." He tucks a loose strand of hair behind my ear. On wobbly legs, I pull back from licking my lips.

He guides me into his bedroom. "Passion is life's feast," he calls to me over his shoulder. "Inhale the rising vapors! Cauldrons of excitement are brewing! You know, they are concocted with erotic spices," he says rubbing his hands hungrily together.

His eyes crinkle. "I hope sex is all over your mind," he whispers, a smile teasing his lips. He reaches for me. I darken. I'm not ready to embrace his ignited imagination just yet. "Don't be cool to my touch," he says. "A wet and glorious finale is forthcoming." I blink and turn my head. "My, but aren't we wonderfully expressive tonight?" he quips. "Can you only speak to me in fantasy or is panic-tinged reality where you reside?" I bite my lip.

Frustrated, he rakes his hands through his hair. "Do you care to share a kiss, or caress, or something more?" he asks. Bashfully, I lower my eyes. He strokes my face. "I can give you all the comforts of home, and more. Even charging bulls can be hospitable," he whispers.

He is keenly expressive, displaying the perfect code of enraptured conduct.

"Passion brings rare delight," he says with a charming grin, and my body goes limp with fear. Clearly, he has a sexual agenda in mind.

"I believe words that emanate from a person should be utterly devouring. Is it wrong to disrobe another's soul with hot talk? I am painted with frolicking. So tell me, are you up for sexual indulging? Don't tell me you are afraid of capturing this feeling," he says and I gulp.

"Perhaps the fruits of exploration are stuck on the tree of virtue," he utters, having trouble suppressing a smile. "Excuse me! I am full of riveting romantic expressivity."

He sits on the bed and stares at me expectantly. "Welcome to my world of worn-out pillows, handmade comforters and cotton sheets. Intimacy can reside anywhere. You'll notice my bedroom is perfectly pleasant in champagne and charcoal." Looking around, I see his bedroom is excessively mirrored. "It is important to catch the reflection of life's lustful gaze," he says, and my hands fidget in front of me.

"Ready, set, predict! Shall we roll the dice on reality? I warn you, I am a heady combo of imagination and origination. There is opportunity in the air! Let our sweltering heat turn the sheets into a raging sauna," he whispers, and I am not sure if I can keep up with his plans.

"Are you waiting for the sky to rain ash or are your pouty lips off-limits?" he asks and I wince.

"Now, don't tell me I'm filled with inappropriate thoughts. You know, it takes a certain fearlessness to be sexual." He turns back the covers on the bed. "But know that I am intimately affectionate, so no supplements please." He pauses. "Do you know I am sexually invincible? A simple nod will do," he chortles. "Now tell me, is my eye on a difficult prize?"

I sigh. His expectations are clear.

"Perhaps you are a high-stakes woman. You know, passion can be sensually satisfying," he says, stroking my hair. He smiles and gives me enchanting whispers. His hot breaths caress my neck. I close my eyes, for I have entered sensual heaven and soon I know I will be gone.

"Passion is within your easy reach, right here, right now. Are you sure it is the last thing that you want to have happen? Volcanic sensations creep within me, Jenna. Just what resides within you? How can you remain passive? Passion is the great enthusiasm of life!"

I dig my hands into the pockets of my raincoat.

"You know, your silence could stomp a blooming flower. Shed your sleepy sensuality. Flirt and chase and tease me!"

I tremble.

"It is hardly about insight and explanation," he says, touching my face. "It is about the tantalizing fire of human heat. You don't need a credible explanation to feel the way you do. Have the courage to go beyond your imagination. Being naked is exciting!" He winks. "Unload your wailing image, Jenna, and give me some outlaw attitude!"

I pick up the quietude I've dropped on the floor and utter the unthinkable. "I have to leave."

"What?" he exclaims.

"I have to go."

"I am not asking you to contemplate eternity. Does it take countless boxes of chocolates for you to discount escape?"

As lust wrestles to set itself free, I wonder if I am wedged in moral dilemma or fearful of ravishing intimacy.

"You, Jenna, stand as a timeless monument of virtue," he says, barring the door. He traces my closed lips with his tongue. "How does one nudge you to life?" he asks, stepping free of the door. "How long will you choose to hide behind the mechanics of your existence? How long will you hide behind your lips?" he shouts and I feel fate smiling upon me.

"Do you kiss erotically?" he asks, composing himself.

I stare at him tight-lipped.

"Do you touch with shocking intimacy? Will you let yourself spiral out of control?" He takes my hand. "Do you know I have a knack for sensual pampering?"

I pull my hand from his. He breathes hotly against my cheek. "Imagine yourself sexually provocative," he whispers. I bite my lip.

He cups his ear. "Do you hear that rustling sound? That is the sound of sexual electricity."

My stomach tightens.

"I believe you reside on the fringes of your life, Jenna. Somewhere in you is a delightful sense of playfulness. Allow it to have its charms."

I let out a cumbersome sigh.

"Do you know what you are? You are a drifter, an emotional drifter!" He pauses. "Excuse me, I am testosterone-fueled," he chuckles. "But I am not going to stand here whispering sweet nothings into your muzzle." Anger spills across his face. "The best part of life is its intimate moments. It's okay to experience a few lapses of logic, you know."

I let out a deep breath, wondering if my moments with him have been accidental.

"Unbutton your corset!" he shouts. "Your passion has been mothballed!" And then with precision, he throws the ultimate emotional dart. "Perhaps you have stumbled upon something too intimate." His words draw heavily upon me.

"You have consigned yourself to a passionless existence." He points a wagging finger at me. "Raise the blinds on your life or are you windowless? You can't hide from me, Jenna. I see you slinking along your shadows."

His words promptly deflate what's left of my spirit, and I dart away. Running past his thickly foliated abyss, my vibrating soul stops for a moment and I look at his house. It is lined with bedded flowers and pruned shrubs. A mysterious wind blows. It is fast moving and complex. I focus for a moment on his freakish musings about how life should be.

"People register their protests by storming out," he shouts from the door. "My home is not a place of indignation, I'll have you know." He pauses. "Throw rocks at my windows, Jenna, for wanting to be rapturous, but mark my words, your stoic exhibit will bustle through your character and have you become a woman with droopy nylons."

With his speech over he slams the door. Consigned to the quietly humiliated, his magnetism pants after me, escorting me into my car. I peer out of the windshield. A rainy ocean breeze rustles the palms. Juggling contradictions, my deflated spirit turns the key.

Motoring along under erotica's rumbling, I know not where I am headed. With my thoughts recklessly wandering, I enter emotions straightaway and watch virtue fly by. Intensity is constant. Dodging emotional daggers I zigzag down first one street and then another. Fraught with powerlessness, I skid on the transition road of my soul, for my feelings don't stop on command. Clouds of pessimism gather on the horizon as I remain an unfocused form of expression and protest. Consumed by my thoughts, I floor it and swerve to the right. Sliding on my morals I slam on the brakes of my soul, but it is too late. A crash is inevitable and I collide with reality. Wrestling with the sexual creature within me, I pulsate out of control and crack the glass of destiny.

A whiplash of senses takes place, and I am overcome by flashing red lights. I look away and cover my ears, but I can't block out the siren of life. A loud speaker sounds from somewhere above, and I am instructed to pull off to the side of the road. Dazed, I sit in my car, the windows down. Hot sultry air hits my face and in my rearview mirror I see shadows. I throw my hands up in the air and wonder if my fevered imagination has taken control.

In a space that juts over the ocean, two goggle-wearing motorcycle officers proceed to dismount. White-gloved and dressed in snappy blue uniforms they trudge alongside of me, their thick-soled boots crunching my moral gravel. Approaching me with little more than nods and smiles, they begin to read me my rights. "Keep your hands on the steering wheel of your existence," they command. "We are all in search of the good life."

I sit behind the wheel upright, my hands clenched in front of me, my eyes darting nervously back and forth. The fallout of their superman aura is anxiety, and I am having trouble keeping calm. Squadrons of stiletto-wielding emotions zip through me as I make a final attempt to hold on to my disappearing self. Pinged with jitters, I lose the battle of composure and the fool within me blooms.

"I always try to obey the speed limit," I stammer. "Actually, when driving at a slower speed I always stay in the right-most lane. I guess I was just in a hurry, but I certainly understand the detrimental effects of road rage."

"You weren't speeding," they retort.

"I haven't been drinking. Of course I am well past the minimum drinking age, and I've never supplied any alcohol to minors. You can trust me on that."

"This is not about violations."

"I am a true believer of seat belt laws," I say, pointing to my fastened belt. "But I do tend to be a bit verbally aggressive behind the wheel. I mean, I can't deny that. Sometimes I get annoyed with people turning in front of me or blocking intersections. And quite often the roads are crowded with slow-moving trucks, and I do get a bit agitated while trying to pass. I am not a daring eager driver, aggressively making my mark on the road. I don't dart between commuter traffic either. I am law-abiding," I say, gripping the wheel even more tightly. "I don't have great fun racing between lanes like some people. But I suppose I have weaknesses while driving. I mean, I'm not perfect. I'm only human. You know, I've only had one parking ticket in my life, and I still feel terrible about it."

"This is not about community standards, noise ordinances, truancy rules, and no-trespassing signs. We are not into lineups, over-the-top car chases, fiery explosions or speed racing."

"You're not?" I ask, surprised.

"No. We are not police officers. We are sentiment enforcers."

"Sentiment enforcers?" I query.

"We are the enforcers of extreme feeling. We understand a hungering soul."

Immediately, I turn moral. "What have I done?" I ask, easing slowly back in my seat.

"We are citing you for apathy."

"Apathy?" I gulp.

"Yes. We can't think of any human behavior that enrages us more," they say and I take in a deep breath.

"You know, there is a huge fine for lifelessness."

I wipe my brow. "What is the fine?" I peep.

"You must furnish us with the registration of your soul."

"What? The registration of my soul?"

The sentiment officers watch for signs of resistance.

"Would that information be in my glove compartment?" I ask, unfastening my seat belt and leaning over to unlock it.

"No, that information would be in your eyes."

I look down.

The sentiment enforcers are kind. "Are you afraid of your predictable fate?" they ask.

"What?" I inquire. They appear to be listener friendly.

"You spark bedlam. Why, you have illuminated our radar!"

"I have?" I gulp. "Me?"

"The readout of our radar gun says you are an erotic traveler."

"Yes," I say, proudly. "I am an erotic traveler embarking on a most exciting travel destination. I am on a quest for fire!"

"How fascinating! A quest for fire is the farthest goal of all travel! What are your sightseeing plans?"

"Well, initially, I'd like to make love in a bed topped with down comforters and feel the shiver of my hot essence."

"You know, the view of one's essence is spectacular!"

"So I hear!"

"You realize, as an erotic traveler you must prowl your soul."

A hot breeze rushes across my face. "What does that mean?" I ask.

"Prowling one's soul is when fire walks the Earth."

I look at them, mystified.

"It is a time when one hotly floats between past and present, reality and imagination. Now, will you be traveling on tinkling bells or in the comfort of a sleek jumbo jet? And if it's the sleek jumbo jet, make sure you forage among the nearly unreadable fine print at the bottom of the airline ads. You know, lurking there are taxes and fees."

I turn bashful. "I am not traveling on a sleek jumbo jet, but I do feel as if I am sexually driven, almost as if I am breathing the sultry air of another time."

The sentiment enforcers smile. "My, but you are sexually driven. It definitely sounds as if you are surging across the amorous lines of desire. Are you seeking wish fulfillment?"

I blush. "Yes. I am trying to get on the road to lust. Does it pass through here?"

"Occasionally," they answer.

"What a stroke of luck! I must have stumbled upon it then."

"You can only chance upon it by hints of destiny."

"Well, perhaps I have been forced to look through life's funhouse."

The sentiment enforcers grin. "Is that a challenge for you?"

"Yes," I answer. Their question spins an enchanting mood.

"All that you seek is in your backyard. Be free! Wander the windswept steppes of your soul. Inspiring moments await you!"

"How do I arrive?"

"Well, that may be a bit difficult. You appear to be a lady-in-waiting."

Tears shamelessly run down my cheeks. "Why must there be uncertainty?"

"The road to lust is a craving road and it can be a bit bumpy. You appear to be having problems steering. Is that due to your rising and falling tempo?"

"I admit I am directionless. My mortal censors appear to be unclear."

"You need roadside assistance. You lack sultry confidence."

"I think passion's intensity is obscuring my vision. I am having trouble keeping my feelings on the speedometer of life. I seem to be caught between wonder and despair."

"Your emotions are in the red zone. Your thoughts are shifting and swerving. It appears that you are toiling in virtue."

"I believe I have lost my sense of direction."

"That can come with taking unfamiliar turns. You have the right to pour out your uncertainties," they counsel.

Immediately I plead my case. "I am lost in revolutionary thought. I don't know what happened. Suddenly I swerved into animalistic yearning, and then I skidded on moral gravel swerving back and forth between craving and virtue. Perhaps I am being transported by sheer sexual energy," I say with a shrug. "What are the laws of chaos?"

"You are thinking recklessly. Slow down. You are speeding into indecision."

"I have an intimate confession," I whisper. "I want to be rapturous, but I'm frightened. Perhaps I am a flawed woman trying to live a double life?"

"Perhaps you are papier-mâché and you want to be paint-slathered," they grin.

"Am I in a manner to escape?"

"You cannot escape yourself. Feelings are burning within you."

"These feelings are an abstraction. I am scared of them actually."

"Are you frightened of your fearsome power?"

"I am frightened and fascinated."

The sentiment enforcers smile. "You are experiencing animalism."

I blush "Me?" I yelp.

"Yes! You!"

I cover my face. "I am wild with feeling. The sensations are untamed. I am bashful about them."

The sentiment enforcers are consoling. "There is fear upon any transformation. Why don't you look at these interests as an exciting part of your life? Look at them as part of being human."

"I believe I am engaged in a moral crisis. I have only been intimate when there is love and now I have thoughts to engage in something different." I look down. "Pardon my animalism."

"There is nothing wrong with poking around life. Rousing the animal inside of you is more than okay!"

Taking a deep breath of sultry air my mind drifts back to firefly shrimp and sipping margaritas on a crowded boulevard. "I am a complex creature full of apprehension. I've got all this mental clutter going on inside my head."

"Yes," they say, smiling. "It is infusing the air."

"Passion is haunting my thoughts! My mind is hotly occupied," I groan, getting out of the car.

"The kiss of legitimacy flaps its wings around you and you are restless in its clutches. Do not cease to exist. The kiss of play may be your magic spell. Let yourself go. Dab your feelings behind your ears and run around in a skirted bikini. Let reality take you to places unimaginable."

"I don't want to be a scandalous, libidinous soul. I just want to get a tad racy."

The sentiment enforcers stroke my hair. “So, you are tired of conventional relationships?”

“Yes. I am on a quest for fire. I want to be magically cured.”

“The only way one can be magically cured is by hunting for one’s truth. Don’t be afraid to purr.”

“Tell me about passion,” I whisper.

“Passion hardly comes to us on little cat feet, settling in so silently you barely know it’s there. Oh no! Passion is the great fire of life.”

“What does passion look like?”

“Passion can be shirtless and covered in grease. It can be beaded hems and goddess gowns. It can be sultry bed dances, dropping boxers, and swirling panties. But in essence passion is the grandeur of your inner self emerging. It is the language of goose bumps.”

“I am running from it.”

“We know.”

“I’m scared. How do I handle fear?”

“Come to terms with your magnificence.”

“I can’t. I am lifeless.”

“Don’t lock up your spirit. Touch your fantasies.”

“You mean, become human?”

“See what you can do.” They wink. “You are a woman forever hunched-over in contemplation. Have you ever considered hauling the thinker away in you?”

“I don’t know if I can. But the listener in me is growing.”

“Stop leaning back against routine. Sink into an armchair of rapture. Settle into a world where your spine tingles and your blood rushes. Stop gasping for composure. Let your eyes widen in a radiant haze.”

I tingle. “Where am I?”

“You are here, there, and everywhere. You are frolicking in emotional wakefulness.”

"I am sprawling wildly in all directions."

"Feelings can be daring company. Now if you want to be a true erotic traveler, you must trap your moments of anticipation."

"It is difficult to journey in this way. The world is not compassionate. The world is full of emotional snipers."

"Emotional snipers?" I query.

"Emotional snipers rifle through sentiment. They are dazed cowards. With their guns of deception drawn, they spray the world with lies and deceit."

I gasp. "I don't want to be a lifeless character. I'm actually looking for a curvier version of myself."

"Within you resides an amorous creature. Sensually stretch out in life. It can be an amusing world."

"I have never been frolicsome."

"Go after the small moments."

"I always seem to stand a safe distance away."

"Do you know what sleeps inside your soul?"

"What?" I whisper.

"Passion!"

"How does passion differ from love?"

"Love is the sweetness that bubbles your skin. Passion wiggles your soul!"

I shiver. "I have another intimate confession. I am a bashful craver."

"Is your stomach tied in knots?"

"Yes."

"Do you long for scorching lips?"

"Yes. I have images of my skin hotly nibbled upon."

"A scandalous soul can be fun from time to time."

"My soul is hardly scandalous. I hardly sprint into bedrooms of spilled champagne."

"Sliding on frilly bubbles will give you a smoky smile."

"You have fun in your eyes."

"So do you! You are filled with sexy sleepiness."

"Oh no! Can I rid myself of this condition by swaying my hips?"

"Perhaps revealing a blush of cleavage may help."

I raise a questioning brow.

"We'll compromise. How about swishing in a sexy sundress? There is nothing wrong with rubbing shoulders with temptation. A gentle finger running along the edge of your black satin bra is nice too."

I give a delicate blush. "I suppose I should get one."

"Sometimes you have to turn to the fun page of life."

"You do?"

"Yes. Have you ever had a pillow fight?"

"No. Should I put that under things to do?"

"Yes! It will have you on the floor with a chuckle. There are more things to put on your list. Holding pillows on a cushy, round bed and making shadow puppets. Putting on your fuzzy slippers and chasing after your swirling energy. Oh! Gasping-for-air giggles are high priority too."

My tongue wets my lips.

"The dark is full of suspenseful capers. The lights are dimmed and you are in a soft muddle of whispers. Trampling through paradise, you are momentarily stunned by something magical. You knock on a door filled with wind chimes. You look around. There is no one there, but the mystery of your soul."

My heart thumps.

"Hunt for life's exclamation points! Embrace your mussed-up hair, smeared lipstick, and slept-in clothes. Lips are powerful. There is fun to staying up all night."

"The stillness in me is disappearing," I whisper.

The sentiment enforcers slip their arms around my shoulders. "There is a reason we've talked under the soft filter of life. We have an unused monorail ticket to ecstasy. We are presenting it to you. Will you accept?"

I lick my lips.

"Become emotionally sumptuous!"

"I will," I say, waving my ticket to ecstasy.

"Venture well, erotic traveler! Green-light your soul and remember to cup your ear to life's sultry whispers." Doling out air kisses, the sentiment enforcers vanish into a silhouetting sky.

With the windshield covered with rain, I shift gears and whiz past my inhibitions. Passing my morals, I run the light of my soul and my moment of truth approaches.

In front of his beach house Bravery grabs me by the scruff of my neck and pulls me out of the car. "It is risky to linger. Have you forgotten the concept of playfulness?" it hisses. Impulsively, I'm moved to action. With the swords of passion drawn, I allow Bravery to lead.

A steady rain dabs at my face. It is soothing and becomes my trusted partner. Puffing on anxiety, I pause at steps that ascend on their own. Sadly, I cannot lift my feet and Bravery is gone.

"Hello. May I help you?"

I look around. "No. I don't think so."

"Why is that?" asks the voice.

"I am fighting panic."

"Life is full of distress signals."

"I am a lost erotic traveler."

"I've heard. Have you missed your flight to ecstasy?"

"No. I've just decided not to board."

"Can't you get through security?"

"It's not that. I'm on a vacation from apathy. I'm trying to let loose, but failing. You see, I want to discover pleasure. And I think I have the opportunity to do so, but now I am running scared. I guess I am an erotic traveler who is abandoning her fantasy trip."

"Your body is dancing a form of madness."

"Tell me more."

"A hand will move slowly up your leg. You will curl your toes. A whimper will escape your lips."

"And then?" I whisper.

"And then, you will melt into being human."

I gasp.

"He is waiting."

"I know."

"You are waiting."

"Yes. My heart is beating wildly."

"Are you afraid he will make your clothes fly off?" asks the voice.

My eyes twinkle.

"A journey of discovery is not easy. Just listen for the purr in the air."

I nod. "What was your name again?"

"I am Experience. I've been there before."

A low purr in the air entices me. Guided by the twinkle in my eye, I ascend the flight of rapture and knock on a door of wind chimes.

"Why, you could be mistaken for a faint star in this downpour," he says, opening the door. "Are you in the business of illusion?"

I stare at him in the doorway. He has changed from his soft-tailored attire to worn jeans. An unbuttoned green-and-black flannel shirt with sleeves rolled up to his elbows hangs loosely over his pants. He is filled with laid-back intensity.

"The air is purring like a kitten tonight," he says, wiping a few raindrops from my dampened face. I close my eyes. His hands are fingers of fire.

"The storm clouds have broken. This is well beyond a darkening drizzle. Are you getting wet?" he asks.

I gulp.

His chin is sheathed in dimples. "Not good weather to build sand castles and forts. Why it looks as if it's raining sideways. The mist has definitely deepened well past a drizzle. Yesterday it was sunny; today it is raining. Life is so unpredictable. Did you find your sexual passport?" he asks.

"My eyes are no longer cloudy," I say. "I am much breezier!"

"Oh, so you have emerged from your tweedy cocoon?"

"Yes. I have removed anxiety from my pockets as well as sensible behavior."

"Those are some pretty deep pockets."

"Yes. They were stuffed with traditional values."

"And so now you are spontaneous, brave, and uninhibited! Welcome! You sound like you are new and improved!"

I nod. "Something has happened underfoot and I am experiencing a wildly different interpretation of myself."

"But are you ready to show your newly found knowledge? I warn you, I don't want your scaled-down version. You can leave your costume and mask for box-office thrills."

"I have arrived without inhibition."

"You won't crawl under a blanket of apathy? You will be yourself, unrestrained?"

"Yes."

"Your real self? No silent howling."

"I will be emotionally expressive."

"And fearless?"

"I will be explosively original."

"Are you sure you have recounted your life? I warn you. The heat may get unbearable in my steamy asylum. You could lose control."

"I have taken my high-powered binoculars and looked into my soul. I am a festival seeker. Trust me, it is a clear-eyed recognition."

He looks at me warily.

"It is not just a glimpse," I utter.

"Good because I don't chase after eclipses."

"I know."

He steps from the doorway to wipe a raindrop from my lips. I quiver. His touch delivers an energy that I have never experienced.

"I apologize for my insensitivity earlier. Typically my impatience sets in when I am forced to wait. I am not good at playing the game of sexual cat and mouse."

"I want you," I say with smoldering defiance.

"What?" he asks surprised that I am so blatantly vocal.

"I want you."

"Is this a costume change? If so, please stop unpacking your images before me."

"I have engaged in tense contemplation."

Looking handsomely rumpled, he steps from the doorway with his hands shoved in his pockets. He has a sun-kissed glow about him even in the rain.

"Do you know while you were gone I redid the sky? I loosened the clouds and put a rose between its teeth. The sky blushed and turned fiery."

My eyes widen. "I want you," I mouth.

He is quiet for a moment. "Have you removed your halo?" he asks.

"Yes," I whisper.

"Then come in," he says, nudging my lips with his tongue.

Slaying my inhibitions, the magical world appears.

Virtue whispers into the moments,
And I wave goodbye to it with
questing hands.

Chapter 21
Wrath of the Seductress – Part 1

"My house overflows with books and music," he says, as I walk into the sprinkling of blues. "And there is more. I am a mad collector of copious illustration. Even a trite production demands my attention. Perhaps this is a testament to my dysfunction," he chuckles, turning off the porch light. "Look at my array of annotations and short stories," he says, taking me to a showcase of literary selection. "I have a genuine love of the cinema. Yes, even the most featureless epic catches my eye. Welcome to my other life," he says, grinning.

My panic gone, my eyes glance at his home as if for the first time. Movie magazines lie strewn about like floating creatures. Vast bookshelves hug endless depths of space. Wherever I look, wood cabinets bulge with film soundtracks.

"You seem fascinated with creativity," I utter, eagerly squeezing his hand.

"Inventiveness is the genius of life," he says, winking.

My skin ripples. "Your words give me goose bumps. You are indeed a writer."

"Perhaps so," he says, jokingly. "But I warn you, I will leave behind no interviews and no written material." He smiles shyly. "How do I let the Hollywood gods know I am king of the wind?"

"I will do all I can to help you," I say.

He cups my hands in his. His nearness plays with my affections.

"I really enjoy the company of books. As you know, I am very private about my writing. But I must admit, I do fantasize about my work lining the shelves." He grins. "Imp-like from my pages, I will emerge as a great author. Icicle lights will canvass huge posters of me and fill bookstores throughout the land. I will be in the hearts and minds of Hollywood with real-world relevance and the universe will have its nose buried in my jackets of obscurity forever," he says, his eyes glimmering.

"I don't need my work to scream off the shelves. I just need to seduce the reader with a book cover fuzzy to the touch. Seduction is carried out in plumes of smoke, you know. Now, don't look at me like I am some half-masked freak but I just seek out bookstores and hang out! Yes. In a bookstore, you will find me smoothed in a chair, lost in words carefully chosen." He pauses. "Do you know that a potential book-buying weekend in a place with so many choices has to be planned with the utmost care? I must take a suitcase with me for my bulky purchases and then jet away to read in the breaths of the sea."

Out of the corner of my eye, I see his bedroom door is slightly ajar. My heart beats wildly.

"Do you know I am an early riser? So, as you come to know me, don't be surprised to find the light on in my study before dawn. And don't be surprised to find me sitting in a pool of lamplight surrounded by books from my library and scribbling into my infamous notebook." He pauses. "Do you know where the timekeeper muffs protocol and I become a connoisseur of idleness?"

"No," I whisper.

"Do you know where the outside world becomes a galaxy far, far away?" he asks and I shake my head, no.

He takes my hand. "Let me take you to a place where my spirit goes hot. Come with me to my picturesque window. It is here that I dust off my crystal ball and issue predictions of magical lust!"

Eagerly, I take his hand. We stroll down a hallway dotted with tall, exotic plants that seem as if they are slowly dancing erotically around each other. "Welcome to my cool, noiseless forest. All that is missing are the chase birds," he says, his eyes caressing my face. "I love greenery. Nature coos seductively," he whispers. "Do you know I am a yard gnome?"

I cover my mouth. "Oh, no!" I say, playfully.

"Yes. I happily rip weeds away from my pathway."

"Goodness!" I exclaim.

"And there is more. I like to touch the dew on the petals of my flowers." He puts a finger to his lips. "And do you know something else? On occasion I can be seen pushing a wheelbarrow. But only up close am I a source of hilarity. From far away I look like an actual human being."

I giggle.

"Nature is full of illuminating moments. I love the feel of the Earth against my feet and blades of grass squishing in between my toes. Why, the sensation is incredible. Have you ever run through a muddied hollow?"

Listening to him speak, I slowly withdraw from the world. "What is happening to me?" I think.

"You are allowing yourself to be dazzled," whispers the wild beast.

"He is exciting," I pant.

"Yes, and you are nowhere to be found. Keep it that way. Let me emerge."

"I bet he is very sexy as he happily rips away weeds from his pathway."

"Let me emerge," repeats the wild beast.

"Your dream life must be exceptionally rich. You are somewhere far away," he whispers.

"I am back," I blurt.

He takes my hand. "Now this is my kitchen. Here you will find me struggling to make a pancake. You can go inside. It is visitor-friendly."

I finger his warm cherry cabinets. They are handcrafted. "You did all of this?" I ask.

"You didn't know I'm a cobbling fool? Usually my kitchen is a sun-dappled alcove. You must come back on a day when L.A. lives up to its great weather reputation."

"Your kitchen is beautiful. It really flows."

"Oh, it is just functional reality. If you look a little bit further, you will see my windowed nook. Here you can read the sports section and vanish under a sea of green."

"It is so peaceful," I say.

"You haven't seen anything yet. Come with me," he says, curling his fingers in mine.

We walk to the end of the hall. "Are you ready for a breathtaking view?" he asks, opening a pair of French doors.

"I'm ready," I answer, my heart thumping.

We enter an ocean-view room with a crackling fire. "The smell of wood burning is nice," I say.

"Savor the scenery," he chimes, taking me over to a window that appears high in the sky. "It is here that I put on my worldly turban and consult the experts on the extraordinary." He sits down on some oversized throw pillows and pulls me close. "It is here that I stretch out in cool breezes and contemplate the world. It is here that I chuckle at life's ironies."

With fascinated eyes I watch the chalky white caps darken the water.

"Even in nighttime rain the ocean's spirit is infectious," he whispers. "Look, the sky has turned to black velvet." I take in an enchanted breath.

"The clouds roll through and people are huddled under umbrellas wondering if they will ever bathe in sunshine again. It angers me," he says, massaging my hands. "Why can't they take in the exquisite surroundings a single raindrop creates? Why is it that humankind has such a problem making the best of it?"

The glass doors to his terrace are open. The rain-laden breeze plays upon his hair, sparkling his eyes. He strokes my cheek as we watch the chalky white caps darken the water.

"Each morning, just before dawn, I come here to view the show of the Earth and the sky." His eyes twinkle. "I watch the clouds stack up on the horizon and drag their shadows across the glistening Pacific. The waves move in softly and then thunder into the wind-sculpted rocks. I find it pampering," he says softly kissing my cheek.

"Jenna, I think of life in great sweeps and how it is strangely chaotic. I am urbanized and I find myself staggering in the toss of the mountains. The scent of wheat grass curing in meadows is now alien as is my backpack flashing in the sun. Hiking through a climax of flowers has long been replaced by mall parking searches, and my jokes to fellow fishermen have also been discarded for entertainment-center boasting. My life is one of bounding into doorways, racing up stairs, catching elevators, and loitering under archways while guzzling down power drinks. Such is the agony of being citified." He grins. "Candles with a wood-mist scent are as close as I get to camping these days." He rests his hand on my arm.

"I could spend my whole life listening to the deep hoots of an owl." He sighs. "In the tidy world of fill-up stations and mini-marts, we have obligations. Construction sites avalanche us at every corner. What matters are luggage tags, dashboard tans and bargain breaks. The best we can hope for is gazing at the sunrise from an office building."

He inhales deeply. "Do you know the suffocating slickness of corporate culture and its pretensions are stifling? And the ecological insanity of our advertising-driven world can really make me rant. Everyone complains about littering, but does the world get any cleaner? It makes me want to quit the Earth and take with me the gas-guzzling vehicles that rule this oil-driven planet." He squeezes my hand.

"We are a drive-thru society, Jenna. Pull up to the window of your choice and you can order a burrito and make a bank deposit. Make a lane change and get a T-bone steak! And, let's not forget about those tri-shaped executive buildings topped by flat-ribbed domes of ice-blue glass that light up in beautiful fluorescence. For inside their supersonic interiors are the most dangerous human beings on this planet: lethargic desk-dwellers with horrible joke-telling skills, and computer-glazed office drones living their dreary lives. Enter my cubicle of hell. Join me at an angular table of fabrication or if you prefer, we can exchange our dialogue of façade on a concrete floor strewn with white and red roses. Here we can sip cups of chamomile tea and admire the busy room of glistening glass, shiny marble, and polished cement." I nod, dazed.

"Give me the ocean, Jenna. I never grow tired lingering in the swell of waves. Drenched with the spray of the surf, the wind whistles through my hair and blows it in all directions. I take a deep breath of salty air and it is as if I am in the throne room of the beach gods. I love watching the surfers boogie boarding. It is cool to see T-shirts and shorts paddling into the water on old surfboards snapped in half. Those poor surfer dudes surf until they are drained of energy, their arms limp. I like when summer is gone and the beach is not so crowded. The scent of suntan lotion fades away, and I can inhale the exhilarating scent of the tides. Of course the straw-hat beachcomber with pants rolled above his ankles never dies. With a taunting gaze that does not wander, he just seems to slip into the eye of the wind, and not even the dimness of fog diminishes his impression." He places his palms on my cheeks.

"Do you know that pure imagination excites me? With my vision fluttering on the ocean air, my face goes anxious as bits of imagined ship wrecks wash up with the waves. In a maze of empresses and jeweled-thieves, the wind-vexed water is cast of gold and dotted with rubies and emeralds. And in my hands are fistfuls of treasures secreted away in the wild blue yonder of my soul." He pauses in thought. "I look out at the ocean, Jenna, and I am a conjurer of life!" He smiles mischievously. "I'll have you know, I don't run from my fantasies, covering my eyes and shrieking. I just kick back, imagining the rush. Yes. As long as I have my wild imagination, I am fixed forever in some distant place of sensual enchantment." He smiles. "Do you draw magical dreams?" Shyly, I lower my eyes.

"I look out at the waves and think of my locker-room fantasies; they certainly had their ambiguous charms! I can only conclude that I must have rubbed a brass lamp and let a genie out of a bottle to come up with such imagination. Rest assured that I am up to something far deeper these days." He thinks for a moment. "How do you truly deliver what you are from the inside to others? I like silly little jokes and nose rubbing." He pauses. "Do you know that you enchant me?" He raises his eyes to mine. "I wonder what you would do if I were to lean over, without warning, and lick the nape of your neck. Would you giggle?"

I plunge into his grin with bashful eyes.

"If I were to cup your ear in my hands and whisper that I want to bathe your body with my tongue, would your eyes widen with wonder?" I look down. "If I should lightly brush my lips across the top of your hand, would it make you want to snuggle into my chest?" he asks and a wild blush creeps into my cheeks.

"If I should rub my nose to yours, would my hot breaths burst you into flames?" He looks at me questioningly. "If I were to wipe a stray tear of ecstasy from your cheek with my finger, would you purr into my neck?" I shrug timidly.

"If I were to prop myself up on my elbows and just look at you, would you get the hint that I am ready?" He takes my hands in his. "Here, by the ocean, there is a special quality to the nights. They are sensual. Perhaps it is the roar of the surf. It allows for repeat listening." He stares at me. "My god," he whispers, "your lips are only inches away." I wipe my tear-drenched cheek.

"Do you know that my fantasies have always been faceless, until I met you? Now, they are of smoldering brown eyes and sensually sculpted lips." He closes his eyes. "Your nails trail down my body. I moan your name and our palms touch until the delicate fingers of early-morning light awaken us." He leans in closely to me. "I want you to know that I don't allow reality to interrupt my fantasies." He drops his voice. "Do you know what commands my attention?" He presses his soft lips to my neck. "Affection commands my attention."

I raise my eyes to his.

"Do you know where I want you to touch me?" he whispers. "I want you to touch my mind. Touch my mind and I will forever be yours." His words plunge into the depths of my soul.

"Do you know you quirk a smile and it rustles me? I can feel your smile digging me in the ribs, slapping me on the back and knocking the air out of me. But do you know what I feel the most? Most of all, I feel your smile slowly nudging me toward you. Grabbing me around my waist it makes me playful. Why, your smile charges the air, slips around my body and scoots me next to you! It actually rubs shoulders with me. Never mind that it has to get up on tiptoe to do it. You keep on smiling and I will wind up in your lap." His lips linger at my earlobe.

"So tell me, are you a spa enthusiast?" he asks. "I'm not talking about being greeted by body wraps, eclectic scrubs, and mood lighting. I am talking about stepping into the tide. The surf is a spa of revitalizing powers unseen by human eyes. It is the gift of enticement. Come on! Let's feel the ocean splash into the palms of our hands!"

"It's raining out," I say.

"Logic tends not to be my first consideration."

"But it's raining out!"

A grin tugs at his lips. "You don't always have to exercise good judgment," he whispers and my eyes widen.

"Look beyond the ordinary, Jenna. Write your name in the wind. You are ready to get wet," he says, tapping the tip of my nose. "You've yet to take off your raincoat and settle in."

"I had forgotten I still had it on," I say, digging my hands into my pockets.

"Whispers of ancient legends roam the jungles of our soul, Jenna. Become as alluring and exotic as your imagination. The night makes a perfect blanket."

I take a deep breath.

He puts his mouth to my ear. "Have you ever been kissed by wild, untamed lips?" he asks.

My fingers curl into his. We walk out into the darkness. There is no escaping temptation.

Timidity's child removes her halo,
And fireballs fall from the sky.

Chapter 22
Wrath of the Seductress – Part 2

"Come on," he whispers, letting go of my hand. "Let's hopscotch across the sea!"

Under peals of thunder, I run after him.

"Looks as if we have just tumbled out of a time machine," he calls over his shoulder. "Look!" he says, pointing into the beacon of light.

All I can do is stare and stare. "What is it?" I ask, my mouth dropping open.

"Perhaps, it is the light of curiosity."

Fixated, I stare into his insight with fascination. "Something is out there," I think.

His gaze drifts off. "The giant has opened its eye. The lighthouse has found us."

"Where is it?" I ask, captivated by the light shining in the darkness.

"It is way off in the distance, probably resting on some craggy rock embankment."

The ocean pauses as I take in the beam piercing the sky.

"Do you know that lighthouses blow in fabled winds? They are firmly embedded in folklore," he says, peering into my eyes. "Beyond a lighthouse are big-winged reptiles that fly across the ocean! Yes. Beyond the sea it is all mystically lit. Esoteric dragon riders escape evil-hearted villains, and oddly gendered firedrakes lure the sea to their playful dungeons of feigned charm. Jenna, you can live in complete fantasy or you can ground yourself in reality, but know that darkness can't hide its face." A shiver runs down my spine.

"I feel as if I am back in the 1800's," he says, gazing off into the distance. "Do you know, long ago there was a lighthouse keeper? In the old days, a lighthouse keeper stayed on guard all night to make sure that the kerosene lamps stayed lit. With shoulders hunched and hands dug into his pockets, he was the story of life's triumphs. But we are modern folk now and those keepers have long since been replaced by bright beacon beams." He stares off at the light billowing in loose waves. "I would have liked being a lighthouse child," he says and I nod, entranced.

"I would have given most anything to grow up with smooth stones crunching under my feet and water lapping at my house. I can see myself now. Every morning I would run for the door, test the water with my toes and wave to the tugboat captains. I would fish at the docks, soar free in the sunshine and play in the boats that washed upon the shore. And in the mysterious dark, I would make shadow puppets on its thick walls. Have you ever made shadow puppets?" he asks and I shiver.

"The lighthouse would have been my sacred place, my fort of protection, my guardian of secrets. We all need a place of security," he says and I become a whirling mass of emotion.

"Lighthouses were designed to stand watch so we didn't slip into the shining sea. But I think they are the secret portals to forever." He winks. "A lighthouse has its own code. This lighthouse in particular is charmingly flirtatious, the way it winks its light upon us. Perhaps it is curious about rapturous spectacles." He pauses. "Perhaps, it is the keeper of magic." He looks skyward. "Legend has it that the inviting glow of this lighthouse didn't always shine peacefully on this darkened beach." My eager eyes follow his lips.

"Legend has it that one wild and stormy night, with the horror of darkness around them, the boats at sea were bewildered and the lighthouse came to their rescue. It shined its beam of light upon them and gave them safe passage. But under its guiding light, eyes glowed in masked faces. Scarred by trickery the lighthouse turned the beach into a cauldron of fire. To this day it trusts only the mysterious speech of the ocean, and destiny watches from the lighthouse window for undeserving faces." He kicks off his shoes. "Now, let's skip rocks."

A sea of mist drifts through me, and I am nudged by the wild beast. "Free yourself from judgment. Imagined notions are more sensible than logical ones. Toss the tassel of sensibility into the breeze. The inner truth is devouring. Perhaps it is you who is the keeper of magic."

Erotically tuned, my sensual being tinges the sky and I am blue light, dancing. Silken tendrils pull greedily at my mesh lacings and I am flowing ribbons drifting in the world of play. Ruffled in silk, I am a seductress leaping across a lusting sea. I am where the wild wait.

"Come play with me," he calls.

I take a deep breath and then, under the guiding beam of the lighthouse hopscotch across the sea.

"It's not exactly warm bath water," he says, as the ocean spray sprinkles his face. Pausing, he wedges his hands into his front pockets and draws from them some tinkling pebbles. "You can see your breath in the air," he says, tossing them into the water. "Hear that splash? That is their forsaken cry into the unknown."

My body trembles.

He wrinkles up his nose. "I have a secret. I know where all of the flat-sided rocks are. If you give me a kiss, maybe I'll tell you. Come on, follow me."

I am a step or two behind him when an irresistible force captures me. Somewhere in the starless void, he calls my name. I don't answer. He pauses, searching for a glimpse of motion. He sees none. He calls me again, this time more frantically. I don't reply.

My lips are passive as my translator whispers. "Don't quell your lustful side," murmurs the wild beast. "Glimpse yourself! Your lips are burning the night!"

Shyly, I stare into the mirror of enchantment. Instantly, I am charmed by what I see. My eyes shine like dark gems. My lips are upturned in a smile, and pinches of play blush my cheeks. I peer closely at my image. Long hair tumbles down my back, giving hints of enticement; a clingy robe elicits a look of undisguised wonder; and a lacy fan is in my hand, cooling the magic within. "I breathe the fire of the dragon," I whisper. Feeling the fire of ecstasy, I fling the mirror of enchantment into the foaming sea and stand in strength, unknown.

"Are you okay?" he asks, appearing in front of me. I stare hypnotically at him.

He blinks at me in surprise. "Your eyes are deep and mysterious."

I lick my lips and then, like a tantalizing creature, I slide my fingers over the buttons of my raincoat.

With the face of a hunter, he stares at me, bulging at the brows.

I unbutton first one button, then the next, then the next. And then, my coat opens and I emerge satin-robed.

His face flashes with excitement. "You are petal soft," he whispers, "but you could fire the sun."

With glowing eyes, I step from the rocks.

He scuffs the wet sand.

Shimmering in silk, I approach him. I place my palms against his cheeks. My body ripples.

"My god, have you descended from flames? You are blazoned in sapphire," he whispers, fingering my robe. "You are human after all."

"Yes. I kiss and see stars. And there is more. My body burns."

He looks at me coyly. "The fear may come," he says.

"No. It has been shooed away by enticement."

For a moment his gaze appears far away, almost as if he is peering somewhere else, at some distant horizon or a place in the past where he dare not go. He kneels down on the wet sand and grabs my hands. "Without morals or qualms make love to me! Without second thoughts, without holding anything of you back, make love to me. Make love to me, Jenna, not because I'm begging you, but because you are begging me."

And in the midst of the darkness, with the wind upon me, with my breath rising, I dodge the Earth and take him. He gives out a cry of delight.

Electrifying rhythms sweep through me, and in the shadow-casting darkness, I set free my sensual spirit. The feeling is thunderous. With the charge of a goddess, I bite at the grin on his lips.

"Your lips are no longer elusive," he says.

"Pardon my animalism," I whisper.

He grins. "Your hot breaths are shaking the air."

I run my hands through his sun-kissed hair, my fingers tingling in its dampness. He closes his eyes. I caress his face and gasp at the feeling. My body quivers.

"I have an intimate confession," he says, "I have been fantasizing about the movement of your hips since we first met." He nuzzles me with his nose. His breath is soft and warm upon my neck. My body shudders as I crawl on top of him. We both share a momentary look of conspiracy.

"Your lips are burning. Is there a low fire within you?" he whispers. I tingle. And then with a force unknown to me, I slant my mouth over his. Slowly, our tongues twine and then tangle teasingly.

"Do you have an appetite for electricity?" I ask. My lips playfully touch his jaw. He purrs teasingly. I flick his ear with my tongue. "Do you really want to get to know me better?" I whisper and a faint blush reveals his reply.

"I'm not here to keep you out of mischief," I say, bringing him closer. Eagerly I run my tongue over his mouth and, with a sly grin on my face, playfully tug at the buttons on his shirt. "I want to feel your lifting hands," I whisper. He licks his lips.

Drawing myself up I straddle his hips, sensually pressing my body against him. I unbutton his shirt and spread it wide. It is open to his navel. With my fingertips I swirl circles through the sweaty hair on his chest and then my nails slowly travel down his body. Quivering, I take a deep breath.

I slide his shirt down his shoulders and his pants down over his feet. He is naked in moments. Mewing softly, I stare at the stranger. His shoulders are broad, his waist thin. I smile as if I know him, but his sprawling nudity before me is unknown and mysterious. I finger every inch of his exposed skin. He gives me a heavy-lidded, shadowy look of expectation. My eyes hungrily roam down his body. I nip at his lips, and an amused grin shapes his mouth. "Touch me," he whispers, "or I will forever toss in restless sleep." My mouth wide, my senses almost leaving me, I drag my tongue down his body. I don't miss an inch of his seething skin. My hips rise. His fingers in my hair tighten.

"You are leaving me breathless," he whispers.

I flatten back down upon him. Through the satin smoothness of my robe, he caresses my back. I arch at his touch, catching his heated breaths in my parted lips.

"I was waiting on the bed for hours wondering if you were going to come back," he pants.

Caressing his lips with my tongue, my hair falls wildly upon his shoulders. Shimmering in sweat, the quiet night awakens and grabs at us hungrily. Slipping my lips over the silkiness of his skin, he growls into my hair. "I want to kiss your fire," he breathes, his eyes glittering.

And then like a wildcat ready to play, I swoop down upon him with hot, heavy kisses. My body bent toward the Earth, I cling to his sweat-slicked skin before lowering my mouth over him. Billowing and fanning, rolling and falling, I wrap around his knees and drown in the heat of his breaths. He gasps, his eyes closed. My fingers sink into him and tumble wildly down his back. "We are riding the tide," he whispers, his body rising with mine. And then, shrouded in mystery amid the moans of the wind, I shift my pulsating body away from him. He arches a brow. I freeze for what seems like forever. And then, in the blackness of the night, in a voice no louder than a whisper, I speak. "Tame me," I breathe. His eyes flash.

Slowly, I tug on my sash. My robe falls open and slides gently over my shoulders and down my back.

"Your moisture glistens," he whispers.

Gliding the wind, I dive the air.

His tongue slides along my body, pausing at my teal mesh panties. He peels them from me with his teeth and brushes them lightly along the curves of my skin. "Do you like your belly button whispered upon?" he asks, parting my legs. A purring growl escapes my throat.

Streaking the sky, the rain of my essence thunders, and I cry out a wild cry that has no words. Splashing the universe, my toes curl into the wet, feathery sand and the spirit of the sea is the only reminder that I am still of this world.

I am a delicate ballerina
Dancing through life's forgery.

Chapter 23
Passion Hangover

A slight breeze blows my sheer curtains. "It's raining orange blossoms," I whisper, curling my toes in scattered rose petals.

A cool voice joins me. "My, but don't you have a passion hangover."

"How do you know about such things, Conscience?" I ask, watching the candles illuminate my petal-filled bath.

"Oh, I've attended a few of your fantasies."

"Have you now?" I say, my fingers gently caressing the water.

"It's amazing what a few human touches will do."

"Ah, it was much more than that," I say, letting the suds cascade down my neck. "The Earth rumbled beneath my feet."

"Uh-huh."

"My lips wandered. I was purring."

"It was a fantasy encounter."

I tuck a loose strand of wet hair behind my ear. "No Conscience, he just made me feel human, that's all."

"He smiled sweetly. It is a common ploy."

"I sighed against his bare skin. The heat of our bodies collided."

"You need to balance your mind."

"I was full of unlimited surprise, Conscience."

"Uh-huh. You were looming and magnificent."

A few sensual suds slide down my breasts. I watch them for a moment, trance-like, before my lips blow them away. "There is more, Conscience. I arched my back and the blaring sound of my erotic being inundated the night."

"It could have been most anything."

"No, Conscience. The world exploded."

"He had a panty-dropping effect on you."

"Conscience, I was a woman in a sleepy gown. He had me tease, peek, and smile. My goodness, I haven't missed your cold presence."

"The lure of fantasy never wanes."

"Ingenuity sparkles in everything he touches."

"He is a gaggle of acts."

"You know, Conscience, life is sexy whispers."

"It is all enchanted fakery."

"I don't know, Conscience. My heart fluttered against his fingertips. I stared at him panting."

"Who can detect the tail wind of delirium?"

"Conscience, I am in a pleasant haze of bewilderment and anticipation. Please let me stay there."

"Haven't you shed your saddle shoes, bobby socks, and barrettes?"

"I let enticement fall past my shoulders."

"You've stripped yourself of sanity."

"I'm keeping my dreamy pose."

"He touched you and the jaws of his trap swung open."

"I straightened my clothes after a night of madness."

"He is a quiver of deceitful arrows."

"You have snatched the clouds from the sky, Conscience. Congratulations!"

"I wish I could be here incognito, but I can't. I have to tell it like it is."

"Conscience, listen to me."

"I'm listening, as always."

"I no longer feel like lusting for the sane life. I have an intimate confession. I did more than smooch behind virtue's back last night!"

"Go on."

"Fire sprayed from my lips."

"Lord, have mercy."

"And there is more," I whisper. "My body followed him without hesitation. Are you still with me?"

"Barely!"

"His hair was silky against my fingers."

"Uh-huh."

"He lifted my hair up off of my neck."

"Uh-huh."

"He placed his lips inside my thigh. I was at the mercy of the ocean."

"Is he going to have you sneaking through windows?"

"No. But I'd like to feel his body press against me in rose-scented suds."

"Uh-huh."

"Do you know his touch still lingers upon my skin?"

"Uh-huh."

"We rubbed noses," I say, giggling.

"Uh-huh."

"Do you know that while I was upon him I whispered into the minutes? I became a pulse-racing woman. And do you know what else? I nibbled his lips."

"Did virtue ever tickle your mind?"

I pile a piece of soaking wet hair back on top of my head. "I thought I fired you, Conscience."

"I'm leaving. But let me ask you this. Will you fight pangs of disappointment if he doesn't call?"

I pause for a moment. "Okay, Conscience. You have succeeded in creating hesitation, creeping doubt, and fear."

"Did you listen for warning bells?"

"I was so hot I couldn't hear a thing," I say, sliding deeper into the bath water.

"So, there were no warning bells?"

"Conscience, you never cease to amaze me. I was sensing my building release. I buried my face in his neck. Afterwards, I covered my eyes with my hands for he had just taken me into a world I had only fantasized about. He licked my tears. Trust me! This is no time for a moral invasion."

"I'm not trying to take you down."

"Conscience, you need to push away your world of stone and become a sensual believer."

"Uh-huh."

"You are a lightning rod of criticism."

"Uh-huh."

"There is absurdity in everyone, not just me."

"His masterful gestures turned you into wide-gaping eyes and a crumbling heap of admiring giggles."

"You have an unfair attitude."

"You are out in the cosmos."

"I was a sweat-soaked clump of hair."

"And so now you claim the future you desire."

"I never want the flush in my face to fade."

"You were seeking daring whims."

"He electrified the stillness. I was happy."

"You were a spectacle."

"His hands slipped down my sides."

"You won't be walking off into the proverbial sunset with him, let me tell you."

I lift one leg up and rest it on the tub and I stare at my painted toes. I raise my other leg out of the water. Suds dribble quickly down my skin. "I wrestled to remain moral, Conscience, but I had to let go."

"You will crash and burn in your erotic world."

“A sensual mist dripped down my skin, Conscience, and a tantalizing woman emerged. I squinted into enchantment.”

“Enchantment?”

“Yes. Gliding fingers ushered me into a world of electrifying rhythms, and in the shadow-casting darkness the Earth shuddered.”

“Uh-huh.”

“Hot kisses splashed my breasts.”

“Uh-huh.”

“There was the rustle of fabric. My breaths came in ragged gasps. My tongue playfully flicked at his lips.”

“Uh-huh.”

“He wrapped himself around me. It was magical. It was everything I imagined. On top of him I ached. The power of his hips turned me into a thigh-grabber. My fingernails cut into his flesh.”

“He will have you running after the weary heels of sadness.”

“My world has changed, Conscience,” I say, flicking the bath water. “Our lips crashed together and in the beads of sweat that flew through the air I caught my erotic being. I became myself, at last!”

“You are a work of breathtaking imagination. You should be carted off to an institution where you can be nursed through your dreams.”

“I want to place another kiss on his tummy.”

“He is a fairy-tale ogre, and I fear that you have slept too long.”

“His soft breaths exhaled in the cool air,” I say, lazily rubbing my curled toes. “It was mesmerizing.”

“He will have you stewing in sorrow.”

“Sweat was flying. My hair sprawled in the wet sand.”

“He had sly touches.”

I sink into the rose-petal water. A flush creeps up my neck and colors my cheeks. I wriggle my fingers gently breaking the bath water's hot vapor. My eyes barely slit, I watch the tiny puffs of steam rise. "Conscience, do you know before I met him I was yawning through life?"

"And now you are a magnificent creature."

"He chipped the ice off my nose. I no longer babble into the frigid air."

"Bring your attention back to Earth. Has he called?"

"No."

"Isn't he known for his early-morning calls?"

I slide into the darkened water. The suds seem strangely creepy. There is a kind of madness to them. Phantom ships ply the apocalyptic waters and slide off my skin as though I were a mangrove swamp of concealed monsters. A ghostly parade of dread illuminates me and the world seems strikingly eerie. "Excuse me," I ask the sudsy creatures clinging to my arms, "do you prey upon those enticed?" An incandescent brew of wonder invades me, and my elation swiftly fades.

"Conscience, you are a great cure for a passion hangover."

"Well, someone has to snap you out of your intrigue."

"But our smoldering bodies left streaks in the sky," I say, weakly.

"Uh-huh. You don't have to convince me."

"Our bodies fused," I mumble. "He kissed my hair."

"Uh-huh."

"I was a spirited rocket."

"That's what they all say."

"I had a delicious tingle."

"You were staggering in vulnerability."

"I awoke to the soft sound of dawn."

"You are not an affair woman. Affairs have us swinging in the cradle of uncertainty, you know."

I groan.

"There was a dark edge to his laughter."

"What?"

"There was a dark edge to his laughter."

"Conscience, you are frighteningly out of touch with the ordinary world. Your interpretation is all wrong."

"Then why hasn't he called? I mean, he cupped your cheeks in his hands, right?"

"Yes," I answer softly.

"His warm voice greeted your ears."

"Yes."

"You became lionized. You purred with contentment, right?"

"Yes," I say, brushing away tears.

"Perhaps you are no longer his ticket to fame."

"You mean he was just using me for connections to shop his book?"

"Welcome to the world of ulterior motives."

A feeling of sadness pits my stomach.

"Perhaps he realized you couldn't give him the bubble-wrapped life he was looking for."

I sigh.

"What else could it be? I mean, the sex was extraordinary, wasn't it?"

"Yes," I say, meekly, my thoughts softly glowing in the flickering light.

"You were awe-struck at the amazingly loud sounds you were making, correct?"

"Yes," I answer, my eyes wet, my lower lip trembling.

"The passion was unimaginable, right?"

"Yes. It was Heaven."

"Are you warped by the sun? His jaws were gaped wide open to charm you. His kisses were all a façade."

"The kisses on my nose too?"

"It was all make-believe."

I finger the dainty bath petals floating around me. Like spider webs, they etch my skin. "Unloosen your grasp on me," I wail. "You are not full of the best intentions." Eerie, sumptuous drones land on my shoulder. I focus on their invasion. "Your shadows mingle," I cry over their crooning hum. "How many of you live amongst me?"

Flinging accents of menace, night monsters with flat, lusterless eyes usher me from my bath. My soul creaks open. I look sideways at my hairless companions. "Your eyes make me shudder," I say, snatching a towel and wrapping it around myself.

"Welcome to the world of human beings," they chortle. My body rumbles. "You don't seem to have fever," I utter. They glare at me. "We feel the wild beast," they chide. My lips tremble. "How many souls have you awakened with desire? How many souls have you destroyed with your false tenderness? You are full of fake joy," I whimper. They laugh hauntingly and vanish. "We feel the wild beast," they hauntingly repeat, their laughter chilling the air.

Warily I gaze through the darkness. "Who is out there?" I call. "Are you dressed accordingly so I cannot recognize you? Is this a doomed attraction? I can't hear you," I say, my voice fading into the silence. Hoax monsters soar above my head. Their fiery, colored wings flutter at my wobbly knees. "Greetings! We are shadow monsters. We are visible only in beacons of light." The room hovers oddly. "Blink twice and we don't look the same. Blink three times and we are bony, deep-eyed skulls lying in the black dunes of slithering lizards." I glance at the coven of crooked noses. "Are you immoral?" I ask.

Deeper I go into the villains of play, their clutching fingers burning my cheeks. "Monsters get lonely too," they shout, their breaths torching my skin. Hissing creatures creep toward me. They flick their forked tongues from side to side. "Are you up for some good seducing?" they pant. "Come with us and shake the air!" They slither closer. "Stay away from me! You are cold-blooded." They repeatedly flick their forked tongues. "Give us the password to life," they roar. "I don't know it," I cry. Their green slimy skin slithers upon me. "Where are your face and eyes?" I squeal. "I can't see them." Long, dangling arms grab me. My legs rise. "There is nothing behind the mask," they chortle.

Foggy figures rustle the darkness, their scrawny necks nuzzling my throat. I shiver from their ghostly touch. "Do you come from sensual mist?" I wail. "No," they chuckle. "We come from the chill in the ground." Thrusting their long, slimy fingers up my legs, they smother me under blankets of spiders. I gulp for air. "Your heads are dragonish," I say, swatting at black-coated bats. "Sample our cauldrons of trickery," they say. "It is sweet to your lips." I bury my face into the shadow-darkened trees. "When will evil disappear?" I cry.

Dwarf-like monsters invade me. Fiendishly, they poke at the horns on top of my head. My lips twitch. "You cannot see our scars and wounds," they chant. "Words are the sharpest daggers to the flesh." "Are there character sightings in life?" I ask, trying to break free of the climbing plants. "Yes. Feel trickery nibble your ears. Deception lurks in snow-capped palms," they slyly grin. Shadowy figures with steaming skin paw at me with their eerie extensions. "What is behind your masks?" I scream.

"Trickles of emptiness," they chortle.

Evil chars around me, its hellish fury burning into my flesh. "We are a haunt of demons. Come snuggle closer to the flames," they chide. Deceit howls into my ears. There is no escaping its wicked breaths. And in the clutches of fire, with phantoms eating me whole, the haunting moans of my abandoned soul wails, "Oh god, Dal, please call me." The Earth hisses and the twinkle in my eye is gone.

Life is a shimmering mosaic
Of painted faces.

Chapter 24
Out of the Fire

I glance at the traffic signal, suddenly realizing that it has turned green. Quickly, I step on the gas. A bloom of pink charges my cheeks and I drive forward with sudden speed. Flinging my hair out of my eyes, I peer through the sun-speckled windshield. An explosion of blue fire bursts before me. "It is his eyes," I cry. "My god, it is his eyes!"

Magically, he appears on every street corner. His mystery is hardly locked away. I reach out for his hand. A feathery kiss brushes just below my fingertips, and I try to keep my robe in place. He darts me a look of sweet madness. A wistful sigh escapes me and I pull back from licking my lips.

Over my shoulder a set of car headlights appears and gets continuously closer. My heart leaps. "It's Dal!" The driver rolls down a half-opened window. "You are driving slowly," shouts the female motorist, speeding off. My hands clench the steering wheel with knuckle-whitening force as my dark gaze sweeps over L.A. I can't get him off my mind.

"You've got to get your act together, my dear. You are on your way to a huge power meeting at the studio. Today is the day you meet the infamous Ross Heaverton. He is a major heavy."

"Well, it's not that huge, Conscience. It's just one of JB's casual, Sunday-morning huddles. But Ross Heaverton is definitely a major heavy. I guess I should get my act together. It will be good to see JB after all this time. I guess I can tell her I found my sip of Cognac."

"You don't want your heart to interfere with your job. You have to eat, you know."

"Dal is a dynamic writer, Conscience," I say dreamily.

"His words swept you off your feet."

"I was going to try to introduce his writing talents to the studio's vibrant mix of industry executives and maybe even to Ross Heaverton. I hear he unleashes power wherever he walks. I have an intense confessional. If I weren't so consumed with Dal, I would be petrified to meet someone as movie mighty as Ross. I mean, you just don't meet people like him everyday."

"You always get nervous around the bigwigs."

"I was helping Dal think of a title for his book. I had visions of seeing him slouched in a comfy chair watching his work in development."

"Were you curled up on his lap?"

I sigh. "I just can't seem to pull myself out of the fire. He was irresistible. Ideas that were unimaginable to me became real with him. He made my head spin."

"Understandable. He was lots of things all at once. He was a beautiful fairytale, an erotic fantasy and an emotional renaissance."

"He could outrun the wind. I held my breath when he fingered my chin. My cool lips warmed under his touch."

"Oh my goodness!"

"You can gasp all you want, Conscience, but my shoulders are drooping without him."

"You know, I'm trying to work with you."

"There is more, Conscience. Out of nowhere, his kisses land on my skin. I cannot swat them away."

"It is a demanding task for you to get rid of his image. He was tremendously exciting to you."

"Conscience, he has a way of seeming present everywhere. His eyes are all over the road, like blue fire."

"This too shall pass."

"I try to tuck my emotions away, but they rifle through my pockets. Do you know he shakes me from sleep?"

"It's just life's caress blowing through you, nothing more."

I move the stray strands of hair off my forehead. "I'm glad we are on talking terms again, Conscience."

"You will get on to something more meaningful. Trust me."

"If I can't trust you, Conscience, whom can I trust?"

"That's what I've been trying to tell you. Listen, you'll be okay. Your emotions will land a few right hooks and a couple of left jabs every now and again, but you just jab back at their madness."

Bundled up in my synthetic fleece, I race through the streets of L.A. My tires bounce on the little white bumps as I roll down my window and let the wind blow back my hair. There is definitely a nip in the air.

Zipping past an array of parked cars, a truck's bumper and grill fill my rear window. Heat ripples through me. The tailgater looks like Dal. The truck changes lanes and the tailgater sticks his plaid sleeve out of the window. "Is your windshield steamed against the cold?" shouts the trucker, flicking his cigarette. "Are you in another world, or what?" He impatiently rakes his hands through his spiked ponytail and, after a bit of eyebrow raising, takes off. I fiddle with the radio although I'm hardly up for singing along with my favorite tunes. At least there is no nightmarish traffic. It isn't often that I can cruise to the studio without shuddering halts due to traffic jams.

Rounding the corner into the studio, I see the parking lot is under construction. Stone and gravel pop out from under my tires and I receive a face full of dust. I roll up my window. L.A. seems to always be outlined in the haze of construction. My brakes squeak as I wheel around the parking structure. Parking my car in the concrete avalanche, I congratulate myself on arriving without any more motorists booing my driving.

Drumming my fingers against the steering wheel, I sigh deeply. "He had a sensual mouth."

"You'd better calm your turbulent thoughts, my dear. Focus is becoming an issue."

"My mind keeps taking me back to an enchanted beach, Conscience."

"You must stop imagining his body."

"He was absurdly sexy."

"You were instantly smitten."

"He was potent moonlight."

"And now you have brooding eyes."

"I am emotionally exhausted."

"He was a passion-clad stranger who took you far away from the daily grind."

"I kissed the lips of the sun, Conscience."

"He had choking arms."

"I was scratching the walls."

"He crept in upon your closed lids."

"He devoured my quivering body."

"He glimmered in veiled obscurity."

"I surrendered to the ravishing of time, Conscience."

"Ah, so you did."

"I have an intimate confession. I would have shared a bedroll with him, anywhere."

"C'mon."

"He blew strands of hair off my forehead. Our lips were slippery with kisses. We left trails of fire. I fear I am smitten for life."

"Here we go."

"I nuzzled his shoulder."

"Give me a break."

"I kissed his tummy."

"Face it there will be no rocking chair reminiscences."

"He has snuck into my presence with mind-altering kisses. Do you know, with him my eyes twinkled in the windswept night?"

"He was cleverly camouflaged."

I tap my fingers once again against the dashboard and clumsily get out of the car. Spiritless, I collect my notebook and with sloping shoulders and an awkward gait lumber to the elevators.

"Try to walk briskly."

"I miss his breaths."

"Don't slouch."

"I have dreams of catching his hair in the wind."

"Focus!"

"Yes, Conscience."

With the cold edges of my car keys pressing into my fingers, I watch him leaning back on the hood of his car. A smile plays on his lips.

"Focus!"

"Yes, Conscience."

The up elevator chimes and, with wistful hunger trailing after me, I step inside.

A voice pours over me suddenly. "Hold the doors open!" Without peering out, I press the panel's request button.

Roy Saxton jumps in and hits the button's release. "Welcome back," he says, smacking my face with a kiss. "How did your quest go?"

A blush tints my cheeks.

The doors open. "Guess we'll leave that for another conversation." He grins.

"Everything looks beautiful," I say, walking off the elevator with him into the studio's executive offices. "You've been painting," I say, wrinkling up my nose.

"We renovated from wall to wall with cheery plum and snowy white blossoms to create a feeling of spaciousness and light. You know, illusion is everything!"

I nod.

"We've even renovated the whole place with floor-to-ceiling windows so we can all guiltlessly bathe in the late-day softness. I've taken it upon myself to transform this place. Why, I've even put down some flooring. My jeans were paint-splattered for weeks," he says, chuckling. "You know, Jen, when you get bored with your current stance in life, renovate!" His face drops for a moment. "Do you know I've missed our chats? I was hoping that you'd call your quest off and come back a little bit early."

I breathe in an inhalation of paint fumes.

"Typically the dust and paint make you feel a little more ill than your typical hangover, but nothing more than that. It wears off just like the buzz from a few beers!"

I follow him into his office.

"I'm going to put a unique paint finish on the ceiling in here. Do you know that when I paint, my tongue pokes out slightly as I concentrate?"

I giggle.

"Painting is a bit fatiguing, but I find it soothing. First, I madly search through the color charts, looking for just the right hues. Then do you know what I do?"

"No," I say smiling.

"I close my eyes! Yes! I close my eyes and I listen for the colors to lead me. I visualize them in my head. I feel their exuberance. And then, I begin to discover what I want by realizing what I don't want. Perhaps a shade is too aggressive. You know, I cannot settle myself in my chair if a color is too dominating."

I listen, amused.

"And I also don't need a color that is so bright that it nods to everyone that it sees! I don't need to be greeted with emotion, but I also don't need to be put in a position to defend my space. The colors I choose, Jenna, must collaborate! They must connect deeply, not consume my curiosity, not seem like they are invaders and not be intrusive to the rest of the room. They just need to give my office a bit of dignity and not take me off into strange directions because of my imagined vulnerability."

I smile at his words.

"Yes! Welcome back, Jen. Now, we don't have to double up anymore, and we can all go and hide in our lazy cocoons!"

"I'm glad to be back."

He glances at his watch. "Oops, you've got to go! You've got a meeting with the heavies. I fear I've kept you too long. You better head to JB's office at a run." He kisses me on the cheek. "Just go right on in. You're expected."

I walk down the hallway to JB's office, bringing with me the warm aroma of belonging. It will be nice to get back to the ordinary issues of everyday life. Still and calm, I step into the doorway of her office and peer in. The morning sunshine streams through the windows, caressing a beautiful walnut table in between two chairs. "JB has been busy decorating," I think, eyeing the abundant flower arrangements in each corner. "JB," I call to the unseen image shrouded in chrome swivel stands. There is no answer and an eerie silence surrounds me. Breathing in the dead atmosphere, I slowly enter the room. "JB, are you okay?" I whisper. "Where is your quiet smile?"

At the tone of my query, the high-back leather creature on chrome legs awakens! It swivels around so quickly that my reflexes spring into action and I grab on to the edge of the desk. Chaos floods my mind as shock rushes toward me. All I can do is stand there and watch the mushroom cloud rise.

He presses his fingertips together and smiles. "It's not easy getting booted out of paradise, is it, Weyburn?"

I do a head-shaking double take. "Dal?" I whisper, my mouth falling open at the site of him.

He is distinctly formal. "I am Ross Heaverton," he says, rising.

My jaw drops. My cheeks flame. Intense panic fills me.

Possessing piercing blue eyes and an intense demeanor, he cracks a smile but appears to be soulless. "There is no Dallas Curtis," he says, sinking back down in his chair.

I gasp and brush the hair from my face with trembling fingers.

He takes a stick of salve from his shirt pocket and slathers it across his lips and chuckles. "Where would we be without lip balm, Weyburn?" he asks, motioning for me to sit down. In shocking silence, I take a seat.

"Everyone's dark hair was spiked fuchsia this morning. Did you notice that?" he asks, yawning. "I'm exhausted. I've been air-kissing people since daybreak. There seemed to be a burgeoning number of wannabes fluttering the streets this a.m."

Lifting my eyes from my death stare, I see he is constructed of fashionably designed faded denim.

"Did you notice the high-speed traffic on the freeway this morning?" he asks, his question interrupting my gaze.

I bite my lip.

"It's Sunday morning, but it's another gas-guzzling day in L.A." He scoots his body closer to the desk. "Do you know I pulled into the parking lot this morning when it was still pitch black? It's a ghostly feeling getting up so early and seeing the sunrise over your shoulder. I don't get up early even with an alarm clock. You know, I stagger out of bed," he says, smiling. "You won't see me walking around with bags under my eyes, my robe belt dragging along the floor. Oh no! I am too powerful for that! I am a champion sleeper." He pauses. "Is that peachy-rose lip gloss you're wearing?"

My stomach tightens.

"Excuse me, while I bring a little coffee heaven to my lips," he says, taking a gulp from the cup on his desk. He stares into his espresso. "Pardon me for not being up on the latest coffee concoction. I'm not a caffeine loony. I go for juices and decaf teas."

I brush a stray strand of hair from my forehead.

"I drove alongside the path of the bulldozers to the studio this morning. I certainly didn't need binoculars to see them. They are quite visible among the blooms. And they are noisy creatures! Why, their heavy stomps rampage the city! They have an excellent sense of place. No dubbed versions of them! They are continuous reality. You can't stop the bulldozers. No one steps in their path. If I should be reincarnated, I may opt to be a dozer and haunt this city with my demolition claws," he chortles. "I love their self-confidence. I love the fact that they are so mechanical. They don't feel regret, sadness or desperation." He chuckles. "Perhaps, I have already mastered their powers!"

His smile dances wickedly on my shoulder.

"L.A. is sprawl weary, Weyburn. Tinsel town is one big construction site. Why, there is no overgrown brush left in this place for us to skin our knees on. L.A. is choking its cities with traffic. Everything is a honking affair. Drivers squeeze past, sitting on their horns, revving their engines, desperately searching for a side street to make time on. Don't they know that they don't exist?" An angry edge is heard in his voice. "There should be a law against traffic noise. It is deafening."

I can't help but melt under his gaze. His shirtsleeves are rolled up to just above his elbows, and I wonder if he has sprayed the crook of his arm with cologne.

He sits back in his seat and swirls his espresso around in its cup, and then gives me a glacial stare. "My wife and I were looking at oak tables all week," he says matter-of-factly. His words tear at my flesh.

"We spent the last couple of days picking out the tiles for the kitchen and bathroom countertops. It was relaxing, sitting in our rose-marble atrium, browsing catalogs of sumptuous fabrics, luxury linens and hot tubs. Ours is a colonial-style brick house with a sloped roof and shingles. You were there. It is where we met. We've got a guy finishing the interior wood trim along the baseboards, giving every room a warm, antique feeling." My body trembles.

"Prior to that, we spent the whole weekend strolling among giant pots of flowers and odd-shaped cactuses. Then we put on our aerodynamic helmets that make cyclists look like space aliens with enormous brains, and we pedaled through tons of marshland." He looks at his tanned arms. "Do you know that I am a pseudo sun worshipper? I hang out at emporiums and tanning booths to get my twenty-minute face tan. Prices have gone up to get a customized, head-to-toe spray tan and it only lasts for about a week anyway. I may have to go back to the dunes, but I am so damn busy."

The moisture from my forehead skims down my flushed cheeks. He is married. My heart races. He senses my astonishment, but appears undaunted.

"The wife and I spent last month shopping for diamonds and sapphires in Paris' elegant boutiques. It was quite a fabled time watching everyone strut around with designer bags. Prior to that, we were in Cancun trinket shopping. We snapped the occasional photo or two, wading in sun-dappled seas and snoozing away on the sandy beaches, but after a while you feign interest," he says, his voice cold and far away.

"And then, of all things, a combination of delays on our flight from LAX to San Francisco plus unyielding traffic on the Interstate had made the wife and I nearly four hours later than we'd originally planned for a weekend rendezvous. My wife feared that everything would be closed before we got off the cable cars. But our jet-fueled sleigh landed in plenty of time, and we were able to dodge the mist on time. San Francisco is always tourist-trammeled anyway. Would you like some water, Weyburn? You look a bit flustered."

"No," I cough, while visions of him kissing my calves whirl the room.

"Do you know this coffee table appears to be a hunk of walnut when it is actually made up of hollow, modular units? Welcome to its other life," he says, grinning.

I swallow hard.

"I come back to work and I have a glut of voicemail messages. My cell phone never stops ringing." He stares at me icily. "The world is water soaked and artificially flavored, Weyburn," he says and I shiver.

"We have to form opinions in advance. We have to be five steps ahead of our competition and ten paces ahead of our informers. Everyone wants to catch the wave of success." He folds his hands and leans back in his chair. "Money doesn't talk in this business. It screams and hums and whistles. It is a high stakes world full of secret handshakes, anxious frenzies, and thick wads of cash. Society is peopled by the tough and the desperate. We constantly look over our shoulder to stay on top."

He leans forward, his hair aglow by a shaft of sunlight. "It seems that even when we gaze heavenward, we are looking directly into the camera." He lowers his voice. "It is all about grand entrances, etched-on eyebrows, and painted on-grins. There will be no sensual reminiscences here. This is hardly a place for a fairytale although we do film tearful scenes," he chuckles. "I am a high-salaried studio executive. My strength is game management. I have the morals of a thief."

I shiver.

"This is a planet of phony leaflets, false documents, and quick getaways. The world is made up of prowling, ghoulish shapes clutching coiled parcels." He pauses. "Are my sleeves too wide, my cuffs too tight? Am I missing a button?"

I stare off from him. Somehow I cannot quite reach his eyes.

"Shall we sit down and rehearse our impeccably predictable opinions?" His eyes twinkle wickedly. "I am swaggered drapes, high-waist pleated pants, zany crochets, and fine woolen knits. I am manicured nails buffed shiny as mirrors," he says admiring his fingertips. "And there is more."

I lower my head.

"I am tasseled pulls for flushing the commode." He grins. "I am a pretension buff of sinful flesh."

The darkness whispers to me. My lips tremble. I cannot break free from his spell.

"I walk in halls of power, Weyburn. I am a series of maneuvers, a wolf in designer threads. I am a fraud."

"A fraud?" I mouth.

"Yes! Me and virtually the entire constellation!"

I shudder. "Are you soul destroying?" I whisper.

"Let's talk softly. I don't want the cynics among us to start talking." He pushes his cup of espresso to the very edge of the table and takes his hand away. "You see," he says, eyeing the cup, "it's playing with me; it's a tease. But where is its power? Will it fall off the edge? Who will fall into the unguarded cup?" He chuckles. "I draw fast from the human soul, Weyburn. Meet the stone-cold lunatic in me," he says, sticking out his hand. "The world is scheme-hatched. You were ambushed by passion." He laughs evilly. "I haven't a touch of decency to my soul, Weyburn. Don't try to topple the mighty," he hisses.

His hot kisses tantalize my body. I laugh and rub against him. He breathes deeply in my ear. My nipples press through my satin robe to meet his eager hands. My body flushes. I grip his hips. He pulls down my panties and trails my body with his lips. I nuzzle his cheek and surrender.

"Humankind is a natural place for trickery. There are few outbreaks of honesty on this Earth. Of course from time to time you have the traditional do-gooder who doesn't play fast and loose with the truth but over all there is intended deception. It is an emotionally messy world, Weyburn. Nirvana is gone in the blink of an eye."

He shuffles some papers. "You knew our secrets. We couldn't take the risk that you were out to capture fame. Betrayal stings deeply, Weyburn. We had no idea if your quest for fire was a fancy dress for personal celebration. The mere fact that you would leave us during Oscar season was crime enough."

Numbness takes over my body.

"You don't trot out on a quest for fire during Oscar season," he says, rushing words at me.

I stare at his icy demeanor.

"You had your chance to think better of your endeavor. There were clues along the way."

I gulp. "Was it all a façade?"

"I had to feign interest. I had to keep you occupied."

My eyes tear.

"Of all of the things I will be held accountable for in hell, this will surprise me the least."

I nod.

"We sleep with spiders, Weyburn."

"Are you a professional seducer?" I whisper.

"Let's just say I am strategically charming." He grins. "The art of seduction is carried out with plumes of smoke."

I wipe my eyes.

"I have an intimate confession," he chortles. "I moonlight as a human being."

My body trembles.

"Stay away from the play gods, Weyburn; you are not cut out for affairs. Stick to love."

I sniffle and wonder how I stare down devastation.

"This dialogue does not come with a pack of tissues." He pauses. "I suppose I have filled more than a few lives with emotional wreckage."

I choke back a sob.

"We are a cheering civilization, Weyburn. It is all about applause." He chuckles. "Humankind is mentally toxic." Trembling, I bite my lip.

He brushes a speck of dust off his desk. "I have an infernal load of paperwork." Acting on reflex, I unsteadily rise.

"Was there ever a book, Dal?" I ask.

He raises his brow amusingly. "There will be no pages wrapped in jackets of obscurity. I can't write worth a damn. But if there were a book, I've thought of a title."

Wearily, I lift my eyes.

"I would call it *The Human Masquerade.*" He laughs eerily. "You know, The Human Masquerade lives in The Pink Forest."

I drop to my knees.

It creeps slowly toward me, half crawling, half walking. It is only inches away, the sunlight melting it like a candle. It casts its hot breaths upon my face. Blood pulses in my ears. It arches up to kiss me. I raise a weak hand.

"I was life's pale bouquet," I whisper. "You turned me into a blushing rose."

It darkly laughs.

I gasp softly at the ghoulish look in its eye.

And then, like a fiery angel descending to Earth, my spirit awakens. Puffing out flames of hot kisses, I turn my back on illusion and my tinkering with reality ends.

Humankind spends eternity
Waiting to enter the Forbidden
City of Emotion.

Untold, Until Now

"Are you looking for flying silk?"

I stare at the straggly bearded man toting cans. "Yes. And big-winged reptiles too!"

His mouth crinkles at the edges. "You only find those soaring beyond beacons of light."

"A long time ago, the night appeared as a black silhouette and a lighthouse tinged the sky," I rustle softly. "Waves dashed against its rocks, and the wind moaned around its tower."

"Did you see the sun dropping yesterday? It was a red ball falling into the sea." He blinks into the mist. "It is becoming more difficult to tell what the real world is these days."

I bite at my bottom lip.

"I've been on this powder-soft beach for twenty-five years. Only moonlight dances upon it." He smiles. "Life is an illusion. Did he fill you with Earth-changing insights?"

"With him, I discovered the ecstasy of a whisper."

"Even the palms can become snow-dusted trees. We all have the right of myth."

"A distinguished looking soul eyed me once. I stood behind my noble stone castle and waved." I tremble. "You see, I once was an erotic traveler."

"Did you bring back any emotional souvenirs?"

"Yes, his soft breaths exhaling in the cool air and the sparkling raindrops caught in his long soft lashes."

"He made your eyes swim."

"With him, I didn't hear music. With him, I felt the symphony. And even now, I am too choked up to wave goodbye to the passing moment."

"It is hard to come down to Earth once we have streaked the sky."

"I think if I could have been with him longer, I would have learned to feel the night grass. You see, he woke me from a sound sleep."

"Perhaps fantasy sent you into his embrace. You know, imagination lifts the veil of our mind. We are but drops in the haze."

I cock my head.

"The greatest mystery lies within us. It is the source of our magic, our seductiveness, our lunacy."

"His eyelashes tickled my nose."

"He gave you a momentary connection to life."

"I would have been mesmerized seeing him drink from a squirt bottle."

"There is wonderful fascination in simplicity. Do you know, I've always thought the wet sand looks like sequins?"

My eyes drift to the silky warmth encircling me.

"Do you know, when I was a kid, I used to dig potholes on the beach to trap water? I was a five year old with sticky hands. And there is more. Wading through the emerald waves, sifting the sand, I was a treasure hunter pretending rocks were impressive gemstones. Joshing my friends, I would spend endless hours showing off my tiny, glowing heaps while the sand crabs scampered about." He grins. "I used to run on the beach and then sink to my knees with sandcastle dreams. I was the king of soft breezes."

I give him a soft nod.

"I used to like watching the birds with long, angled beaks digging for sea creatures! They would race along the water's edge on matchstick legs, and I would admire them toe dance in the crashing waves." He pauses. "Do you know the sand creates images? Look at it long enough and it curves very lightly in a gentle smile. Sometimes I watch it, simply mesmerized. Sometimes I sneak up to it just to listen. Running my fingers through it brings out another presence in me, and I am climbing out of bed with a little boy's wonder."

I stare at the endless grin on his face.

"Under my mother's unsuspecting nose, I would grab my spoon from lunch and ceaselessly dig to reach the end of the world. I would spend days brushing the glow of the sand from my fingertips." He smiles. "Trust me. You are standing in magic."

Nodding, I pull the blanket of the Earth closer around my shoulders.

"I used to peer out at the world through my little elf sunglasses. Scowling furiously from the shadow of my big beach umbrella, I would stick my tongue out at the hordes of people invading my space. But the steep path leading to life beckoned me. And look! I am measureless! But know, I would give anything to scoop that little boy up in a hug."

I take a deep breath. "Do we ever get over people who hurt us?" I quietly ask.

"No. We just learn to go on."

"Do we just live with the ache?"

"We can make an attempt to bury the magic but we cannot bury the spell."

"You have burning blue eyes," I gasp.

"Perhaps, I have emerged from the imagination of paradise."

"Once my cheeks were reddened with fire," I whisper.

"We are all descendants of wild rivers."

"His tongue danced upon the bare edge of my shoulder. His kiss was from another time."

"He gave you a crush on life."

"He creeps into the corners of my memory. He remains more than just a moment's existence."

"We all exist in the moment and then we are gone."

Tears splash my eyes. "I miss my dog."

"There is no masquerade in a wagging tail."

"She reigned her life with truth, goodness, and beauty. She was my loyal shadow. The sun no longer brushes the Earth," I say, wiping my eyes. "I miss her so much."

"Dezerae is only as far as your pulse."

"How do you know her name?"

"She is written in the wind."

"Does anyone look after you?" I ask.

"Just the shaggy-headed fan palms and their feathery shadows." He stares off at an unseen horizon. "The world is full of emotional snipers, but the atmosphere under my leafy umbrella is peaceful and calm. I rest my head on an ocean of pillows and awaken to the sun glinting off the waves. And I'll bet you thought all I do is go grazing in the trash and gobble up lunch." I stare at my vacant image.

"I come to the ocean, not for the salty air and not for its crashing tide, but for its endlessness." His eyes twinkle. "I am a magical realist. I spend time with my impulses."

I listen to him, captivated.

"Society is measured by timers. But in my leaf-covered world, I am measured by the fire of the sun through the heavens. I try to stay up until not a shred of daylight is left. Even as a small boy, I lived for the dawn."

I stare at him, wide-eyed.

"I find revelation in unexpected places. To glance eye to eye in a moment's revelation is enticing." He pauses. "Do you have a willingness to see the unseen?" he asks. "You must, if you want enchantment to touch your presence."

I bite my trembling lip.

"The mysterious charm of the night blankets the tide and lulls me into an unguarded sleep. Pulling the darkness up under my chin, I am able to sleep on the breeze where my dreams tuck me into the falling stars." A smile climbs to his eyes. "You know, in a bedroom oasis we sneak out of disguise."

"Yes," I whisper.

"In my leafy world, I have experiences I can curl up with. Society has fallen into a fitful sleep. Of course that is bound to happen when you tear off a piece of the sun."

I let out a deep breath. "I once had an impulse to be myself. I don't know what came over me."

"You wished upon life."

"Ah, so I did!"

"We are the magic of our enchantment."

"I closed my eyes. He lifted the waves."

"A stray breeze carried his smile. It pecked you on your cheek."

"I placed my palms against the wind. Blushing flames kissed the sky."

"Life thundered your ear."

I gasp.

"You snuck into the heat of your soul. You became human."

My lips tremble. "I have an intimate confession. I have an impulse to fall into your arms. I am filled with unspoken thought."

"We never know whose shoulder we'll cry on."

A tear trickles down my cheek. "You see, for a brief moment my life was mystically lit, but a gust of wind flung sand in my eyes and I fell into the jaws of illusion."

"Allow your tears to warm the Earth. Sometimes, it takes an eternity to enter the forbidden city of Emotion."

"What is the password to life?" I cry.

"Love," he whispers.

"Love?" I tremble. "Not passion?"

"Passion is the spice of life. Love is the touch of peace."

"How do I get to love?" I ask.

"By following the twinkle in your eye."

I look down. "I danced in clouds of woven leaves. I've never done that before."

"In the pink forest painted toes rise like spires into the night sky."

I gasp. "How do you know about the pink forest?"

"I have been rumored to live in lands of magical refuge."

"I was filled with discovery," I whisper.

"Fascination puts us in the moment."

I smile. "The sensual genie within me appeared."

"It is you who delivers your wishes."

"Me?" I ask, shyly.

"Yes. Enchantment breathes upon those who step from the Earth's shadow."

"You have sprayed the crook of your arm with cologne," I whisper.

"Even a glass slipper squeaks of surprise."

Lifting my head from the pillow of his shoulder, our eyes lock.

"Do you know the rain falling on your cheeks is the sincerest form of flattery?"

I reach a waving hand out toward his voice.

He throws me a graceful kiss from the ends of his fingers and then, with furrowed brows and searching eyes, continues along the bicycle path, toting his cans. I watch him until his image fades into a shadow of silvery mist.

Stilled in the morning's sharp air, I stand alone on the beach. It is utterly vacant except for a few seabirds waddling at the water's edge. I look into the fog. His breaths fall in the curve of my cheek. "Passion is the face of enchantment," he says.

I stare at the wind-battered folding chair facing the tide.

"I can watch the rise and fall of the ocean for days," he whispers.

A tear falls from my eye.

Glistening in the silky dress of the shore, my fingers brush my parted lips. I blow once more on the flame awakening me. And then, lifting my mask I slip into Eden.

Upon a million grains of sequined sand, I cast
my intimate confessions. If you've read these
pages, they've been found and published.

Where have all the humans gone?
I think it fair to ask.
They are all right here in front
of you.
They are just hiding behind
their masks.

Epilogue: The Human Masquerade

They are cab chasers, bus riders, bike pedalers, and horn honkers. They are at airports, trains, and trolley stops. They begin their day with an early morning newspaper tucked neatly under their arm, sit at the bars for noontime pick-me-ups, pick up dinner tabs, and kick back at backyard barbecues. They catch a meal and glance at their watch. They gather around martinis, dress up for grand openings, and prop against pillows with their shoes kicked off.

They wear wet suits, hard hats, goggles, and headphones. We see them digging, trolling, wading, and chasing. They are gear freaks, ski demons, soggy-glove wearers, and armchair enthusiasts. Straight-faced and the clown of the party, they listen, watch, and wait.

They hold handrails, push elevators, and skip stairs. They skid into early-morning meetings, make it to early-evening workouts, and work late into the night. They nod, wave, and shake hands. They drink jet-lag-fighting smoothies, bathe in cold towels, and snuff out the warmth of your eyes.

They come from here and there. They are noticed or hardly noticed. They are worn jean jackets, suits and ties, tennis shoes and jeans, and T-shirts and plaid. They are high heels, midriffs, and low plunging necklines. They are backless gowns and shoes of suede. They are bow ties, cummerbunds, and tux shoes. They wink and blink and pinch in the right places.

They are coded messages and hidden gestures. They are the soft laughter behind you, the chuckle that is not your imagination, the whisper you think you heard. They are flowery notes and carved initials in the bark of spindly gray trees. They kiss. They linger. They love. They are all a part of the human masquerade.

Starchly polite, they are faceless people whose automated smiles are demoniacally on cue. Lurking in the thickets of masked deception, they know the right words and arrive at the right time to twist your face into their bizarre mask of insecurity. Laden with schemes, they hug your presence like hungry vines and then wave goodbye to you with sand-filled shoes. Their well-orchestrated images anchor them in a soul-destroying land where they would rather tell a good story than do good in the world. Ducking through sincerity, they get into you. Smudging into the ridges of your skin, the human masquerade electrifies you with an ambiguity that vibrates well after their ominous image is gone.

Tapping the mic of deceit, tactical creatures who creep to their conclusions tune up for their pitch-perfect performance. Diabolically sung, their classic-screen storytelling is told with cold calculation. Shaped, polished, and gemmed, they utter a living voice that crafts your existence. Their protocol is deception. Slipping their masks only superficially, they wink sweetly as you lower yourself into their realm of delusion.

Rising calmly to their feet, they are always there with open arms and ready to lend a helping hand. But cross their peering faces and they will wrench the burning incense from your grasp with their soft-served charm.

With fingered cards, these emotional forgers ruthlessly impersonate sentiment. Riddled with trickery, they are in love with their own cleverness. Open the door to them and they will review your wish lists and diaries and become a mystery in your life that hinges on illusion. They turn your head cunningly. But they are staring at you through leafy vines. They craft the world, and nothing escapes their hooded eyes.

The human masquerade is a ghastly court. It betrays any ideal, any promise, and any moral. Its cynicism is boundless. Its lust to dominate consigns it to a world of lies. The human masquerade is cold, ambitious, calculating, and believable.

I thought I saw him behind the gleaming hood of his roadster, cruising down Pacific Coast Highway, designer shades in the eyes of the sun, cell phone in his hand. I thought it was him. But I think it was a mask of someone else.

I stood in a forest once that was kissed by a rose.